DEAD
COUNTRY

DEAD
COUNTRY

Max Gladstone

TOR PUBLISHING GROUP
NEW YORK

DEAD COUNTRY

A Tordotcom Book
Published by Tom Doherty Associates/Tor Publishing Group
120 Broadway
New York, NY 10271

www.tor.com

Tor® is a registered trademark of Macmillan Publishing Group, LLC.

Library of Congress Cataloging-in-Publication Data

Names: Gladstone, Max, author.
Title: Dead country / Max Gladstone.
Description: First Edition. | New York : Tordotcom Book, 2023. |
    Series: The craft wars ; 1 | "A Tom Doherty Associates Book."
Identifiers: LCCN 2022041368 (print) | LCCN 2022041369 (ebook) |
    ISBN 9780765395917 (trade paperback) | ISBN 9780765395900 (ebook)
Subjects: LCGFT: Novels.
Classification: LCC PS3607.L343 D43 2023 (print) | LCC PS3607.L343
    (ebook) | DDC 813/.6—dc23/eng/20220829
LC record available at https://lccn.loc.gov/2022041368
LC ebook record available at https://lccn.loc.gov/2022041369

Our books may be purchased in bulk for promotional, educational,
or business use. Please contact your local bookseller or the Macmillan Corporate
and Premium Sales Department at 1-800-221-7945, extension 5442, or by email at
MacmillanSpecialMarkets@macmillan.com.

First Edition: 2023

Printed in the United States of America

0 9 8 7 6 5 4 3 2 1

To my family

DEAD
COUNTRY

1

Tara walked out of the Badlands to her father's funeral, trailing memories and dust.

The last stars failed and the sky hung blue above her and the ground cracked underfoot. She kept to the path, a sunbaked run-off trench left by the thunderstorms that scoured the land each season. Black-green moss clustered in the shade of the rocks beside the trench. The moss grew slowly and did tender work, turning the bones of the world to something livable. One false step could erase a century of progress, so Tara followed paths already destroyed.

Years ago, after the Hidden Schools kicked her out, she had followed this same path, half-blind and half-dead, caked with sand and her own blood and the blood of the carrion birds she'd caught and killed to make it through the desert, home, to Edgemont. Home to the town she'd run away from, years and a lifetime before.

She had left an eager angry witch-girl, drunk on sweet hope and intimations of power that would have soured if she stayed. She had returned a sorceress and a shell, betrayed by her teachers and by the world of Craft she'd hoped to master. They used her and cast her out, but she refused to die.

She had walked across the flats for weeks, alone. Each step hurt. She'd remembered that walk many times in the years since, in the life she'd built back east in the great metropolis of Alt Coulumb as a necromancer and counselor to gods. There, on the sidewalk, in her small apartment, in boardrooms and at cocktail bars, the memories felt safe, like a story that was over. She had told dates about this walk over drinks—she was bad at dates—told them how many miles she'd crossed, how she dealt with blisters, how she used to fake death to lure scavengers in reach of her hands and knife. Two Aviations into the night, she was tipsy enough to laugh about it all. She held the story as lightly as a student might hold the answer to a thaumaturgy problem she'd memorized off flash cards. Bloodless.

Her dates didn't take it the same way.

Here, now, with dirt shifting underfoot, the memories did not feel safe, did not even feel like memories: the agony of her raw throat, her cracking skin, her swollen tongue. In pain there had been a clarity of purpose. The desert was not dead. It was honest. Everything here—the cactus, that circling vulture above, the dune rat whose tracks she passed, the bugs that sang at dusk—moved to survive. Just like her.

Forward. Farther. In the end she'd made it home. To her family, who did not understand her but pretended they could. To a life she never understood, either.

Then the world took her up. The job offer came through. She left again.

And now her father was dead.

———

She had packed in a hurry. Clothes, toothbrush, tools of the trade, and, of course, the black folder tied with black string that she brought everywhere these days. The room was dark, as dark as Alt Coulumb ever was, the great city sprawled outside her window and the letter a moonlit ghost on her end table. Her mother's pen had worked the paper in fine angled whorls of measured black. If she turned on the light the ink would have had a color, but the light hurt her eyes.

Just that afternoon Tara had been helping Cat with mortgage paperwork. Cat, punchy after too much coffee and more sitting than she tended to do when she wasn't on stakeout, poked fun at Tara's handwriting, schoolhouse-mannered after all these years. *Why can't you just scribble like a normal person?*

Her mother was why.

When she got home, she found the letter waiting.

She felt sick when she saw it on the desk. She felt sick when she looked at the jackets, slacks, and shirts folded in her suitcase, between the little brightly colored organizers she had bought to keep her clothes from wrinkling, which she always used even though they never worked.

If she had to pack and make it to the airport by will alone, she would not have made her flight. But she wasn't a teenager anymore.

On the night she'd snuck away from home to join the caravan that would take her to the Hidden Schools and a life of sorcery, she'd held violent debates with herself about each object she might bring. Would this knife help more than that? How much dried meat would she need for the trail, which books? By the time she used, gods help her, a rope of knotted blankets to climb down from her bedroom window, she'd given more thought to her kit than most surgeons she had met in the years since gave to theirs.

She could pack by habit now. Habit had filled the suitcase, habit used those stupid brightly colored organizers, habit snatched the letter from the end table and stuffed it in her inside pocket without reading it again.

City lights burned too bright. She sat beside her suitcase and did not remember what was in it or how she'd reached the curb. She looked away from the moon, from Seril who was its goddess. The Silver Lady wanted to talk to her, but she did not want to talk back. Habit hailed a cab.

As Tara's cab passed the Ashen Quarter, something heavy landed on its roof, with as much delicacy as possible. The horse whinnied in terror; Tara pretended not to notice. When she looked down she realized that she'd clenched her hands into fists, and the glyphs cut into her arms were glowing.

A stone talon tapped the window.

"Go away, Shale," she said.

The talon reached down and opened the door, and limb by limb a lanky winged statue coiled himself into the cab. His furled wings pressed against Tara's shoulder. He watched her out of the corner of his faceted emerald eyes.

The first time she'd met Shale, in human disguise, she'd thought he was cute. Not long after, she had stabbed him in the stomach and cut off his face. He'd saved her life since, and she'd saved his, and somehow they'd ended up something quite like friends.

He said, "You don't have to tell me what's going on."

"I know."

"But whatever this is, you don't have to do it alone."

Shale's eyes were clear, brook-like, as if he'd never met a task that was not easy. She had seen him hurt. She had hurt him herself. When he felt pain he showed it.

She shoved the letter toward him. Her grip crumpled the paper, already creased by its slow passage from hand to hand across a continent. He pressed it flat between his palms. Her mother's red wax seal winked as he opened the flap.

"I," she said, and stopped herself before her throat could betray her, and took a breath. "I should be gone a few days, a week at most. Can you tell—" Abelard and Cat and my ten o'clock and my one o'clock and, hells, tell all my appointments and tell Aev and tell that woman from the Two Serpents Group and Cardinal Bede and Matt and the Rafferty girls and Ms. K and Kos and, and Seril, and everyone, tell everyone, otherwise I'll spend the next year, the next rest of my life telling them my pa is—

His arm settled around her shoulders. His talon-tipped fingers were long as her forearms and his flesh was stone and his muscles steel, but there was a warmth to him and a weight greater than the weight of his body testing their carriage shocks. He was older than her. She always forgot that, because age hung so easily on him, while for her it was the muddying of a pool and the knotting of a body with scars.

But a goddess had carved him before the world was marred, and he had seen so many of his fellows die.

He got her to the airport. Habit took her across the dragon-bridge to her cabin, and the beating of great wings lulled her to an approximation of sleep, and late at night when the dragon's porter woke her to ask how she'd prefer to descend—they had opter-ans and balloons and short-flight Craftwork to let off passengers whose destinations fell outside their usual landing route—habit helped Tara wave off the porter's aid and roll her suitcase to the hatch.

The desert spread beneath, endless and unbroken as ever, stippled here and there with gnats of light.

Just like old times.

She stepped out of the hatch and fell.

Falling was the best teacher. The ground never lied to you.

Neither did the desert.

She lay coughing beneath the deep stars as the dragon flew west. Then she stood, slapped dirt off her suit, popped the handle of her rolling bag, and started to walk home.

Dawn came.

The sky was clear, save a dark smudge eastward, and the sun was vicious. Tara wished she'd brought a hat.

When she closed her eyes she saw the Badlands with a Craftswoman's sight, all the outer lies peeled away to reveal the souls of the place and their relationships: a black expanse hung with loose dusty cobwebs of life, the tiny threads that were mice and cacti and insects, microorganisms in the soil, and that one circling vulture far up. A dry and lonesome sight. Back in Alt Coulumb, she could walk the streets with her eyes closed, guided by the light of the gathered masses' souls, by the obligations and contracts that bound them together. Life here was spread out, desperate, and small.

She followed the runoff bed east and south. Soon the Badlands would ease into scrubgrass herding country and then farmland, and she'd make the post road, and Edgemont by nightfall. Camel Bluffs rose dead behind her, and she could just see the Needles to the north, limestone formations worn vertical by ages. Around this bend and another mile along she should find Blake's Rest, four farmhouses and a few hundred goats near a brackish spring, settled by a bitter family who did not answer to the name Blake and claimed they'd never known anyone who would. Their cistern and the irrigation stonework bore ancient Quechal glyphs, so perhaps Blake's Rest was an echo of an echo of a lost name. She'd fill her canteen there and buy breakfast if they were selling.

Her suitcase wheel caught on a rock as she rounded the bend, and she cursed and knelt to set it right. When she looked up, she saw the smoke.

Raiders.

Impossible, was her first thought, before a calmer, older voice cut in. Ms. Kevarian's voice: her old mentor, her old boss. Don't trouble yourself with what's possible, Ms. Abernathy. Analysis proceeds from observation, not preconception. Even from this distance she could see blackened farmhouses still smoldering, the soil carbon-scored, rotting hoofprints torn in the yellowed grass.

Yes, the sun was up. Yes, Raiders seldom left such a wreck behind—Raiders preyed on settlements, they stole and menaced and killed, but you could not raid next month a farm you razed today. But the signs were right. Raiders, and recently.

She'd been so scared of them when she was a child: bandits infected with rotten misfired God Wars ordnance, half-shadow and half-bone, riding out of the dark wreathed in curses. They were villains in fireside stories at first. Later, when she began to explore her interest in the Craft, they were everything she'd feared she might become. The other kids used to chant rhymes in the village schoolyard, Raiders gonna call you, Raiders gonna get you, Raiders gonna turn you inside out.

She could walk on. This did not have to be her business. But the farm was burning, and she was not a scared child anymore. She had power, and she was bound to use it.

She left her suitcase behind a gnarled bush. She brought her purse. She wasn't dressed for this. Road dust streaked her charcoal suit. She shuffled sideways in her flats down the scrubgrown hill to the dry yellow plain that used to be pasture for the goats. Wind rolled back past her, out toward the Badlands. Grasshoppers ticked.

The farmers had built a rough stone wall around the pasture since she was last here. The Raiders had toppled it as they rode through. Dead goats lay scattered on dry soil. Skulls and ribs showed through broken skin. The bodies should have been dead a year, but if the farm had been raided a year ago the buildings wouldn't still be smoking.

The goats weren't all here—or if they were, the herd had shrunk while she'd been gone. Tara hoped some of them had fled through the hole in the fence. A Raider's curse was a bad way to go. She'd never met a goat that deserved it.

Down past the ruined farmhouse, she heard a woman scream.

Tara ducked behind a wall and peered out. The yard was still. Another scream, from the barn, this time cut short—a slap, a roar of pain almost like a man's, followed by a third scream.

A space inside her chest turned sharp. She didn't know why the Raiders were here. Her mother had been so clear on the when and the what of the funeral, but she had not bothered to say how, or why.

Tara was supposed to feel confused and shaken and scared. She was not supposed to feel furious, so she went with that. She rounded the collapsed barn, mad and ready.

There was a Raider in the yard—a man, or what was left of a man. Half his body rippled with the slick black oily shadow of his curse, the darkness writhing with maggoty white thread. He had three arms, the extra grafted on his left side below the ribs, and here and there bone showed through gaps in his skin; one of his arms was half-cursed, the remaining flesh plump with rot, the skin split in places.

The Raider was dragging a girl by her hair from the barn—a young woman, seventeen or so and blond in a homespun dress, twisting against his grip. She recovered her footing to kick him hard in the knee, and tore free as he stumbled. He caught her by the wrist with his black right hand, and his curse bit her flesh. She crushed her scream between her teeth, and clawed for his eyes as he heaved her toward the assembly of bones and metal in the shape of a headless horse that he'd left waiting near the well.

Tara reviewed her options. They were alone: Tara in the shadow of the barn, and the Raider and the girl. Nothing stirred for miles save wind and this growling barnyard fight, tiny figures against endless ground. The Raider was close to the girl. If Tara scared him, he'd kill her. Drawing her work knife, invoking her Craft, gathering shadows for the kill, that would scare him. She had her suit, her sweat, the contents of her purse, and an anger so strong that she shuddered as it stretched inside her.

Tara stepped into the light.

The Raider swung to face her. One of his eyes was a pit of black with a white dot, the other bloodshot red around a dark pupil. He had no lips in the half of his face the curse covered. His teeth burned white as facts.

The girl saw her, too. "Help!" She strained against the Raider's grip but could not break free again. He tugged her back against his body, caught her neck in the crook of his cursed arm, and wrenched her wrist behind her. The girl's eyes were wide and staring and cornflower blue. She writhed against him but she might as well have fought cold iron.

The Raider snarled. Those white threads pulsed within the curse, thin as piano wire. She didn't remember the threads. Had the curse always looked like that, and she just never noticed before? Or had the curse changed?

She held out her hand, palm down. "She doesn't want to go with you."

"Walk on, stranger." The Raider leveled his extra arm at her, and the bones of its hand clicked open. A cursethrower barrel nestled in the wrist where the nerves should have been, its mouth round and hungry. "Walk away."

He tightened his grip on the girl's neck. She gasped, but no air came.

"It's okay," Tara told her. "I can help you." The girl was so scared. What had she seen, in the last few hours? What had she done to survive? "I need you to trust me." Tara tried to seem stable, in control, a pillar for the girl to lean against. The clouds of panic parted. The girl nodded. Tara, to the Raider, then: "Let her go. I can cure you. I can break the curse."

His rot-pale face went slack with hope.

No one was born like this. Where had he come from? Who had he been, before he wandered into the Badlands, before he listened to the whispers on the desert wind and found the curse and gave himself over to the slick and eager promise of a dying weapon?

Whatever was left inside him, the curse would not tolerate

rebellion. Little wisps of black smoke rose from his skin, and he bent over mewling as black tendrils corkscrewed deeper into his flesh. The girl gagged for air.

Tara took a step closer. Her hand dropped into her purse, to the knucklebones she carried there. The Raider's will broke then, and the curse raised him up, still and sharp and alert, rigid and loyal. "Stay back."

"The souls I have on me will feed your curse for weeks. You won't get half so much from her." She drew her hand from her purse, clutching a knucklebone she hoped the Raider could not see. She did not like working Craft in the daytime. The stars were set, the soil barren. She had no power but her own reserves. She could only afford one shot.

She couched the knucklebone in the crook of her forefinger like a marble, tensed against her thumbnail. "It's a good trade." She hoped she wouldn't need the bone. Say yes, she told him with her eyes.

His face twisted in scorn. "No deal, Craftswoman." The curse on his arm sharpened and serrated, its hundred tiny points biting the girl's throat. But the girl did not seem to notice. When he said, "Craftswoman," the way she looked at Tara changed. She was scared, yes—gods, Tara was tired of that fear—but she was hungry, too.

Interesting.

"Last chance," Tara said—then, before he could answer, she woke the glyphs in her hand. The knucklebone flew. There was a flash and a crack of thunder and a scream.

The girl lay bleeding on the ground; the Raider had fallen, bleeding, too, the curse's black oil mixed with the normal sticky red stuff. But the blood, to her, looked gray, and so did the desert and the ruined farm. The sun was cold. Tara had pushed too much of her soul into that knucklebone. But she did not have time to faint.

She forced herself from her knees to her feet, and scrambled to the girl.

Just one shot. Couldn't afford to miss. So she'd shot through her, to get to him. Her, she could fix. Probably.

The girl lay curled around the wound in her shoulder. Tara's aim had been true, and she knew the inside of a human body better than the inside of her apartment—but an error of arcseconds, the slightest flinch, could mean the difference between life and death. Tara checked her vitals frantically, six pulses, temperature, airways.

The girl was alive.

The exit wound was well clear of the spine. Tara wadded gauze from her purse against the bloody gap, and rolled the girl onto her back. The girl whined, but pressed her hands against the wound. Good. Her face was all teeth now. The pain cut fresh lines onto smooth features. So young, even for seventeen.

Shock is the first enemy.

"I need your help," she said as she turned out the contents of her purse. The Raider wasn't dead yet. If she could stabilize the girl, she might save him, too, find out what was happening. What had changed. Raiders in daylight. Those white threads. "Can you hear me?"

The girl's face creased with pain. Her eyes were slits. The sun glinted off her tears. She was afraid, and not of death. "Craftswoman." A whisper, a rumor, a ghost story. *Raiders gonna turn you inside out.*

"I'm Tara Abernathy," she said. "What's your name?"

The girl growled when Tara reached for her wound. Her eyes focused on the sky, the sun, Tara's face. She seemed confused by the question, but her lips twitched and she found breath, and a voice. "Dawn."

"Dawn. Good. It's nice to meet you, Dawn. You're very brave."

"Gone," she growled, or something like it, "all gone."

A better world would have let her mourn without bleeding. "Stay with me, Dawn. You're so good, so brave, I need you to hold on a little longer. I can close your wound and stop the pain. I need you to take your hands away." In her youth, Tara would have paralyzed the girl, or seized her mind and moved her hands for her. But times changed, and so did people. "Can you do that for me?"

The girl managed to nod, and pull her shaking hand away. Dawn could barely breathe, taut with pain, but Tara could reach the wound. She slid on silver bracelets from her purse, sparked them together, and let the surgical shadow cover her hands. Dawn trembled.

Tara drew her work knife from the glyph above her heart, and cut a bloodied pane out of Dawn's dress. Dawn whined through her teeth when Tara peeled away the fibers stuck to the blood; the knucklebone had dragged one long thread a finger's depth inside her. "Just a little more."

Dawn bucked against the ground, and lines of muscle shifted in her jaw and neck. Her hands, balled to fists, struck the soil. Tara's knife blade split to tweezers, and she drew the thread out.

It was done. Dawn went limp, ragged, panting.

"You're great." Tara banished one of her gloves and wiped sweat from the girl's forehead. "The wound's clear. Now I'll close it up. This will hurt more, a cold heat. Then we're done."

Dawn shook her head. "I can't."

"You can, Dawn. Just a little more."

"I need." She drew breath. "I need something to bite."

Tara took the pocket square from her jacket and twisted it into a rope. "It's clean."

Dawn's hands trembled as she pressed the cloth between her teeth and bit down. Fear tightened into resolve. She nodded once.

Tara woke the glyphs in her wrist. They drank light, glowing as she gathered power. The Badlands sun still shone overhead, but the shadows of the burned farm deepened as color left the world, leaving blinding cutouts of white and black. Tara could only draw on the light to power her glyphs; the soil here was dry and nearly dead and the Raiders' curses had hurt it enough already. An instant's careless Craft might turn it all to ash.

She made a small sphere of searing light and held it above Dawn's wound.

Craftwork wasn't made for healing. It killed what it touched. It would be easier, cheaper to end Dawn's life and raise her from the dead. But Tara could knit severed veins and tissue, give skin a lattice to regrow. It was a mortician's art more than a healer's, but it would keep Dawn whole until they reached Edgemont, and everything else Tara had spent the last few minutes ignoring. Like the letter in her pocket.

Focus. You can only do one thing at a time.

Not Ms. Kevarian's voice, this time. Her father's.

"Are you ready?" Tara asked.

Dawn wasn't, but she nodded, thumbs-up, and bit down on the handkerchief.

Tara pressed her Craft into the wound. Dawn's eyes snapped open, and they were full of silver-blue flame. That, Tara thought, was not supposed to happen.

Then Dawn screamed through the handkerchief, and the world went wrong.

Darkness slammed out from her with the force of a crashing wave. The sun vanished and Tara could not feel the world underfoot, could not feel gravity, could feel only an immense weight pulling her down and in toward the wound beneath her palm, her heart drawn like a splinter from her chest, her breath torn from her lungs, the Craftwork light she'd made pried from her grip. Her wards and glyphs strained to guard her soul from this desperate hunger, but their light was drawn, too, down and down.

"Stop!" The words flew from her and were devoured. She could not breathe. With agonizing effort she pulled her hand from the wound, and glared into the silver-blue flames that were Dawn's eyes. "Stop it, Dawn." She put what little she knew of the girl into that name. The strength of her kick; the lines of muscle in her jaw when she bit down. Her tears. Dawn, that specific person, a shape greater than this weight of need. "Please."

The weight eased, and the darkness and Tara collapsed at once. She wasn't sure which of them had won. When she opened her eyes, she was lying on top of Dawn; the girl's hand rested on Tara's neck at the line of her hair. She was breathing. They both were. Dawn repeated, softly and over and over, "—sorry I'm sorry I'm sorry I'm—"

Tara pushed herself off the girl. Dawn's wound was closed. The ground crumbled beneath her as she moved. The soil was dead and ashen gray.

Tara forced herself to her knees.

The barnyard was an ashblow, and the barn and stable and houses dust, the Raider a skeleton. The parched trees were ruins now, the wind dead, and there were no grasshoppers anymore. White splinters rained onto the ash: bones that had been a vulture once.

Tara closed her eyes and saw, for the first time in years, nothing. The gray stippling life of the Badlands was gone. As far as she could see, the world was black, the pressing, present weight of a cavern underground. There were only two lights: Tara, and the girl curled now onto her side, stammering, "—sorry I'm sorry I'm sorry—"

She was terrified, and she was powerful. She was a Craftswoman. Or she would be.

Unsteady, Tara knelt, set her hand on Dawn's shoulder, and breathed with her until she stopped trembling.

How long had the girl kept it secret? Tara looked down at Dawn and saw herself, unsure and thirteen, afraid of the power she sought. What had she needed to hear then, that no one was there to tell her? Tara herself had left her home and fled across the world and mortgaged her soul to evil men in high towers to learn the Craft. What could she say, now that time had brought her back around to this?

"It's okay," she lied. "You're going to be okay."

2

One mile south of Blake's Rest the ash stopped, a border sharp as a surgeon's cut across the road. When they staggered onto dry packed dirt again, Tara kept walking until the air was clear, then took the scarf from her mouth and set her luggage back on its wheels. Dawn shifted against her and looked up, her gaze vague. The girl had settled into a revenant's slow shuffle as they left the ruined farm. Tara knew that pace. You moved forward on momentum. There wasn't enough left of you to stop.

"Look back," Tara said. "We have to know what happens when we lose control."

Dawn's eyes snapped into focus when she said "we." "I know what happens." But she did look back. She lowered her own scarf and crushed it as her hands formed fists. "It's so even."

"It's geometry." The wind was already filling their footprints. "See how the border climbs that hill? If you scooped out the ash until you reached healthy soil you'd find a perfect sphere centered on Blake's Rest, carving through earth, roots, bedrock. The Craft doesn't care what's underneath. It works through transcendent claims, clear definitions. That's why we use so many circles. They're an easy shape. Stable."

Dawn did not speak. She watched Tara, tense with hope and fear. Tara had used that word again: "we."

Slow it down, Abernathy. This girl isn't you, even if she is young and angry and confused and you remember what that was like. Try again. Try to be human for once. "It's okay to cry," she said. "If you want, I'll go over there until you're done." There were grasshoppers again, out here in the land that wasn't yet dead. "Or I can stay."

"I can't cry." There were salt tracks on her cheeks, hard to see against the pale skin. "I tried when we left. I just choked."

"That's the ash. It's finer than sand. Gets in your lungs." Tara watched her. There had not been a blond girl named Dawn at Blake's Rest when Tara was a kid, but sharecroppers came and went. Don't assume. Ask. "Who did you lose back there?"

"No one much." She sounded bare. "It was me and my dad on the road. He found work here, for a while. Then it was just me. The Farnhams kept me on after. Their boy liked me. He was— nice, at least." There was more. Tara could tell. But there would be time. "It's all gone now, I guess."

"How long have you been learning?"

"I never—I never did anything so big. Learned small charms from women on the road, mending things and making deals, you know. But at night the charms worked on each other in my head. The glyphs would talk to each other. I got to keep them with me, when they'd take everything else. When I broke my ribs, falling . . ." Her eyes swept up and to the left, wet and bright, as if expecting Tara would press her on how she had fallen, or whether there had been anyone else involved. "When I broke my ribs, I went out to the goats, and one of them came up to make nice because I was always nice to them and I just breathed her in, you understand? All of her. She fell to pieces, to dust, and my bones knit up. They thought she'd run off. That's when I knew there was something wrong with me. So I tried to stop, stop the numbers and the charms and all of it. I wanted to stop thinking that way. I wanted to stop thinking at all. I tried, for a long time. I'm sick."

Years of curling inward, hating herself, afraid of her own mind. Tara felt sick, too. If the farm and all its people hadn't been a pile of ash she would have stormed back there and set after them with lightning and whips of fire.

"You're not sick." She took Dawn's hand softly, not wanting to scare her, but Dawn clutched it like a lifeline. Tara was doing this all wrong. The girl didn't need someone else's anger now. She needed comfort and warm arms and silence and space to figure out how she felt. But anger was what Tara had to offer. "It's not like there's some gene for it. The Craft's a way of seeing, of knowing. Everyone trades soulstuff and prays to small gods. Everyone takes from the world and gives back. We just do it more. You weren't cursed. You didn't break anything. You're good at this kind of thinking, the way some people are good at farming or music or math. *That's bad"*—she waved at the shifting ash—"but that's why we train and study and teach, why we don't make girls scared of what's inside their own heads. And it's not like the Craft has a monopoly on massacres. I've seen priests kill and artists twist the truth and settlers split the godsdamn world in two, but somehow Craftswomen get the blame." Dawn's mouth was open. Stunned. Kos and Seril, Tara was usually good at this. No, scratch that. She'd never been good at this, but she was usually better. Usually there wasn't a letter in her pocket. Her father had never been dead, before. She held Dawn's hand. "It's a big world. It's not all bad, but everywhere you go you'll find the mobs with their torches and pitchforks waiting. You don't have to keep them inside your head."

Dawn said, "Teach me."

Tara felt cold. She wasn't a teacher. Her own studies at the Hidden Schools had not exactly been a showcase of good pedagogy. She remembered Professor Denovo's arrogant hands, remembered laughing as she burned his lab, remembered the Disciplinary Committee gathered over her in grim judgment, her graduation and her fall. She wouldn't even know where to start.

But Dawn could not survive on her own. With her talent, her need, it wasn't a question of whether she'd hurt someone if left untrained—it was a question of when, and who.

Teach me.

Gods.

She drew breath, not knowing whether she would say yes or no. But before she could say either, Dawn collapsed.

Tara caught her on the way to the ground and felt a stab of guilty relief at being spared the need to answer. Trying to keep her alive was so much easier.

Dawn's skin was smudged with curse near the wound, white spiderweb lines pulsing like tiny grubs inside the slick black oil. The Raider must have splashed her, and the curse had been growing this whole time. Tara had missed the signs, that feverish eager gaze, the dulled emotions. She'd put them down to shock. Amateur hour.

She drew sunlight to her and slowed the curse with a counter-glyph. The world's shell trembled. Not cracking yet, but close. Tara had to be careful, so close to the wreck Dawn had made of Blake's Rest. Demons moved out there in the dark. "We have to get you away from the farm. Can you walk?"

Dawn dragged in breath. "It hurts." She'd sounded almost imperial before, "teach me." Now she was young again.

"Come on," Tara growled. "My students don't die before I'm done with them."

Dawn stared up through her sweaty ash-streaked hair as if the world held no pain. And Tara tried with all her courtroom art and skill to look like she knew what she was doing.

3

Tara limped under Dawn's weight.

"I can walk on my own."

"You said that last time."

"I can." Dawn drew a pained breath between the words, and she laughed without humor. The pain did not inspire confidence, and neither did the laugh, but Dawn's face was set. She needed to try to do this on her own, needed to fail and suffer before she could let herself believe she deserved Tara's help. They'd done this twice already. Tara, tired, wished the girl would just lean on her and let it be.

Phantoms gathered around the road as the noon sun baked down: Ms. Kevarian, and the moon goddess Seril, and Aev and Cat and Abelard, teachers and friends, watching her with flat and schooled expressions. So. You wish she'd accept her own limits, do you? You wish she'd stop fighting and let you help. Frustrating, isn't it? We've never met anyone like that before, have we?

Good thing they were phantoms. She'd have to think up a comeback otherwise.

She let Dawn try to walk. The girl made it three steps. Tara's arm was waiting when she stumbled.

They stopped often, for water and so Tara could change the ward she'd set around the curse. Each time the smudge beneath Dawn's skin was larger, deeper, closer to the spine.

Dawn craned her neck around, trying to see the wound. "How is it?"

Tara judged the horizon. Sand and salt and worn limestone canyons to the edge of sight. If they didn't make the town by midnight she'd have to risk lancing the curse out here, and who could say what her power might draw. They weren't far from the Badlands.

She weighed all her bad options. She felt the girl's cold forehead, took her rapid pulse, measured the burgeoning curse. Worrying over Dawn felt easier than worrying over what she'd find when she reached the town that was no longer home.

"You'll make it to nightfall."

———————

The sun set, finally.

They were left with the stars and the moon and the road, the world etched with a razor on black-painted glass. By the mountains to the east Tara judged them another two hours' walk from Edgemont, but Dawn was slowing. She had not said a word since dusk.

Tara stopped them beside the road and set her down.

"I'm not tired. I can keep going." Dawn sounded as if rising from a long sleep.

"The curse is growing too quickly. I have to contain it until we reach Edgemont."

When Tara looked up from her preparations, she saw Dawn watching her. The girl said, "It's going to hurt."

"You catch on fast."

Dawn laughed and winced.

"It won't hurt for long." One way or another, was what she would have told a friend—a bad joke. But that felt wrong with a student. Not that bad taste would have stopped any of her own teachers. Which was part of the problem.

Dawn settled herself against Tara's gaze like a wall. "Do it."

A shadow unfolded over the sky as Tara gathered starlight to her parched soul. She drew as much as she could hold, and when she stopped, the light slunk back.

But the girl was gone.

After a moment's panic Tara found her. Dawn had scrambled away and curled into a shuddering ball behind a cactus, making a sign Tara did not recognize across her chest.

"It's okay." Dawn did not stop. "It's all right, Dawn. That was me." She crouched, held out a hand. "That's just the Craft. It's not scary." She considered the objective facts of the Craft, and tried again. "I mean, it is scary. But it's our scary."

A coyote yipped out in the dark. Dawn took Tara's hand. Her panting slowed. "My dad said the stars are the dead watching us. When we can't see them, we're on our own. You blew them out."

They're just balls of fire, Tara almost said, fires impossibly huge and ages old and so hot the word "fire" is a gross understatement, and all the cold worlds like this one we walk upon are the ashes they leave when they burn out. They watched before we lived, and they will watch after we die, and if they care no one's seen a trace of it. That used to comfort me, until I learned what walks between them.

It occurred to her that the truth was rarely reassuring.

But a student who asked a question was owed an honest answer. At least, that's what Tara had always thought, though most of her teachers didn't seem to feel the same way. "We drink starlight to work the Craft."

"I thought it came from death. Each time I . . . did what I did . . . something died. Flowers sometimes. Sometimes the soil. The goat."

Gods. She really was new at this. But even Tara had started somewhere. "We use souls to power the Craft. Others' souls, often, but we can use our own, too." How to explain a soul? People traded pieces of their souls all the time, to pay for cabs and meals and rent, but they so rarely thought about what it was they traded. "Souls are patterns. Of thought, of matter, of energy. Patterns on chaos. A blade of grass has a soul—the pattern-work of its life. Sentient creatures, things like us that think about the world, we create more complicated patterns. The stars are just scattered points, but we see shapes between them. When we look at them intently, we gather their light to us." She wasn't doing this right. Everything was all out of order. "You can take soulstuff from other people if they let you, or if you're strong. You can pull it out of plants, animals, even base matter. But the stars are always there. When you call on them, the darkness comes. But you don't have to be afraid of the dark."

Dawn looked unsure.

"You don't have to study the Craft if you don't like it," Tara said. "There's no shame in stopping, once you know enough not to hurt yourself."

The girl's hand closed around her wrist. Her eyes were points of sharp and vicious light. "I have to learn." Her grip was fever warm—no, Tara's skin was cold. Were those threads of curse in the whites of Dawn's eyes?

"Then you'll have to go into the dark, and out the other side. You'll leave Blake's Rest behind, and do things that scare you worse than you've ever been scared before. If you're lucky, you'll live long enough to lose your flesh and joy and love, one by one, and then you'll lose your death, and you'll think that's the end of it, only to learn how much you still have left to lose. With each step you take, it will be easier to take the next, because you'll be one step farther from what you left behind. That's the path."

"That's what I want," she said. "I've got nothing left."

Tara felt guilty then. She had left Edgemont of her own will—one step ahead of a mob, yes, but there still was an Edgemont to come back to. Dawn had nothing. Was she jumping at the Craftswoman's life because she wanted it, or because she had nowhere else to go? Did it matter?

Did anything matter, except that the girl looked at her and said, "I want to learn," and meant it?

"Hold still," Tara said. "This will hurt."

She circled the curse with moonlight wards, and drew some of its ichor to ease Dawn's pain. Screams followed, but not for long. The girl was steady after. Not just steady: eager.

They walked on.

4

Dawn had been quiet for a mile, hardly conscious, and Tara thought they were alone.

What at sunset she had hoped would be two hours' walk had stretched to three under the stars. Her arm and shoulder hurt from supporting Dawn. She needed a drink—water first, lots of it, then liquor—and a bed.

She limped on, thirsty, cold, and tired. She had not slept much the night before, walked straight through the desert to distract herself from that letter in her breast pocket, from memories of her father and the last night she'd seen him, the night of the mob, when she left town on the wings of the storm. She'd meant to walk all night and reach home tired. But she had not planned for Raiders, or Dawn.

She was half-asleep, lulled by her footsteps and Dawn's and the monotonous roll of her suitcase wheels along the road. She was tired of watching the packed dirt a half meter in front of her feet, but when she looked up, the sky was a yawning black gullet lined with tiny glittering teeth, and she could not see the moon at all. Snakes slithered out in the desert. Something she thought might have been an owl slid past overhead. Bugs and vermin burrowed underfoot.

"At least let me take your suitcase," Pa said.

She didn't know how long he'd been walking by her side. She had not heard his footsteps. She could not hear them now.

Turn to look, was her first instinct. If you're going to hallucinate, at least go all the way. See him how he was, or how you thought he was. Her last clear memory was of a man who would have been cadaverously slim if he had not spent his life hard at work, a man who had been carefree before the cares got to him. He leaned against the mantel of a fireplace. One hand held a cup of whiskey, the other reviewed the contours of the face beneath his beard. That was the night she'd left. He had tried to convince her to hide her power, to warn her that if she used her Craft to help Edgemont she would turn its people against her. Stay small, stay safe, stay free.

He was right. But if she had listened, she never would have left.

Back then she had not argued, though anger burned clean inside her. Now she would have suffered all that and everything that came after just to turn her head and see him grim and worried beside his fireplace.

But if she turned her head, he would not be there.

"You can't take my suitcase," she said. "You're not real. I miss you, and I'm tired enough to let myself pretend." They walked together in silence. "It's good to hear your voice."

"Let go of the handle." He sounded gentle. "I'll catch it."

"I'm so tired," she said, "that I might catch it myself with Craft, and think it was you who did the catching. Because . . ." She trailed off and without turning her head or eyes she saw him beside her in the night, a childhood memory deathless as marble, from when he'd brought her to watch the meteor shower: he'd played fiddle for her and her ma around sunset, and Tara fell asleep listening to the songs. When he nudged her awake the night was deep and quiet, and he sat next to her, with Ma, beneath a sky crossed with streaks of light. "Because I want you here." She could not say, "alive." "But that would just wear me out. And we have miles to go."

"You always did think you knew best." He sounded pleased. She stared fixedly ahead, but the tone of voice called another face to mind, his wondering half smile when she made a point he couldn't refute; when she moved a pawn, revealing check. "Even about death."

She knew what he expected from her: the easy follow-up, the gentle dig. "Death is literally my job, Pa."

"So a man can't drop in on his daughter at work?"

"That's—" But before she could finish the sentence her throat closed, her eyes went hot. She didn't think she was crying until she tasted the first tear. "That's not how it goes."

"Embarrassed to show off your old man to your new friends?"

"No." Her voice broke.

When he spoke again, the teasing note was gone. As if he could tell he'd gone too far. As if he was there to tell. "I'm sorry, Tara."

"When . . . when you're gone, you go. That's all. We're all connected: to each other, to the land, to the sky, to history. We're all . . . knots in a net, and when the knot that's us unravels, the rope remains. Nobody comes from nothing, and nobody ever goes away. But we don't stick around. Not like this."

"So what am I?"

One step, and another. Keep moving.

"Memory," she said. "Extrapolation." The long words were easier: clinical, made to cut and classify and not to feel. "A vibration on a plucked string. A story. What the rope remembers when the knot unties."

"But there's more of the rope than there ever was of the knot. People aren't just flowers, Tara—we're stalks, leaves, roots. You were a bright kid, a brilliant woman, and you always watched your mother and me close enough to see more than we wanted to show. Say that I am an echo, a memory. You've been remembering me your entire life, painting a sort of picture of me in your head, and you think you're talking to that picture now. But how different is that, really, from me being somewhere else, somewhere you can't imagine, and reaching you the only way I can?"

"I don't know." She swallowed, tried again, and understood in that moment why he was pushing this point, and why she was pushing back: she could bear this sort of bull session more than she could bear the words closer to the heart. "I don't know how you died. Ma's letter didn't say. You couldn't tell me if I asked."

"But you won't ask."

Footsteps and the roll of suitcase. She tried to breathe around the lump in her throat. At last, she admitted, "No."

His hand settled on her shoulder, heavy and strong and warm even through her suit. She needed that weight right now. Her breath eased, her heart calmed, and the night that had seemed so close unfolded from horizon to horizon.

He said, "You didn't have to come back."

She almost looked at him then, almost spoiled everything. "I did. I should have come before, I was just too godsdamn busy. Everything's moving so fast, ever since Alikand. Ever since we learned . . ." She cut herself off. She didn't want to talk about the black folder. Not now. Even if this wasn't real. There were, for once, more important things to say. "I should have come back."

From the shift in his touch on her shoulder she could tell he was shaking his head. "This town was my place, and it became your mother's. I hoped it could be yours. We'd seen so much worse out-side, in the Wars. I wanted you safe. I should have listened more. When you left—"

"You didn't know I'd be okay," she said. "I wasn't, for a while. I might not be now. But I had to keep going. I had to figure out who I was. What I was."

"When I was a kid, you know, ten years old, twelve, I read so many books, I read newspaper serials about how a poor kid from the country could strike it rich, and I ran away from home and found myself in the middle of a war. I didn't want that for you. But when you wrote home, and told us where you were, what you were building—I was so proud, Tara. John, I thought, your girl won't stop for you or for anything. I was so afraid, but . . . There you were. Shining. And I thought, she doesn't have to hide anymore. Maybe it will get dark in the days to come, darker than any of us can dream, but she'll be ready, and she'll fight, and she might even win. You'd love to see her home, and safe, but it would be wrong for her to stay."

"Ma would never forgive me if I didn't come back for this."

He laughed. "Well. There is that."

A desert insect sang. They were climbing a long low hill. "What do you mean, darker than any of us can dream?"

"So you don't think I'm just a memory after all?" He was smiling, teasing her. She could tell from his voice.

She budgeted her breath. If she used short sentences, she could keep the tears inside. "You don't know the future. You can't.

You're saying things I always hoped you'd say. Things I tried to read between the lines of letters. I wanted so much for us to talk like this, and we never could. I thought there was time."

"But you can't let yourself believe it. Even when I'm standing right here."

The joke of all this grasping irritable reason caught her then; she laughed, at herself, at him, at the long low hill, at the Badlands and the night.

"I love you, Tara," he said. "Stay strong. There's so much ahead that's hard."

He kissed her on her tear-wet cheek. His lips were soft and dry.

And out of the corner of her eye she saw him, or saw some movement somehow like him, and before she could stop herself she turned.

He was gone.

They stood at the top of the hill, and below them lay Edgemont, and the barricade.

5

There had been no wall near Edgemont when Tara left, but they'd built one since, a low packed rampart near the road and circling south, a line against the Badlands.

She was so tired that when she saw the wall with its gate, saw the glint of steel and the holy light the Pastor wove about the guards to arm and strengthen them, she just pressed on. A slow and steady march. Even from this distance she could hear the guards' songs and hushed chatter. They were distracted. They might not notice her until she knocked on the gate. Hells, she could knock the gate down if she wanted. She felt tired and raw and unsettled and weak, and this last obstacle fused all those to fury.

She tripped halfway to the wall, and looked down to see what tripped her. Her toe had caught in a thin trench carved across the road and into the dirt to either side.

A bell rang out.

They'd set an alarm. Of course. Not that there was any first-principle reason for Tara to expect one, save that its presence would be maximally inconvenient.

A muffled curse came from the wall, and flashes of torchlight off metal as guards found their feet, their bows, their aim. She let go of her suitcase and raised her hand. "Don't shoot!"

Dawn surfaced from her stupor. Tara had given her painkillers. They'd worked a little too well. "What's going on?"

"I know these people," Tara said. "Let me do the talking." She turned back to the wall. "It's me! Tara Abernathy!"

An arrow thudded into the ground at her feet, shaft thrumming with the force of its impact. It glowed with the guard-light.

"Hey!" She stopped short. "What the hells was that for?" She snatched the arrow out of the ground and held it up; its light shone on her face. "Who's up there? Is that you, Thom Baker?"

"No." The voice was rough and proud, and the man who stood on the wall above the gate was thicker than she remembered. "Keep still, or we'll shoot."

"Grafton Cavanaugh." She knew him. A hard man, a sheep farmer, heavy on his children, a happy drinker, player of banjos, her father's friend. "Since when do you stand night watch? Where's Thom?"

The helmets shifted on the wall, men whose faces she could not see turning to Cavanaugh for guidance. "Baker's dead."

She felt groundless as a kite loosed in a storm. She'd come here for her father's funeral, and carried memories of John Abernathy with her all the way from Alt Coulumb. She was not done thinking of him, through him, out from under the long spread of him. The liquor she'd hoped to drink once she made it across this killing field was his whiskey, and the fire she'd hoped to drink it beside was his fire. But at least she'd charted the edges of what it meant that he was gone.

More than one man could die at a time. Death, actually, was all around—you didn't need a Hidden Schools education to know that. She'd known Thom Baker since she'd known anyone. Edgemont wasn't so large that people got lost.

Baker. The godsdamn wall. Her father. She was done with changes. She stared up at Grafton Cavanaugh. He looked larger and more grave than she remembered. "You know me, Cavanaugh."

"If that is you, Tara Abernathy."

"Your brother taught me to ride. I danced with your son at the solstice. And you know why I've come."

"You wear the face of my best friend's daughter, but many a monster can wear a face. You come at night, with a stranger, and the curse-bell rang when you crossed the line. Any word you say to prove yourself, the Raiders could have torn from you by force."

She almost laughed at the whole sick situation, but to show scorn for the Raiders' power, to scoff at his suggestion that they might have tortured Edgemont's paltry secrets out of her, would not help her case. Grafton Cavanaugh was not joking. And her father was still dead. "This is Dawn," Tara said. "From Blake's Rest. Raiders hit the Rest this morning. She caught the curse from them."

Murmurs spread on the wall—heads turned—but Grafton Cavanaugh sought no counsel. "Then she's past help. Leave her, and come inside. The Pastor will see she's buried safe."

Tara could not see Cavanaugh's eyes at this distance but she remembered them, small black points in a broad face. "I won't leave her. She's my student. She's not past saving, so long as I have a clean place to work and starlight to work with."

Dawn smiled, drug-dreamy, and waved.

"Edgemont is a good town," Grafton Cavanaugh said. She knew what that meant. A simple town of simple magics, of local faith in a priest of a vague and personal god, untouched by your foul Craft. A place that burns people like you who don't hide themselves behind manners and courtesy. "Your pa knew that."

Tara felt herself go hard. She knew what would satisfy this man. Nothing much: just bow to his order, please him, and disclaim her Craft for a while. He might accept a simple lie about Dawn, that all she meant to do was a bit of surgery, a bit of prayer. There would be no Craft in Edgemont.

But this very nonsense had chased her from her home. Poor dead Baker and the others had faced her across an open grave in Edgemont's cemetery, with a mob behind them, pitchforks and torches in the hands of people she'd known all her life. People she'd only wanted to help.

Admittedly, she'd tried to help by raising the dead to fight on the town's behalf. In her travels since, she'd learned that certain kinds of people could not accept certain kinds of help. She would make different choices now.

But she'd run from them back then, and never stopped running. Because of them, she hadn't seen her parents since that night, for all her offers to host them if they'd visit her in Alt Coulumb. If she'd been here, she could have helped them fight the Raiders. If these people had not been so godsdamn scared of her, maybe there wouldn't be this letter in her pocket.

She was done.

She stepped forward, and pulled Dawn, still waving in drug-induced friendliness, with her.

"Stop!" Grafton's voice, maybe meant for her, maybe for the other guards.

A bowstring sang.

An arrow trailed light through the air.

Shadows rolled from Tara's glyphs to cover her. With a glare, she shattered the arrow in midflight.

Splinters of glowing wood rained onto the soil. The blunted arrowhead bounced and rolled to a stop beside her foot.

Power surged through her, all the softness of the human soul melted away, rendered useful as a blade. She wanted to tear down the stars, to drink the soil, to cast Cavanaugh from his perch and batter down the gates of Edgemont and march through town, revealed in the glorious dark self she'd never showed these fools before, all the way to her father's grave.

Which would solve nothing. She'd just scare scared people worse and prove the Craft no better than Grafton Cavanaugh might think.

New lights gleamed on the wall: guards raised bows and took aim, arrows nocked and burning. What did it matter if they feared her, this particular handful of scared dumb farmers in a world full of scared dumb farmers?

The Craft, she'd told Dawn, was a way of seeing. Like most truths, that one was a prism that cast different rainbows depending on what light you raised it near. Here was the first meaning Tara had learned: you had to see things, people, places, as classes of being rather than isolated entities. This mob of villagers ready to strike her down might be any mob, anywhere, even if she'd grown up knowing them. Their individual identities dissolved once they joined together. She'd learned that truth early. It was the cornerstone of her power and sometimes she felt she'd spend her whole life since trying to see past it.

Dawn watched her, eager, hungry, feverish not just with the curse and her drugs. The girl had spent so long afraid of a power she could not control, a power that promised freedom, or at least revenge. And now she looked for Tara to stand unbowed, to break those who scorned her. To teach her what that power could do. If Tara fought her way into town, the mob would fall. She would pay her respects and leave them cowering, these men and women who chased her from their midst.

But when Grafton Cavanaugh played banjo, John Abernathy joined him on the fiddle, and they kept the whiskey passing round.

She gathered the shadow back into her glyphs. She drank no starlight, she ate no life. She stood straight, but let herself be small and soft beneath their aim. She reached into her coat and drew out her mother's letter. "My father's dead. I came for his funeral. I have a sick girl here who needs my help. Will you let us in?"

He did not say no at once. The archers kept their aim, and the guard-light gathered in their arrow tips.

Then the gate opened, and a voice that did not belong to Grafton Cavanaugh rang out into the Badlands silence. "Wait!"

Grafton looked down in shock no less than Tara's. A young man in haphazard armor emerged from the gate, hands raised. His helmet was off, his black hair in tight curls, and his face belonged to a carving in a temple a long way from here, more than it belonged to his father on the wall. She recognized the man— the boy this man had been. They'd almost slept together, once.

"Connor." Cavanaugh sounded a more private sort of dangerous when he addressed his son. "Get back."

"That's Tara, Dad." He was halfway across the killing field already, closing fast, near enough that a poorly aimed arrow might skewer him if Grafton let the archers shoot. "She's come back."

"She's a witch, Connor. She'll get her hooks in you."

"Then would you trust someone who knows her better?"

Tara's breath caught. That voice was new—to this conversation, at least, though it was as near to Tara as her bones. She turned once more to the gate, and to the shadows beyond from which the words had come. Her breath stopped. Her heart might have done the same for all she would have noticed, or cared.

Her mother stepped out into the moonlight.

6

The house was empty.

Of course it was empty. Stupid girl. You fly two thousand miles because you learn your father's dead, you walk for a night and a day and half a night again turning that news over in your mind, you talk with his hallucinated ghost, even, and still, when your mother leads you, silent, stately, through the village as doors gape and lanterns glitter and silent eyes watch you pass, when you follow her wordless down a road you could walk in your sleep to the peaked two-story house where you were born, after all that you still ask yourself why there are no lights waiting in the windows.

She took the front steps one by one with Connor's help. Her foot slipped, and for an instant he bore Dawn's whole weight. He looked guilty, as if he was the one who had tripped. She tried to smile to absolve him. Someone at least should be blameless in this mess.

Together they helped Dawn across the threshold into the house. The family room enfolded them: the empty fireplace, the book by the armchair with a ribbon halfway through. Her mother stood tall as a statue of a goddess near the kitchen, noble and furious and unable to speak. And still Tara's eyes swept naturally to the stair, to the kitchen, to the workshop door, the root-cellar steps, as she wondered where her father was hiding, which passage he would enter through.

"Take her up to your room," Ma said.

They had embraced before the wall, tight as drowning women, clinging to each other in place of air. But they'd traded few words, and Tara's memory of those was choked with the same wet heat that would not let her breathe. "She needs help," Tara said. "My kind of help. You might see things, hear things while I work."

This was as close as she'd come to talking about the Craft with her mother, and even though she was proud of her work and her life she felt ashamed, as if she'd been found rutting with a farmhand in the hay bales, rather than learning how to rule the world.

The world contained objects that were weak, and objects that were strong. (One more feature of the Craft, one more way of seeing: form precise divisions into kind, use definitions to split the world.) In the first category, place oak and iron and hurricanes. In the second, Tara's mother.

"Don't kill the cornfield."

"That only happened once." She heard her voice go plaintive in a way it hadn't in years.

"Tara."

"I was twelve, Ma. I won't kill the cornfield this time."

Her mother drew breath through her teeth. "Grafton will come once he settles his people down. I'll see to him."

Connor glanced from Tara, to the stairs, to Ma. "I'll talk with him, ma'am. It's the least I can do." He had grown since she last saw him, in ways that weren't obvious; there was a callus in his voice when he talked about his father now, where once there'd been a quaver.

"Help my daughter, Connor Cavanaugh. I'll handle your father."

Once Ma set her word to a thing, it was done.

Tara's bedroom. Gods, her bedroom! With her own bed, still made, and the quilt her dad's mom stitched for her, her books double-shelved in her small bookcase and stacked on top, her empty jewelry box on the dresser beside the carved and painted wooden figurines of monsters she'd bought from peddlers who came through town, with the profits from small jobs. She'd bought an engraving of a dragon at age eleven and tacked it to the pale yellow wall over the dresser and got in a small fight with her dad over the holes in the wood. Now that she'd seen dragons firsthand, she had to concede this wasn't the greatest likeness, but she didn't care. He'd left it up when she had gone.

With Connor's aid she got Dawn to the bed. The girl stayed upright where she was placed—not a good sign. Sweat beaded her forehead, and her eyes showed black between the lids. Tara checked both eyes, and her pulse. Down to the midthirties.

Tara eased Dawn back. She twisted. "Don't." Her voice was ragged. "They'll hear."

If Blake's Rest had not been ash, Tara would have burned it down herself.

She knelt beside her suitcase, unzipped the pocket where she kept her professional equipment, and removed her leather tool pouch and the black folder. She set the folder out of the way for now, and unrolled the tool pouch on the dresser, knocking over her old monsters. A small ghostflame burner would sterilize the instruments, and she decided on a number-six scalpel. Most of this operation she could, in theory, handle with her work knife, but the curse interacted oddly with Craft, and she couldn't risk Dawn having another episode here. She lit the burner with a snap of her fingers. "Connor, get a tarp from the hall closet." No answer, no sound of footsteps. She turned.

Connor's dark and liquid eyes rested on the ghostflame, on the glyphs glowing beneath her skin. His mouth was half-open and his eyes unsure. His tongue flicked pink between his lips. "So this is what you do."

They'd grown up together in Edgemont's one-room schoolhouse, where her parents taught. His father wasn't much for book learning, but he knew that running a farm needed someone with letters and numbers, and the Abernathy school was more than most towns had, and far be it from Grafton Cavanaugh not to take advantage. Connor had been an eager kid, antsy in class, his mouth quicker than his head and the rest of him lucky his feet were fast to match. He was wiry and lanky-strong and sort of sideways confident, and people listened to him, but he never put himself forward, never tried to lead any pickup ball teams after school, just did what people told him. When she learned more about his family, she'd understood.

The first time she came back to Edgemont, she'd found that he was quieter, and calm, and she liked talking to him. She hadn't told him much about the Hidden Schools then. Tara and Ma and her father had decided she wouldn't tell anyone. There were too many shades of ugly that conversation might turn. But Connor, who couldn't talk about a lot of things, had a compass needle's draw toward others who couldn't talk either. It turned out there were a lot more things they could talk about than things they couldn't. He showed her the sheep he tended when he had to and the goats he tended because he liked them, and they took long walks together, and he told her stories, though she was the one who'd been away. It wasn't much, but it was there. One night she lay under the stars beside him and looked up and thought she might drink him in, instead.

But she hadn't, and then she left. He had questions now, but he was no better at asking than she was at answering. "It's a thing I do," she said, as she sterilized the blade.

"I wanted to say that I'm sorry." The words slipped out quick and painful as stitches drawn from a wound.

She tensed, and felt herself bleed inside. She couldn't take this now. Her mother she'd grown a shell against, but Connor had never hurt her. She couldn't break down in front of him, not with a patient on the bed, not ever. When she learned the Craft she'd learned, too, its useful inhuman ways. Why feel what you could not bear to feel? Set it aside. Crush it if you have to. "Get the tarp. Please. And, for this next part, just do what I tell you to, when I tell you."

He got the tarp, and unfolded it at her direction, and rolled Dawn onto it. Tara gave the girl a fresh rag to hold between her teeth. Together, they began the work of saving her.

She told him to wash his hands while she prepared the site. He did not ask questions or argue. He went, and came back ready.

She held out her hand. "Scalpel."

He passed it, and took it back when she returned it to him, bloody.

"Compass, and pencil."

Dawn groaned. Her jaw muscles bulged as she bit the cloth.

"You're doing great, Dawn. Hold still. Syringe." And she looked at Connor when she took it from him. "You'll see a shadow, and feel a heavy weight. Just keep passing me what I need."

He looked ash-gray, but he nodded. That tongue tasted his lip again. "What if I can't see the instruments?"

"You will. They'll glow." She felt guilty. He didn't know much about her world, and here she was dragging him into it with no better reason than that he'd offered, he was useful, and she didn't want to be alone. "You don't have to stay," she said, reluctantly.

"You look half-dead. Let me help." And then, as if stepping onto ice: "If you need a soul, take mine."

There was a grasping hunger in her head, and a horror in her heart. "You don't know what that means." He'd spent thaums to buy goods and earned them by selling, but he knew so little of the Craft that the last time she came through town he'd asked her if the Hidden Schools were actually invisible.

"I do. Some. I read up, after you left."

She needed soulstuff more than she could say. She felt bone-slow and weary from the day's work. Outside, downstairs, she heard raised voices. It wouldn't help Ma turn back Cavanaugh's goons, if Tara covered half the village in darkness to gather starlight for the operation. "Fine." She took his hand. "You'll feel a wind drawing you toward me. Don't fight it."

He'd never done this before, and the first time was always hard. She took as little as she could bear, and his soul rolled into her, delicate and smooth and thick with guilt. She crushed a sob in her throat. He did not know how to keep himself out of the transaction. His eyes rolled white in his head. He sagged against her, but she held him and made his soul her own. He did not fall. She used him and drew starlight through the window. Shadow pressed them down, held them close.

Tara plunged the syringe into Dawn's back, and as Dawn screamed she drew the curse.

Connor recovered fast. He passed Tara tools, and when she sagged halfway through he offered her more soul, which she did not take. There was too much risk that she'd drain him to the dregs. She could not spare the words to explain; she hoped he would understand. Maybe he did. He did not offer again.

The operation lasted forever, and like all forevers it had an end. Dawn was safe. Her wound closed. Tara let her glyphs sleep. Cold and thirst and sorrow and exhaustion flowed in to replace the in-human chill of work. Starlight slunk back through the window she'd climbed out years ago.

She sank to her knees.

She felt a hand on her shoulder and heard a voice, and as she fell she wondered who could there be in this empty house beside her.

7

She woke on the couch in the dark, sweating in a nightgown and a flannel bathrobe and more blankets than the night was cold enough to warrant. Lantern light flickered on the living-room ceiling. In the years since Tara left home she'd found herself under so many unfamiliar ceilings in so many blank medical rooms that it felt strange to wake like this in a place she knew.

"There's tea on the side table."

She scrambled free from the blankets. Ma waited in the armchair by the fire in her nightgown and robe and slippers and shawl, her hair up, a book of poems open on her lap. The tea beside her lamp was cool and dark as wine. Needles winked from the knitting basket by the chair. Ma in that chair had a firmer seat than any wizard in any tower.

Her features changed as the lantern flame danced. Ma did not show age much—gray threaded through her braids and her hands were harder and more lined—and what signs there were, the soft light rubbed away. In that confused waking moment Ma was everything she'd ever been to Tara: the classroom kindness of thin velvet over an iron frame, the quiet ruler of their house who sang songs in tongues no one nearby knew, and read to them after dinner as they worked, the woman who ran through a rainstorm screaming, chasing a daughter who sprinted before her, heedless and hungry to catch the lightning.

Edgemont did not know her. At home she'd laughed, fibbed sometimes, tickled, let Tara's father whirl her through the kitchen and dip her and kiss her like a swashbuckling hero as Tara rolled her eyes. In public she kept herself composed, walked stately and erect with an instinct for command, trailing straightened backs and respect. She was a teacher, she explained, that was part of it, and she understood that respect attached to a role only so long as the role was performed. But Pa was a teacher, too, Tara pointed out to her once she was old enough to spot the difference, and he laughed, joked, slapped his fellows' backs.

John Abernathy was from here, Ma replied. She had come from away. She seldom talked about *away*, as if silence could cover it up, but it was there in the old Glebland stories she told Tara when she was a girl, about rabbits and spiders and other thieves, stories her own parents handed down from their own *away*. Tara hadn't realized until much later that her mother's bearing held a gentle hint of snobbery. Valentine Ngoye's ancestors had been warriors once and doctors later, first in the Gleb and then, after the God Wars chased them from their home, in Alt Selene, before the Wars followed them across the sea. Her parents raised her for high scholarship and masquerade balls and all the aristocratic whirl of expatriate high society in antebellum Selene. Rebelling against the weight of their expectations, she'd gone hunting the low town for adventure and found John Abernathy, runaway on the make, and they'd spent a few enchanted weeks together before the Wars caught them both.

And here she was now, and here he wasn't.

"Ma," Tara said. "What happened to my clothes?"

She placed a ribbon in the book and closed it. "They were filthy. You've torn a knee on the suit, and you sweated clean through the jacket. The shoes need a buff and polish, if there's any hope of saving them. No need to gape. I brought you into this world. I know where all that came from. Except the glyphwork, I suppose. Did it have to be so… extensive?"

Tara sat cross-legged, annoyed, and tried to keep from showing it. "Yes."

"And that patch of your neck, where it's metallic and gray—"

"A scar."

"From what?"

"A fight."

"Against whom?"

"Some gods. Sort of. On a work trip, a few years back. I won." The memory felt foreign to her on this couch, in this room. But it had happened. The scars were real. So was the black folder on the dresser upstairs—and the records it contained, which led her to fight that particular battle. She felt dizzy, thinking that her mother and the black folder were part of the same world.

"Well." That "well," if published, would be a four-volume set in leather, with engravings. "The Cavanaugh boy brought you down after you finished with the girl upstairs. She seems healthy. Sleeping. I sent the boy home. You needed rest, but I wasn't about to let what was on your jacket onto my good couch."

She tugged the blankets off her legs. She'd been practically cocooned. "Your letter was in the jacket. If you washed it—"

"The letter's on the side table. By the tea. Cold now, of course. I can reheat it."

She set the book aside and prepared to rise. Tara grabbed the mug first, and snapped the fingers of her free hand. The fire-invoking glyphs in her forearm gathered light, a blue flame burned in her palm. Steam rose from the mug.

"Can't stir it with both your hands busy," Ma pointed out.

Another glyph lit. The spoon flew from the saucer and stirred the tea for her, then shook itself off and flew back. Tara took a sip.

The tea was her favorite for late nights, not a proper tea, in point of fact (she'd learned the difference from snoots and know-it-alls at school) but an infusion of rich, deep vanilla, dried redroot and berries, a hint of rose. She drank, grateful. Her hand shook with exhaustion. She spilled a little on her chin, and knuckled it away.

Ma noticed, and, of course, she said nothing. That's what Tara deserved for showing off. The Craft could do all sorts of things, but making heat (or drawing it from the surrounding air) was hard, since Craftwork tended to chill. She'd made the flame out of pique, because she wanted to pick a fight with someone and her mother was the closest.

Gods. So wasteful. What would Ms. Kevarian say?

"Thank you" was what Tara said, anyway. "You remembered."

"Of course." Ma did get up, then, and crossed to the couch and sat beside her. Tara tried to ask a question, any question to fill the terrible silence of the room, of the house that held only the pair of them and Dawn asleep upstairs, but all questions fled her save one, and that one she could not ask. "I slept here, you know," Ma said. "My first night. When your father and I finally reached Edgemont. It had been a month since my last shower, two seasons and more since we left Alt Selene, and I'd seen things, done things on the road that I wanted to forget. So had John. It was bad, all of it everywhere. I was sure we'd find Edgemont in ashes, because that was how stories like the one we were in always end. But the town was here. I was just bones then, all bite and blade, and then all around us we had friends and family and food. I sat down on this couch, which felt soft as any bed I ever knew back home, and slept through the night, and woke in the afternoon for the first time I could remember. The house was so full back then. It's been emptying ever since. Your uncle first, then your father's parents, and then you went, and you came back only to leave again. And then." She reached out unseeing, and pulled Tara toward her. "I'm so glad you're here."

That sentence hitched, the smallest crack in the music of her voice. Ma might not have meant to hint that Tara could have stayed away, but in that crack Tara heard doubts Ma had not allowed herself, a fear she might have scorned by daylight but that slunk back through her ears each night in bed: that maybe, after all this, she would be alone.

Tara hugged her mother, and breathed in the warmth of her body. She was crying. So was Ma. The tears left her at last and nothing flowed in to take their place, a nothing that felt close and true. Ma's hand pressed down Tara's neck, soothing.

How long had it been since she last wept? You didn't learn that at the Hidden Schools, how not to cry. That was something you had to teach yourself before they let you in.

The weeping hour passed, and they were still there, on the couch, in the house. She could ask the question then.

"What happened?"

She recognized her mother's indrawn breath. She did that herself, in court and boardroom argument, to break rhythm and steal time for her thoughts to gather. She hadn't thought it came from anywhere, and only realized it was a tell when one of her Alt

Coulumb friends pointed it out with a viciously accurate impression. So: she'd learned it here.

"There have always been raids. In the last four years they've grown worse. This year they started hitting settlements. Not just killing livestock and fields but razing them to curse and ash. Seems they have a new leader. They call him the Seer. Say he cut his own eyes from his head and replaced them with the curse. A hard man. We built the wall to keep him out. Your father joined the watch."

"What? He never fought before."

"We both made done with killing long ago, when we came back to Edgemont. But he couldn't stand by. Not when Cavanaugh asked him, with the Pastor in tow. Not after Baker died, or DuChamp. He kept watch, with the other men. And for a long time, the watch held, and the wall. We started to believe the next attack would not come. We were wrong.

"We thought it was a sandstorm first. Too late we felt the curse in the wind. Raiders coming. The watch stood up at the wall, but Cavanaugh's boy wasn't there."

"Connor." Tara remembered his guilt, what he'd tried to tell her and she refused to hear.

"He was out in the Badlands, in the canyon maze. Your dad went after him. Found him, sent him running back for help. Saved the boy's life. But your father was not the running kind. He let the fight take him. The watch brought his body back."

Tara breathed out.

"That's all."

"I'm so sorry," she said first. "Your letters—you didn't say anything, he never hinted—"

"He didn't want to worry you."

"Worry me?"

"He blamed them, Baker, the Pastor, even Cavanaugh, for chasing you off. You'd come home, you were trying to build a life here, and they were so small they couldn't understand. He was so proud of you, forging your way back east, like he'd tried to before the Wars. Were you supposed to leave all that and come back

here to help people who hated you for what you'd made yourself?"
She sounded like him then—like he'd sounded on that long walk
south, his voice in Tara's mind, his hand on her shoulder.

"Yes," Tara said. "I could have helped."

"I love these people," Ma said, as if she was reminding herself.
"But they wouldn't take your help."

"I was an idiot back then, when they chased me off. I was proud."

"They came for you with torches. They called you a Raider.
That was not your fault, Tara. Neither was this. This wasn't your
place. Your father knew that."

Ma had a tone as final as any spell. But Tara could not accept
it. She sat beside her, and imagined her father, and Connor, and a
curse-flashed sandstorm towering over the canyons.

"That girl upstairs," Ma said. "She's like you, isn't she?"

Tara nodded, too tired to pretend she did not know what her
mother meant.

"What will you do with her?"

"I don't know."

8

Tara slept a little, and in the morning she knocked on her door and waited until Dawn answered, "Come in."

The girl sat upright in bed, propped on pillows, even paler than she'd seemed yesterday. She wore a loose cotton blouse Ma must have left for her, and she'd gathered her hair in a neat braid. A book from Tara's shelf lay on her lap, open to a picture of a griffin. A wicker tray rested on the nightstand: a plate that once held eggs and toast, and a cup that once held water. Good. Dawn's appetite was back. Sometimes, if you got things subtly wrong in surgery, patients lost the drive to eat or drink, without losing the need. That didn't go well. "Enjoying the book?"

"I like the griffins. Your—mom? She's nice. She said you wouldn't mind. About the blouse, too. If you want, I can find something else to wear. Do you need special clothes to be a witch? Do they give them to you, or do you have to make them yourself?"

"I'm not a witch." Tara placed the roses she'd brought on the nightstand beside Dawn's breakfast tray, and settled herself in the desk chair. "I'm a professional. How much do you remember about yesterday?"

Dawn closed the book and looked down, away, out the window.

"I wouldn't ask," Tara said, "if I didn't have to. But you were far gone last night. I need to make sure you're healing."

"The Raider. I remember his hand in my hair." As if it had happened to someone else. "I remember . . . eating him. And Blake's Rest. All those lives, the plants and the bugs and the birds and the little things in the dirt, popping in my mouth, like berries." She shuddered, not entirely from fear. "I remember the road. You helped me. I remember—there were men? Men on a wall. With bows?" She looked around the room, suddenly scared. Shadows in the corners quickened with her anxiety. "They tried to shoot us."

"Dawn. It's okay. It was a mistake. I stopped them."

"A mistake? They tried to kill us."

That anger in her voice was a good sign. A worn or damaged soul tended to give up or give in, as the consciousness surrendered to entropy. Dawn was remembering herself. Remembering that she mattered. "They did a bad job of it. You're safe now. With me."

Dawn touched Tara's hand, gingerly, then pulled away as if her skin were a hot pan. Fearful of contact but hungry for it. Hungry for something to trust. "Thank you."

"I'd like to take your pulse." Dawn offered her wrist, tenderly. Tara found her pulse and, as she counted, tried to think of some excuse to put off the conversation they needed to have. "Is there any pain?"

"Only when I breathe very deep and turn my head to the side." She drew breath until her lungs strained, and jerked her head sharply left. She winced.

"You probably shouldn't do that, then."

"Yes, master."

Tara's ears insisted on the words, but the rest of her wanted to believe she hadn't heard them. "Excuse me?"

"Um. Mistress?" When Dawn tried to read Tara's expression her eyes got even wider, which Tara hadn't imagined was possible. She'd known spotlights with smaller apertures.

The girl's pulse was fine. Tara let her arm go, and crossed her legs.

The silence made Dawn nervous. "Magestrix? Lady? Madame? Professor? Boss?"

"How about Tara?" she said, but Dawn looked less than enthused by that suggestion. "Ms. Abernathy, if that makes you feel better. Look, Dawn. We need to talk about this . . . this me-teaching-you thing."

The girl—Tara might have said she *paled*, if there had been any paler possible. Words tumbled from her, desperate and mouse-fast. "I don't know what I've done wrong, but I can make it up to you, I swear, I promise on my name, I can fix it, I can change—oh gods, this is *your* bed, I should have slept on the floor, I know I should never have read your books without you telling me it was okay and I should have done the dishes already and—"

"Dawn." She'd only whispered, but the girl shut right up. Tara steepled her fingers. She hadn't been this bad with Ms. Kevarian. Had she? But then, Ms. Kevarian hadn't been her first teacher. When Tara arrived at the Hidden Schools she'd been just this voracious, insatiable, and terrified. Yes, the Schools had answered her call, and yes, she'd made it through the Labyrinth in record time, but surely there must have been some mistake. Country girls just didn't go to the Hidden Schools. She threw herself into work. If she was good enough she'd graduate before they noticed she shouldn't have been there at all. When professors assigned chapters she read the whole book; when they assigned books she read three more by the same author. She learned languages when she could have muddled by with phonetic pronunciation. She asked for advice, she attended office hours, she pushed against the horizons of her understanding. That was how she came to Professor Denovo's attention.

"You haven't done anything wrong." Outside of destroying Blake's Rest and almost punching a hole in the world, Tara did not say. Everyone made mistakes, starting out. Tara herself had killed a cornfield. Maestre Gerhardt had shredded the Northern Gleb and started the God Wars. There was precedent. And that precedent was why you didn't leave novices to figure things out on their own. No matter how bad a teacher you thought you'd be. Besides, it sounded like being reduced to carbon ash was the best thing that could have happened to Blake's Rest. "I want to talk about learning the Craft. You need to be sure it's what you really want."

"It is. I do."

Gods, the certainty of her, like an arrow nocked and aimed at Tara's heart. Tara remembered how it felt to aim herself like that. That's why she had to be careful. Because she remembered.

"Most Craftswomen on this continent, if they met someone whose mind was bent like yours—I mean that as a compliment—

they'd send you straight to the Hidden Schools. That's where I learned the Craft. I got an excellent education there. They'd prepare you well for Craftwork. Your life would change. But." This part was hard to say, hard even to admit to herself, but Dawn had to hear it. "It's dangerous. The Craft will kill you, sure, but that's not the worst of it. When I went to the Hidden Schools I worked with a professor named Alexander Denovo." Even after all these years she heard a thread of awe in her voice when she spoke his name. He'd woven that thread into her, and sometimes she thought she'd spend her whole career picking it out. "He was . . . He was a genius. I worked hard to get into his lab, and when he doubted me I worked harder to prove my worth. And he used me. He used all his students. He took over our minds. He drained our souls, used our dreams for his projects, bent our spirits through his will. He worked us like puppets until we broke. And then he threw us away."

Dawn sat very still. Tara wondered what expression was on her face, but she couldn't look. She kept her eyes on the tips of her fingers.

"I freed myself. I set his lab on fire. I broke his hold over the other students. I denounced him before the board. But they already knew. They knew, and let him work, for decades. They guided students from influential families away from his lab—but not even those kids were completely safe. The board protected him. They didn't protect us.

"You have to understand that these people I'm talking about aren't outliers. They're not stuck on the sidelines. They're giants in their field, influential faculty at the most selective, most elite Craftwork school in the world. Professor Denovo's gone now, but the people who protected him and worked with him are still right there. So. You can't trust the Hidden Schools. And if you can't trust them, I don't know who you can trust."

"I didn't ask you to take me to the Hidden Schools." Dawn reached for her as if across a great distance, and tried to take her hand. Tara hated herself a little. Here she was trying to turn Dawn away from something the girl thought would save her. "I asked you to teach me."

As if it was that easy. "What I know, I learned at the Schools. From Professor Denovo. And I learned well. On my first case I had a minder, someone the client posted to keep tabs on me. I wanted her gone. So I reached into her mind and twisted her, just like Denovo twisted me. Not so hard, but I did it, and barely thought about what that meant until it was done. That's what you'll get, with me as a teacher. And when you've learned what I can teach, you'll have the life of a Craftswoman. Which is not much of a life."

"It's your life." Dawn's voice was sharp and eager, and in it Tara heard the determination that had kept this girl going, kept her learning, kept her alive in Blake's Rest through conditions Tara could only imagine. "I can do this. Look what I've learned already."

Her eyes burned white, and the world went cold and dark and the sky bowed and the chill robbed breath from Tara's lungs.

Tara snapped her fingers, and it stopped. Birds sang outside. The fields rolled on undisturbed, and still, for now, alive.

Dawn looked at Tara like she'd just grown a second head. And that look, that awe, made Tara feel a bit like Ms. Kevarian, and proud. Which was dangerous. "Lesson two," she said. "Precision beats generality. I grew up here. I know this place better than you do. I can name it, its whole and its parts. That gives me control."

Dawn's surprise gave way to a smile. "So you'll teach me?"

She realized then that she had chosen. She hoped she'd chosen right. "You have to know what you're getting yourself into. You'll use the Craft, but it will use you, too. And so will the community you're entering—other Craftsmen and Craftswomen. Even I will use you. You have to learn how to name yourself, and name the tools you work with. You have to learn precision, and control." She took a rose from the bouquet, and passed it to Dawn. "Here's an exercise. Drain this flower, and use its life to make a light. Just light, not heat. Focus on the rose, specifically. Don't pull from the air, or from the sun. Look at the flower, smell it, taste it, until it becomes a part of you."

Dawn frowned at the rose, at its curved petals. A thorn pressed into her thumb. The red blossom darkened. It dried and shrank, petals wrinkling.

Then it exploded.

Dawn screamed, shaking ash from her singed hand.

"It's a start." Tara stood. "At least you didn't set the bed on fire. Go out back to practice, but keep close to the house. If you're careful, you can draw a minute's light from each rose. Just light, remember. Don't push yourself. Don't kill anything. I'll be back this afternoon."

"Where are you going?"

She adjusted her tie. "To a funeral."

9

There was a casket near the altar of the church beside the village green, and it was open.

Tara paused at the door. Rows of pews faced forward, broken by a central aisle, clean lines and light, simple tricks of architecture arranged to draw her in. She'd come all the way from Alt Coulumb, and this aisle was the final stretch of road. Except it wasn't, really. Her way led to that casket and beyond, even though she couldn't see the path from here.

She crossed the threshold and let the body draw her forward.

He lay in the casket in a suit she'd never seen him wear in life. John Abernathy owned a good suit and a bad suit, and he'd wear the first to weddings and funerals and the second to services and town meetings and holidays. When he wore through the bad suit, he started calling the good suit his best suit, and when he started to wear through his best suit he patched it with what remained of the old bad suit and still called it the best. When Tara left the first time, Ma had been one quarter through a several-step plan to buy cloth from a passing caravan and sew the man a new suit herself. But this stitching was too regular to be her work.

Tara gripped the casket's rim.

In her Alt Coulumb apartment, with that letter open on her desk and the city outside, she'd felt the world end. She'd walked all this way carrying shock, anger, pain. Standing here in front of him, all those anchors fell away and she stood rootless in a terrible white space.

Emotions formed like rocks, by layers, under pressure. On top of the first giddy flash of purpose she had felt when she took up the Craft as a girl, she'd pressed years of work, sweat, mastery, joy, exhaustion, heartbreak and defeat, subversion, success, despair, self-hatred, all lithified into something she'd call love.

She felt that now: love. All those compressed layers unfolded inside her. But she felt something else there, too, something new and raw, and she fell into it without knowing if it had a bottom. Or if she'd just keep falling.

Here you are, Pa. Here's what's left of you, this footprint of a body, those lines where you smiled, that beard you kept neat and close. Those are your fingers thick with work and your gentle hands that held me. There was a good voice in that mouth, high and clear when you wanted to sing. You sat with me and read the same book over and over until I could read myself. You heard my stories and wrote them down. When I was a kid I'd watch you with people and wonder how you could be so free, joking, touching, backslapping and setting your arm around other men at work, and I tried to study it, to pick it all apart and learn your ease. As I got old enough you shared the books you loved and knew, and when I went beyond your limits you helped me where you could. You took me in when I came back broken, and you sent me worried letters when I left again, but you never told me I'd chosen wrong. I hope you know I loved you even when I left.

And now I'm back. Speaking to your footprint. Falling in the pit that's where you used to be.

A hand touched her arm, and she spun.

She was a more mature person now than she had been on her last visit. She could tell, because she did not draw her knife on the Pastor. But he must have seen some danger in her, the shadow of a threat, because he stepped back and spread his hands as if calming a scared beast. "It's just me, Tara."

"I'm sorry." She told the hairspring tension inside her to go away. It did, eventually. "Thank you for this. It's good work. I don't know many people who could have kept him whole this long." That was a lie—she and most of her classmates could have done the same, as could any hedge witch worth her salt circle— but for a backwater priest with no god to speak of, a soother and a weaver of faith, Pastor Merrott had done well. Corpses weren't his specialty.

"Your mother asked me to keep him for you. I tried."

"And you cleansed the curse. No trace left that I can see."

"I've had more practice than anyone should." She didn't argue. "Tara, I know you don't think much of my calling. But if you need to talk, I'm here to listen."

She let the casket go. "Thank you." He wasn't that much older than her, she realized. He'd been a young priest when he first reached Edgemont to replace their last pastor, fresh from the preaching schools in Albec City. She remembered him as a tall, slim, kind figure with a clear voice. He was seven years her elder, and that gap had seemed like forever when she was fourteen. Even on her last visit home he'd seemed like a creature from her parents' world, not hers; a wall stood between them. Now it was gone. Had they ever been as different as she imagined? He was born in some tiny farmhouse on the vast Kathic plain, and went away to learn his art, and made his life caring for people who were not his own. He had not wed here; he was in Edgemont, not of it. She wondered if he felt alone, too. She should say something. What she said was "Is that all?"

His eyes flicked away from her face before he forced them back. That moment's aversion, in a man so practiced at sincerity, told her what he was about to say. She tried not to hate him for it. "Some folks are . . . concerned. There's talk about what you did last time." The open graves, the reaching hands, the groans.

"They want you to ask me not to turn my own father into a zombie."

"You raised his friends."

I was a kid, she did not say, and I'm sorry, I was angry, I wanted to help, I'd spent six months keeping everything I was, everything I could do, secret from the fools that fill this dusty town for fear you'd tie me up and try to cut me open to make sure there weren't demons inside. I made some bad decisions and your loyal godsdamned parishioners chased me out and now he's dead and how long will you make me pay for being who I am?

He could not read her silence. "We're all hurting now. Pain takes the form it finds in the soul. You don't have to say anything. I only ask that you hear their concern."

"I hear it, Pastor." She turned from him. "Now. Where should
I sit?"

The funeral was terrifying. All Edgemont gathered into the church,
each person wrapped in their own silence, but they did not approach
her. Tara remembered growing up beside them, remembered the
kindnesses they had shown a fierce and quiet girl, remembered
torchlit faces and pitchforks upraised.

Ma sat by her side, proud and tall, and the Pastor stood by the
altar and asked the village for their blessing and their faith. From
the pews, the people of Edgemont gave small pieces of themselves,
and he wove their souls together. Tara offered a few thaums of her
own, and felt the comfort of blessing in answer, easy as a whiskey
shot, no less real and no more.

Speeches were made. She could not focus on them, not on Tra-
vis Cooper's, not on her mother's. But when her own turn came
and she stood at the lectern, under the weight of their attention,
she felt torn and tired. She was part of Edgemont, but they did
not want her, or trust her. She did not say much. She could not
bear to. But they listened. When she finished, old Mrs. Dailey
was crying.

In the farthest pew on the right, Connor Cavanaugh sat watching her, as still and somber as if he were the one laid out in the
coffin. His pew was crowded, but he carried aloneness with him.
She tried to meet his gaze and tell him that she did not blame him
from all the way across the room, that the world was big and hard
and sometimes bad things happened. But you could not say all
that with a glance.

His father spoke. Grafton Cavanaugh looked bigger in his suit
than he had in his armor atop the wall, and he did not raise his
head. He looked at no one, especially not his son. He read the
speech haltingly, from a piece of rumpled paper. Once he took
off the glasses he wore to wipe them dry. He spoke of his best
friend, a man anyone could love, who left home seeking fame and
fortune in a far-off city, a man he'd thought dead when the God
Wars came and the letters stopped. But that man made his way

home across a continent, with the most beautiful girl by his side. You would have thought he was a ghost, but that he'd grown since he was gone. There were many stories like that back in the God Wars. Most went the other direction. But John Abernathy never was a man to do what others would. He chose his path and he walked it home.

Tara watched Grafton Cavanaugh weep and remembered him ordering the archers to aim for her, ordering her to leave Dawn out in the road to die. Where anger should have been, she found barren soil.

There were songs. She sang what she knew. Ma's voice was strong as ever.

After, Tara joined them at the altar to help bear the coffin to the grave. Grady and Thibodault sidled away as she approached, and murmured their condolences, and glanced to Cavanaugh, who did not seem to notice her. But Sam Cooper offered her his place.

The casket rested hard on her right shoulder. She knew how much his body weighed, and the rest was wood.

They lowered him into the grave with ropes. More singing. Another prayer. The preacher took their faith to ward the body against any curse that might remain.

Tara's mother strode to the grave, took the spade, and whispered something not meant for Tara's ears as she pitched the first spadeful down.

Once again they turned to her. There had been little sound save the wind, but now the hush fell total and complete. Even breath stilled. Sam Cooper, Grady, Thibodault, the whole Braxton clan, the Dariens, even Pastor Merrott, and of course Grafton Cavanaugh, all tense, all ready.

She'd told off a mountain to its face, she'd fought a demon in the Courts of Craft, she'd held the walls of Alikand against a desert's worth of carrion gods, and as she walked to the graveside she felt more seen than she had ever felt before. The audiences she'd faced, adversaries and enemies and friends and gods, they'd only seen her as she was then, in that narrow slice of time. These people had known her since before she learned to hide herself.

They all tensed as if they thought she would do—it didn't matter

what. Raise her father as a zombie, sure. Call black magics from
the grave, summon a demon to kill them all, why not. Peel open
the sky and reveal to them the heaven they did not really believe
existed, the grand clockwork of wishes they hoped moved the
world. All the same to them.

They didn't think she was human enough to have come home
just to bury her dad.

Maybe she wasn't anymore. Maybe she really should show
them.

Her mother stood tall and bright in funeral garb. She offered
Tara the spade, and Tara took it, and in that moment she felt an
understanding between them. She thought of her parents as a
matched pair, like the village did—but Ma was not from here.
Tara had studied so many burial rites, so many ways to dispose
of the dead, mostly so she could reverse them if need be. A form
of respect in one city could be a desecration a few miles off. How
would Ma have wanted to inter her husband? Should he have been
rubbed with sacred oils, or wrapped in the skin of a sacrifice, or
burned?

Tara had left Edgemont, but her mother never had that choice.

She sank the spade into the dirt and as she raised it she swept
the crowd with her gaze, accepting the pattern of their suspicion,
drawing it, using it.

The Craft is a way of seeing.

There, at the back, stood Connor—sad, lost, guilty, soft in the
morning light.

When she tossed the dirt into the grave, it made the ordinary
sound.

———

People lingered afterward, in tight clutches. Grandmother Braxton came and hugged Tara and her mother, and as she left, steadying herself on her cane, others followed. People Tara hadn't seen
in five years thanked her for her speech, what beautiful words, I
couldn't see for weeping, and Tara wished she could remember
what she'd said.

Across the graveyard, Grafton Cavanaugh stood with his crew

of coffin bearers and the Pastor, trading stories. Connor stood silent and near. Their black suits looked alien and blocky against the green grass and the too-blue sky, like a part of the landscape the painter had not finished. She thought about Cavanaugh at the front of the church, wearing his glasses, reading slowly and sounding raw.

He did not look at her as she neared, though he must have seen her coming. "Grafton." She'd always called him Mr. Cavanaugh when she was a kid, but it seemed absurd to do so now. His expression darkened as he turned to her, and she didn't need Pastor Merrott's warning glance to tell her she'd made a mistake, but, hells with it. "Thank you for your speech. I know how much my pa meant to you. You meant a lot to him, too." Cavanaugh's brows lowered with every word, and the lines that could be seen beneath his beard deepened. But Tara had come to make peace and godsdammit, peace would be made. "I wanted to apologize for last night. I want to help the town, as much as I can."

"Help." Cavanaugh's voice rolled deep in his chest. "We don't need your kind of help."

Connor blanched. "Father."

But it was Pastor Merrott who set his hand on Cavanaugh's shoulder. "This is not the time, or the place."

"Pastor, I try, gods know I try. I cannot keep this in my heart. It gnaws at me."

Tara glared at Pastor Merrott, then Connor, then, finally, at Cavanaugh himself. She'd come here to talk. She'd apologized. But if he wanted a fight, then by all the gods, she could offer one. "I am not sure I take your meaning, Grafton."

"Oh, you take my meaning, Tara Abernathy. You left."

"You chased me out."

"Because you were raising the dead." His voice got low. "Our dead. Our friends, who deserved rest. And after that night it all went wrong. Raids grew worse. Farms failed, and settlements, and towns, and the Raiders' curse struck like a storm, and even your father, a man who swore off arms, took them up to fight. And now he's dead and you come in with your natty suit and your witching speech and say you want to help?"

The anger found her then, searing and sweet, and sweeter still the clarity it brought, after these muddy days when her soul turned against itself.

Grafton Cavanaugh was an asshole. Tara was a trained mediator. She knew at least six ways to ease this moment, to make him feel heard and safe. She rejected all of them. Let him burn. "He was my father, Grafton."

"He was my friend!" He cut back fast and vicious, on instinct. "All these people knew him, and loved him, and he fought for them when you ran away. Where were you, when it got bad? Off. Somewhere. Making a name for yourself. Your father would tell us the high and mighty stories you'd send home, and he was so *proud*, because he couldn't see the self-involved mind behind them. And now that he's gone you've come back here to spit on all of us."

There it was. The gap in his dragonscale, the soft penetrable flesh. She felt her eyes widen, she tightened her lips to stop the killer's smile from spreading, and Merrott, mistaking the nature of her expression, tried to save her. "Grafton, please—"

"I am a loyal man, Pastor, a gods-fearing man. And she's standing here at John's funeral to scorn us all."

"So that's what this is about." She went cold because it would hurt him more. "I left. I found a place and a power you can't touch. He was proud of that. And at the end of the day for all your talk you're still just the loudest man in Edgemont."

Then, with what the local brawlers would call speed, he went for her.

He didn't throw a fist—just gripped her arm tight enough to bruise. But she was ready. Her defensive glyphs flared, shadow rolled out between them, and he fell back into his friends and then to the earth, clutching his numb hand, a shocked, scared blotch against the green.

He growled to his feet, and in that moment Tara felt not fear but shame. He could hurt her if she wasn't paying attention, but for all his size and strength he was a child before her Craft. She'd wanted him to swing, wanted him to give her an excuse to scare him and break him down, to mark him with her power and prove she existed.

Were they so different?

(Well, yes. But in that moment?)

Before he could speak, before he could come at her again, before she could piece out how to stop this thing she'd started, Connor was between them, his arms spread. He was smaller than his dad, but certainty made him seem larger, like the night before, when he faced the archers of the watch: a slender man making himself a shield. "Dad. Stop. She's just hurting."

"He's right, Grafton." Pastor Merrott's hand on Cavanaugh's shoulder might not have existed at all.

"Hurt? Look at her. She's enjoying this. And then there's you, Connor. Standing against your own father to defend a witch who does not care. She won't stay for you. She's not built for everyday. She would not waste a thought for a dying town and she won't come to bury whoever dies next. If you were so brave against the Raiders as you are against your dad, John Abernathy would be alive today. She knows that just as well as we do."

Connor did not shrink, or hit him, or snap back. He sounded tired when he spoke. "You're more drunk than is decent. Go home, Dad."

And he did. Pastor Merrott and Cooper and the rest drew Cavanaugh back as he glared, first at his son, then at Tara, then away, a great mound leaning on those who would support him. Only once he'd lurched far enough away that there seemed no chance of him looking back did Connor allow his hands to shake.

"He's wrong," Tara said. She wished she did not sound so small. "I don't blame you."

He turned from his receding father, but not to her. "You should," he said, and walked away toward the Badlands.

10

Several million years before, a vast and shallow stinking green algae sea had spread over what were now the midlands of continental Kath. As tectonic plates shifted and meteor strikes choked the sky with ash and spelled the end for the last masters of the planet, those seas died and dried to leave scoured sunbaked soil, what was left of a world once you peeled away the soft.

Lifeless? No, though human travelers down the centuries called it that, the barren landscape a common subject of letters and journals and slapdash adventure tales featuring heroes whose parents, the reader was meant to believe, thought names like "Bat" and "Flash" were practical choices for a young person trying to make their way in the world. A vast and trackless territory. Unforgiving. Maybe it made them feel better to see this bare and blasted land, and think surely nothing can live here, rather than, what's possible here is a form of life that's not like mine. Snakelings nested in some reaches of the Badlands, and the great hive cities of scorpionkind spread in caverns far below. Rocks spoke and dreamed. Lizards skittered up dunes and down. Buzzards circled. What thrived grew small, or kept to shadows and tunnels, shied from the sun and courted the moon. They'd been the Badlands for as long as human memory, in many cultures and tongues: the Forbidden Place, the Place That Is Not Ours, the Place That Is Not Dead.

And then the God Wars came. A hundred fifty years ago, far across an ocean in the Northern Gleb, a group of scholar-theologians cracked the secrets of the Craft, of the power of the gods, and seized the reins of the world themselves. Gods fought back—some to save their place, some against the devastation those first Craftsmen and Craftswomen wrought, some for joy of battle, some because they felt a change in the wind and knew no other way to meet it. The Wars came, plural in grammar as they were plural in their theaters and combatants and battlefields, fought in so many ways in so many lands as alliances and social realities shifted. They lasted a century. A few brief stretches of not-quite-global peace broke out (though someone was always killing someone somewhere) while all the many sides circled like stags whose antlers just kept growing. But always the carnage began again. The Wars were polymorphously perverse. They infiltrated history from the root. To think you stood outside them was to stand at their heart. And for a very long time northern Kath had thought it stood outside.

But one day Kath realized the Wars were already here. By the time they turned hot each side held weapons honed by decades of conflict, weapons subtle and fierce beyond imagining.

Kathic gods—the big, old ones, the Quechal and the transformed immigrant Glebland pantheons of Alt Selene and the grizzly combines of the city called Shikaw or Chikal depending on who you asked—those gods met the Craft in the Badlands.

And the world broke. But the Badlands endured, transformed.

Tara sought Connor in the glass canyons. He'd come this way, said the sole guard on the wall above the open gate, a thick-necked man who Tara recognized with some shock had been two years her junior in her parents' school—what was his name? He said Connor had walked west from the wall, eyes downcast, and brought water with him. Tara hated the wall, but she had to admit it helped in this one way: standing on top of it she could see for miles and miles. But she could not see Connor. Which meant he was hiding in the canyons. So she went there.

Faces lingered in the glass walls. Ghost eyes watched her pass, and melted whorls formed screaming mouths, like in that Skaldic painting everyone had a print of on their dorm wall back at the Schools. As she walked on, those faces faded, only for others to take their place. No great Craft had been worked here—the true battles had been fought deep within the Badlands at the Crack in the World—but unreality seeped out from the wounds that conflict made, and left scars. Sunlight broke into rainbows in the glass depths, and shadows moved within.

She thought the shadows were illusions. The faces, though—the Crack in the World was a gateway to other realms, other histories. Perhaps beings from those alien worlds peered into hers through scrying glass. They might be God Wars dead, holograms caught in the glass like a bomb might sear a shadow on a wall. Or they might be echoes of the future.

Gravel ground beneath the thin soles of her shoes, and the noise echoed. Glass walls circumscribed the sky. It looked bluer through the narrow gap, a trick of the light. From this angle she could not see the spot where the glass stopped and the sky began. She might have been wandering in a cave, a tunnel, beneath a blue-painted dome.

If she had not been a Craftswoman she would have lost herself in the canyon maze, seeking him. She closed her eyes and let his soul's light guide her. She ignored the little darting selves of bugs and snakes, the background witchlight of the glass. Connor's soul was a tight-wound net, and after two dead ends she found him.

The glass walls were cracked here, and splinters tall as Tara sank into the scored dirt. Splashes of black spoiled the rainbow diffraction: curse that sunk into the glass and died there. Rocks were broken and burned. A dead bush in a boulder's lee dripped black icicles of curse, dormant without any life to reach for. Tara's passage drew them like a magnet. She knelt beside the bush, burned the curse to ash, and drifted on.

The canyon widened. There had been a battle here. There was only cathedral silence now. Connor sat on a rock that rose from the crushed glass. He still wore his funeral suit. So did she. Tara picked her way toward the rock. She slipped, set out a hand to stop her fall and almost cut herself on a sharp edge.

"There's a clear path to your left," he said.

"Thank you."

Connor did not seem surprised she was there. She had not spoken to announce herself, but she had not been sneaking up on him either. Not that she could have if she tried. He hunted. Once she'd seen him creep toward a drinking doe, moving through dry brush like a breeze, just to set his hand on her flank. She'd wanted to eat him when she saw that: to swallow him and take into her this thing he'd done that she could not, the joy of this power to pass unnoticed and to touch. She settled for asking how the fur felt, and he said, "Rough."

On the way to the rock she knocked over a tall pane of glass. It shattered, and the echoes were still settling as she climbed the rock and sat beside him. He shifted to make room.

"I was afraid you'd run. I couldn't catch you in these shoes."

The rainbows in the walls cast strange shades on his skin; he did a thing with his mouth that looked like a smile. There were gulches and ravines inside him, places in his heart that he'd scouted for the same reasons he had learned the twists and turns of these canyons as a child. No matter how well he thought he knew the maze he could still lose himself inside. He had a different kind of beauty when he retreated there: the beauty of a closed box or a labyrinth wall. "You could have witched me back. Stopped my legs, or frozen me in place."

Serious, or teasing? A bit of both, she decided, and let him run with it. "I find that's a bad way to start a conversation." She picked up a piece of gravel, and bounced it in her palm. "'Witch' is pejorative, you know. You'll hurt my feelings."

"I know what 'pejorative' means. And I don't think I could ever hurt your feelings."

"You might be surprised."

"What should I call . . . what you are . . . instead?"

"Just call me Tara."

He came out of his maze at that, and she saw the other him: unguarded, wondering, amused. "Where did you get that scar on your neck? The silver one?"

"I was fighting a god. Well. Gods."

"Why?"

"A lot of reasons. My friends were in trouble. And I wanted to learn a secret."

"What secret?"

She thought about the black folder, the crystal records inside, the click of clawed footsteps drawing nearer across the stars. "How the world would end."

"Did you?"

She heard those footsteps in her nightmares. "I hope not."

He laughed at that. "You know, you haven't changed after all."

"What's that supposed to mean?"

"You'd always talk about the weirdest stuff back when we were kids, and act like it was normal, like of course everyone would know what you were talking about. Sometimes your head would be here in Edgemont, sometimes a thousand miles that way, and you never seemed to know the difference."

A thousand miles that way was nowhere special, but she didn't push the point. It felt good to sit here beside him and not argue. "The weirdest stuff? Like what?"

"Like, I don't know, the time Emperor Whoever the Sixth invaded Agdel Lex in the year Nine Eagle, or how some poem was really about Maestre Schatten's three theories on the under-conscious or, like, geometry."

"It would have been Emperor Whoever the Second. Later Telomeri dynasties didn't last long enough to hit sixes and sevens, because the emperors were more or less immortal."

"See?"

"And they called it Alikand back then."

"Does it matter?"

She had to laugh at that. "Yes." She threw her stone, and it bounced off a large piece of curse-stained glass.

"The glass is sturdier than it looks," he said. "Works better if you hit it near the edge." His throw took a chip off. It sparked as it fell.

"You spend a lot of time out here."

"Grandpa taught me. He came out this way for thinking, and hunting. Music. When I was a kid I started to follow him. Dad wasn't much for it, he always said there was work I should be do-ing. Which I guess was how the old man taught him. But after Grandpa died, when Dad would get to shouting, the more he'd shout the more I'd come here—for days at a time when I could." He took some silence for himself. She feared he might collapse back into that maze. "I've been small today. Thinking only of my-self. Of my feelings."

"You? Selfish?" Laughing wouldn't fix the situation. "That sounds more like your dad. And me, for provoking him. I'm sorry. You came here to be alone. I don't read other people's signals well."

"How are you?"

The question stopped her, because she wasn't used to answering it honestly. "Pissed. Confused. Sad. Then angry again. At Pa, at Ma, at myself, at the whole town for the way they looked at me graveside like I was about to spit lightning or grow wings. At your father. He didn't have any right to say what he said. This is a mess and we're all upset. But I don't blame you."

"You should." He rolled on before she could find words to disagree: "When the raids got worse and Dad started talking about how we all had to serve the town together, I thought maybe I could use what I knew. Prove myself. I talked it over with your pa. How if we had to run, we could escape through the canyons, or we could put sentries out here, or traps, in case the Raiders tried to sneak up on us this way. So I scouted the maze, and the tunnels that lead from it."

"And one day the Raiders came." She didn't want to hear the story, but she could not bring herself to stop him.

"The Seer was with them, eight feet tall with eyes like pits. I ran as fast as I could, but they were faster. Your pa saved me. I told him to run, there were so many. He wouldn't let me pull him back. He told me to go, get help, I listened. He had to stand." He drew a ragged breath. "I never saw a man fight like that. When I found my dad coming down the canyon with the others—I told him where to go, and how to get there, but before he went he looked at me like he'd seen some hole where my heart ought to be."

She hugged him. You didn't have weapons, was what she later thought she should have said. The Raiders are full of curses and viciousness, and this Seer is not the kind of thing you face head on, unarmed. If you'd stayed, there would have been two funerals in Edgemont—and they wouldn't have waited on me for yours.

Pa should have run with you. Maybe he would have, if he hadn't fled a bigger war when he was a younger man, if he hadn't felt he'd worn out his lifetime's supply of running. Baker and DuChamp were dead and his best friend had cried through the town for strong men to stand and defend their homes. And I left him there with something to prove and a need, a duty, to protect someone he still thought of as a child. "It's okay" were pitiful words. It wasn't. But she pulled him against her and felt the warmth of his body and his cheek against hers. She trusted that warmth over the voices in her head.

"He was a good man," he said into her shoulder. "He saved my life. But I can't stop running away."

Tara thought about the black folder, about her father, about the Seer. "He didn't want to worry you," Ma had said. As if she were still a child he could save. Connor couldn't have fought the Raiders, but Tara? If she hadn't been half a continent away, fretting about spiders beyond the stars, about the death of gods and the end of the world, about all those big and terrible things that were her responsibility, and yet did not seem to matter in the way that spade of dirt she'd thrown on her father's coffin mattered . . . If she had not been so far away, she could have made a difference. If she'd cared for these people, for her people, like she claimed to care for the world.

If Connor called himself a coward, what was she? She held him in the maze of glass, and he held her, and for all her emperors and geometry she could not say.

11

Tara had only been gone two hours, and the stream of guests and well-wishers bearing casserole had trickled off as folks went home to change and see to their day's work and make ready for the wake. But still Ma's wave when Tara walked up the winding path seemed tense, her smile the kind of fake-easy that, with Ma, meant that if someone wasn't sorry yet they would be soon.

Ma sat rocking on the bare porch, with a cup of tea. Gods, quick, take inventory. You've sweated through your suit, your shoes are a mess of dirt and glass-scratched all to hells, and you've been crying, but she can't fault you for that surely. Now, she will fault you for your disappearance, and that is hard to justify—so start there.

"I'm sorry." She slumped up the stairs, letting the exhaustion she'd kept in check on her walk through the village show through. "If I tried to keep my face up all day, I might have set someone on fire at the wake." An upward curl of the lip answered her. Ma had lived through the same pressure for months, without, apparently, murdering anyone. Or if she had, she'd covered it up. "Connor needed a shoulder. He blames himself. His dad hasn't let up. It's not fair."

"You should have brought a hat."

"I will next time." She wanted to collapse in the empty rocking chair by her mother's side, but Ma remained watchful, the professor granting the strangling student a few more feet of rope. Growing up in this house Tara had learned many gambits and passages of escape from these silences, in the same way kids who grew up fighting learned to fight. Most students came to the Hidden Schools from families more acquainted with the Craft than Tara's, so she'd grown to treasure her every edge and advantage over them, and this was one. But after the canyon maze, after the funeral and yesterday's march, she felt tired. "What did I do?"

Ma spread her hands. "What's missing?"

Porch, tea, Ma in funeral white with her hair up, waiting. Pa was missing—too bleak a joke for even Ma to make. Tara thought about funerals, the way houses looked after, gifts of food that would keep, of comfort, of—"Oh," she said, and "shit," and then realized she'd said it out loud in front of Ma and added, "I am so sorry. I'll talk to her."

"It's not that I mind"—indicating that she did—"save for the rosebushes, and those will recover. But the neighbors have been generous, and it has been a good season for flowers, and there have been questions. Given the general mood, I think we'd both rather keep those to a minimum."

"I'll talk to her," Tara repeated, already on her way inside.

Ma raised her tea and her eyebrows. "Mrs. Leary brought cookies. They're on the counter. Have one."

Tara almost let the screen door slam behind her—then caught it at the last minute and eased it shut. That could have gone better. Not that Ma could tell her to go choose a switch from the trees out back anymore. But Tara was taking a risk with Dawn, and that meant Ma was, too. The least Tara could do was pay attention.

The house was dark. The living room table was piled with empty pots and baskets. The bouquets in the kitchen were empty cones of bright paper.

Dawn sat cross-legged in a blue dress in the backyard, humming a song Tara did not recognize. To her left lay a teacup and saucer, a plate with crumbs, and a wicker basket in which a single tulip remained. The rosebushes were bare. The lawn had been picked free of daffodils and dandelions and clover. To her right there stood a mound of gray ash, shoulder-high.

"Good thing I didn't tell you to practice on herbs," Tara said. "If you'd touched Ma's garden not even I could save you."

"Tara! Look!" Dawn turned, excited, and grabbed the last tulip. She held the blossom cupped in both hands between them, and breathed out. A cold blue light burned in the petals—brighter than the sun, and clearer than the sky. As it burned, the tulip's color faded, consumed. When she let go they stuck in midair, the flower and the light, and they glittered in her wide eyes. "I can keep it going for—I lose count, but I think it's more than a minute."

More like two at this rate. In spite of her frustration Tara was impressed. "I told you to practice with the bouquet."

"I did! I only burned that patch of lawn over there, and I put it out by myself. But I ran out of bouquet just when I was starting to get the knack. It's like trying to peel an orange in one piece, isn't it? You start slow and listen to the flower as it breaks." The petals were shriveling now.

"If you push yourself too hard, you can lose control."

"I haven't, though. And I need to push, there's so much ground to catch up. How old were you when you started?"

"I didn't reach the Hidden Schools until I was about your age." Two years younger, but there was no point telling Dawn that.

"But you started learning earlier."

"Preliminaries. Building blocks."

"Like this."

Tara knelt before Dawn and closed her eyes to examine her work. There were many ways to make a light, though few would do so without heat. You could heat a specific spot until it caught fire. You could rub woven cords of Craft against themselves to generate heat. You could cause bits of a physical object to fluoresce. Dawn had addressed the light around her, which was a kind of pattern, a story told about itself, alive like rocks were alive. And she offered the flower's soul to the light, a bribe for it to gather in one place. Elegant. She knew kids who'd spent their first year at the Schools unlearning their assumption that the world was dead matter, but Dawn had come this far in a day. With the right foundation—with the right teachers—if Tara didn't screw her up first—what couldn't she accomplish? "There's a leak here." She pressed it into the proper form. "An inconsistency in your offer. You were losing a few fractions of a thaum per cycle."

"Oh," Dawn said, and Tara could tell from the tone of voice

that she understood, and was happy to be set right. Another leg up. Most could learn to take correction, but it was easier if you had that instinct from the start. "Thank you."

Tara sat back, conscious of grass and stains. But, hells, this suit needed dry cleaning already. She'd be down to her old skirts before long. "Ma's angry about her rosebushes. And the bouquets."

"She said I could—"

"You're a guest. Of course she did." She passed her fingers through the light, and felt no warmth. Nice work. "The neighbors will ask what happened to the flowers they gave her."

"Oh." She looked down. "I'm sorry. I'll apologize."

"You won't. Because they can't know what you were doing. They can't know who you are, what you can do." Puzzlement on her face. "They know I'm a Craftswoman, and it's tearing them apart. Cavanaugh, the man on the wall, the man who shot at us—he doesn't see a firm line between us and the Raiders. He's not the only one. Edgemont can ignore one Craftswoman long enough for me to bury my pa and leave. I don't think they could deal with two."

The flower's light went out. "Your mother told me what happened. To your father." She curled her hand around what was left of the blossom, and she curled herself around her hand. "It's hard. You keep expecting to see him around corners, through trees. When you speak, you hear his voice in yours. That's how it was for me, anyway. I'm sorry."

She was. She'd lost her own father, and here she was reaching out to Tara, and Tara couldn't take that. She wanted to help Dawn—because it was the right thing to do, and, if she was being totally honest, because this relationship was the one thing in Edgemont that felt like the world she knew. She knew what she was supposed to be for Dawn: a guide, a mentor. Someone who wasn't hurting.

"I will teach you," she said. "I'll teach you everything I know. But you have to be careful, until we're gone."

"It's so stupid! They can't stop the Raiders by themselves. They think that wall's going to save them. They need you, even if they can't see it. Why won't they let you help?"

"They're scared" was the best she could offer. "Their way isn't working, and they can't accept that." And she couldn't stay. Not with the black folder upstairs, and the work of the world waiting for her back home in Alt Coulumb. Not with Dawn trailing ash and dead land. "We'll stay for the wake. Tomorrow, we'll leave."

But that "why" lingered like the aftertaste of medicine, as the sun went down.

All Edgemont turned out for the wake. It was their way to ease the pressure of a death, a pressure that had built as Ma's letter wound from caravan to air freight to Alt Coulumb. Now that pressure vented all at once. Mrs. Leary led volunteers to spread food across the long tables dragged up from the church basement, and Grafton Cavanaugh and Cooper and Barnes and Nell Ott played banjos and drums as the dancers danced.

Old men and women gathered in clutches around the edge of the town green and spoke and drank and whispered and sang because their time had not yet come. When one couple took the center of the dance the old folks would stop to judge the whirls, the flips. Better, or worse than Dana Braxton and her boy twenty years ago? Do you remember that? They danced like water. And John Abernathy himself, before he left, he was finer still. They'd say that even if it wasn't true.

Ma presided, with no throne save the seat she chose, no dais save the space others left around her. That, too, was the nature of the wake. She had been cut off from these people by her sorrow and their echoes of that sorrow, their own fears when they thought of their husbands, wives, brothers, children dead. Now the space began to close. Mrs. Leary drew nearer, and Dana Braxton fetched a drink. Pastor Merrott tried to make a joke that only Ma laughed at, but when he went away they all laughed together, and he turned back to offer a self-mocking bow. As time rolled out in drumbeats and dances, Ma seemed less and less to preside, and the gap her friends allowed her dwindled, or she bloomed to fill it. The town repaired itself, taking back its own.

Tara drank. Mostly alone.

The Berrys had brought up a barrel laid down ten years before, and while it was not great whiskey or even good whiskey it had a rotgut weight and a roundness of age. She sipped it neat. It went down like fire and lingered like a burn.

Men and women she'd known as kids came by, toasted her, told stories about their children, their fields, their failures and small triumphs. She thought she was making the right noises in reply, and laughed at almost the proper times, but none of the conversations lasted long after the point where she had to offer stories of her own.

If she'd been a younger woman—not much younger, a few years would have done the trick—she would have blamed them for that silence. Tell an Edgemont farmer a story about skyscrapers and gargoyles and the vast depths of space, tell her about the movements of oceans of soul into which even Cavanaugh's farms would vanish as a rounding error, and her eyes would glaze over. Describe your own recent work conspiring with priests and gods and Deathless Kings to fight, maybe, if you can, a threat none of you can quite believe exists because its magnitude eclipses even your imagination—you could scare them, but you couldn't make them believe.

That's what she would have thought when she was younger. And in a sense it was true. Their eyes glazed over, sure. She couldn't talk about her work, her life. But they didn't need her to. These men and women she'd once known and still remembered drew close to her for the same reason her mother's friends gathered near. They wanted to bind her in, to weave her back.

Her memories of Edgemont were memories of distance, difference, of being what she, a kid without much experience of hate, thought was *hated*. They sensed her as a thing apart, and they'd had two options, as any body has for a splinter lodged deep: to consume the outsider, or reject it.

She had left them behind to become herself. She was back now. Soon, she'd have to leave again. She could not let herself belong here.

She looked for Connor, but he was not nearby. Maybe he was standing watch.

Dawn danced. Tara didn't have to look hard to find her, a shock of blond among dark hair, dark skin. She wore a dress of Tara's, short on her and loose, but it flared when she turned and her hair flared, too. She said yes to it all, to the music and the night and the dancers, turning to one and then the next, as hungry for this as she was for the Craft, as if she could spin the web of the town all through herself. For all the anger in her voice earlier, she loved the night, these people, new knowledge and promises of mastery swelling in her mind. The girl had known more than her share of pain, but neither Edgemont nor the Craft had hurt her yet.

She was young. She could grow through and past what she'd been, layer by layer, until the bonds that once held her would be no more than a ripple in her bark.

Gods, Tara. Listen to yourself. What are you, thirteen? Eighty? A Zurish poet? What? Tara rolled her eyes and tested the Berry rotgut again, and when the thick-necked young man who'd guarded the wall that afternoon came up and tried, awkwardly, to hit on her, it crossed her mind to take him out beyond the firelight, have a sober conversation about boundaries and safety, and then, that being sorted, spoil him for farm girls. It had been long enough since her last decent uncomplicated fuck.

She was tired and drunk and missed home. Which this both was and wasn't.

So she excused herself for a moment, in a way that perhaps left Farm Boy options open for later, and lurched out into the night to—

Pray. Ugh. She felt dirty thinking the word. She'd become a different woman in the years since she left home, left the Hidden Schools, arrived in Alt Coulumb, but still inside her lived that girl who asked, What can a goddess do for me that can't I do myself?

Some things never changed. But others did.

The moon was up, here and back in Alt Coulumb. Behind her the dancers formed a circle and in their center one by one Edgemonters came forth and danced animal dances, spirit dances, memories of centuries-gone tradition that once had gods in it, that even now sometimes caught the fire and the stars and the clapping beat and smelted it to meaning, to the stuff of souls.

She walked around the church so it would block out the fire and the dancers, and sat on the rear steps facing the cemetery. She poured out some of the rotgut and breathed in the smell of alcohol and turned earth. The moon's silver reflection glinted in the puddle.

And Tara prayed, to Seril Undying, Lady of the Moon, Lady of Alt Coulumb, whose light is justice and comfort, and whose priestess, of a sort, she was. Seril had been an outcast, too, for decades, exiled from her city by her people, proclaimed heretical. What better goddess for a Craftswoman to—let's not say serve, shall we? Stand within, stand beside. They'd each saved the other enough times for the patronage relationship to run both ways.

Hi, she prayed. *I'm sorry I left so fast. I couldn't be with people. Yes, you're people, don't get cute.* Intoxication did not, thankfully, preclude prayer. Or the other way around. *I had to come here for the funeral, but I didn't realize how much I left behind.*

It's bad out here. I found this girl, she's a self-taught Craftswoman and she's been hurt and she's afraid and I'd tear the ones who made her suffer to pieces with my bare hands but they're dead already. If she stays here this town will bring the pitchforks out for her like they did for me, and I hate them for that even though they need my help. And even though I missed them.

I don't need anything. I just wanted to talk. Please, tell everyone in Alt Coulumb that I miss them. That I can't wait to come home. A pause, in which she reflected on deities' general tendency toward literal-mindedness, and this specific goddess's tendency toward sarcasm. *Not everyone in Alt Coulumb, I mean. Just the usuals. Abelard and Cat and Shale and—you know. My friends.*

Silence, moonlight, stars. She waited, and made herself open, which was the heart of prayer.

When the answer came, it was wrong.

—*eed to he—ain, reply haz—n't unde—re are yo—*

Into the openness of her soul a sandstorm came, scouring,

bearing shards of glass and clods of dirt and bugs and lizard bits. The rotgut pool caught fire, and clouds boiled up to block the sky. She recoiled on the church steps, cursing, clutching her singed fingers.

Behind her, beneath the music, she heard screams.

12

She could not see what was wrong at first. The diffuse gathering of villagers, dancing, singing, trading stories, had become a dense knot of crowd, gathered to watch something terrible that she could not see. She heard cries and questions. She tried to shoulder through a wall of burly men and farm-strong women, and thought about the behavior of flocks.

The Hidden Schools studied such phenomena intensely. They sponsored chairs where skullcapped seers sat to peer down from the lower balconies at starlings over sedge fields, black lungs breathing in the sky. Murmuration, nuisance, swarm, murder, parliament, each group of birds responded to wind or threats or food with behavior no less complex than that of single beings in a single skin.

After all, what was an animal—you, your kid, your dog—but an association of smaller creatures to whom a grain of sand would seem a monument, as united in their own way as those starlings, locusts, rooks, and crows?

As above, so below. Call a group of starlings a murmuration. Call a group of cells an animal, a plant, a person. Call the entity that is a group of human beings a god.

And the small god that was Edgemont was afraid.

Once she thought of it like that, she could model its dynamics, and knew where to step. There were holes in any crowd, and currents she could use. She found one and let it bear her forward, and at last when people pressed too close for her to move, she lit her glyphs and pushed. They parted before her like the sea in a mystery play.

And there stood Connor, with a wounded man in his arms.

She felt surprisingly calm. She realized, surrounded by former classmates and not-quite-friends staring on in terror that she felt more at ease in a panicked crowd than she had felt making small talk in the town where she grew up.

Set that aside for now. Think of them as clients, if it helps.

She ran to Connor—she may have called his name. He sank to his knees and settled the hurt man down. The crowd clustered close. She ordered, "Stay back." She did not use the voice of Tara Abernathy the schoolteachers' daughter, and her face wore an expression they'd never seen. They obeyed.

The man was ashen with pain, bleeding from his stomach and from raw welts around his wrists. Pulse rapid and shallow, breath wet. Gods, Tara hated pretending she was a doctor. She saw old man Braxton closest in the mess, holding of all the damn things his tambourine, but still sober enough for her purposes. "I need clean water and clean rags. Needle. Thread. Bandages. Go." He went. Connor's side was wet with blood. Not his. "What happened?"

"I was on watch. This guy ran up out of the Badlands like the whole world was after him. Fell ten feet from the wall."

"Not one of ours." It was half a question. There were new families in Edgemont since she left, though not many.

He shook his head. "They must have taken him. He got away. Those wrists look like they've been tied with rope."

"Wire," she corrected. "Raiders?"

A nod. His eyes wide. "A storm's building out there, Tara." She could see it, too. Mountains of cloud to the west, carved from the dark by green lightning. He was afraid. Good.

Grafton Cavanaugh burst through the circle. "What is this?" Then he saw the body. "Farnham."

"Raiders, Dad. He got away, and they're coming after him." Tara was ready for the big man to sneer, but for once Grafton Cavanaugh seemed selfless, genuine, concerned. He shouted orders to the crowd, rallying the militia, and they moved out to the wall. Connor looked to her. He wanted to stay, he had to go. She remembered what he'd said in the canyon. Always running away. What was running away, now? To follow his father to the wall, or to stay here by her side?

"Go," she said, and he went. Tara missed him, but who had

time to feel things anyway? She worked to stabilize the client. Farnham. Where had she heard that name? Oh yes. The Farnhams were one of the Blake's Rest families. She'd seen this man before. He'd been ten years younger then, and not dying. But Blake's Rest meant—

Dawn and Ma and Pastor Merrott reached the front of the crowd at once, and Ma and the Pastor ran to kneel beside Tara. Dawn drew up sharp, her face a mask. Farnham shifted on the ground and his eyes focused and the desperation in his features took on a new and personal edge. Dawn advanced, wooden. Tara thought about broken ribs and dead goats, and about the clean-burning anger she'd sensed behind Dawn's will to learn the Craft, to get out, to leave Blake's Rest and the Kathic plains behind and be someone, anyone but the girl who'd worked that farm.

But she had also watched the others die, dragged away by monsters. She heard their screams. And here was young Farnham.

Perhaps she wanted him dead. But it was one thing to want and another to see the man there bleeding and broken and scared.

"Dawn," Tara began, and would have finished, *stay back*, but Dawn stepped forward like a puppet and knelt by Farnham's side, just out of that trembling hand's reach. Tara recognized her brittle stillness: great engines locked gears inside Dawn's heart, strength pitted against strength generating stillness and heat. Or else that was Tara projecting herself onto Dawn, and that silence was mourning, or anger she was choking down, or fear. Or an entomologist's detachment, watching a specimen writhe.

Tara turned to Merrott. "Pastor. Can you help him?"

His hands glowed golden on Farnham's chest, but his brow was damp and he looked weary. "Not while the guards draw our faith." Without his blessing, Cavanaugh and the others would be left with their bad homemade armor on the wall, facing Raiders. Sheep before wolves. "I can dull his pain." Which was a genuine help, Tara reminded herself as her first thoughts ran more uncharitable courses: ah yes, so I'll just do it all myself as usual, and, you see, this is why I don't trust priests. Though she technically was one. She'd never tried to heal anyone with Seril's power, but there was a first time for everything. She tried to open her heart—

but the prayer line was full of sand and howling static, and clouds choked the moon.

Gods. Always so damn situational.

"Coming through!"

That was Braxton, with the bandages. At least *this* was proceeding as she had foreseen. "Keep it up," she told the Pastor. Braxton was sweating but he'd brought an armful of clean cloth that would serve, and a jug of water. Her social reflexes thanked him, while the rest of her planned the operation. She could use her work knife—which would mean pulling a blade of moonlight from her heart in front of all these villagers. Not to mention the shadows, the cold, and the dimming stars.

But, hells, they'd spent all day looking at her as if they expected a show. Might as well give them one. They were afraid, and they didn't trust her, but she had no time for gentleness. Farnham was dying—and while she might be tempted to say good riddance, she wasn't about to let all these Coopers and Braxtons and Learys and Cavanaugh cousins watch her fail.

She was about to speak when Dawn screamed.

Farnham's trembling hand snared her wrist. Black oil bubbled from the wound in his stomach and climbed his chest to his arm, sinking hooks into his flesh and reaching for Dawn. The curse's white threads seethed beneath the black, and more threads turned in Farnham's eyes. Merrott recoiled as if from a snake. Ma tried to drag Dawn away but Farnham would not let go. Dawn was lost in panic, prying at the man's grip. She broke two of his fingers but he did not notice. His mouth split in a mindless grin.

Curse tendrils lashed at Dawn, barbed and dripping. Tara grabbed them.

She did not realize what she was doing until it was done. The curse strained against the glyphs on her palm and around her fingers, writhing fishlike, clawing her. The pain struck, electric and searing, but she could not let go, would not let the curse take Dawn.

This was her fight. This was a thing she understood as she had never understood this town, as she had never even understood her parents: this hunger, this darkness, this desire to possess. It was the seed of Craft. She tried to crush the curse, to deny it, but it crawled through her fingers, up her wrist, up her arm. Her glyphs tried to armor her in shadow, but not fast enough—the curse found a gap above her elbow, and pierced her, and began to saw.

She gritted her teeth against the pain as it moved inside her. Her cry was lost in others'—Edgemonters recoiling in terror as strands of curse slipped free of Tara's grip and reached again for Dawn.

Then, from the depths of her fear, Dawn laughed—hysterical, haughty, furious, mad. Her eyes burned white, and shadow rolled from her.

Time did not work the way it should. Gravity suspended. Hunger claimed Tara, her world the inside of a cold cold mouth, as the tongue convulsed, as a gullet crushed her and dragged her down.

Screams somewhere. Not hers. She would have been screaming, though, if she could just remember where she left her voice.

There was no law in this place but need, and will.

Good thing she had plenty of both.

She willed Edgemont into shape around her. She willed the Coopers and the Braxtons and the Learys and Cavanaughs and the abandoned banjo and Ma and Merrott and Dawn. Her glyphs burned, and her knowledge cast its own shadow, deeper, dense, controlled.

The darkness broke and the village green snapped back: torches, bonfire, grass, stars, storm clouds, Coopers, Braxtons, Learys, Cavanaughs, banjo, Ma, Merrott. Dawn.

Farnham was a skeleton, sinking in a bed of ash.

Black dust slipped from Tara's skin, leaving a burned trail between her glyphs. Blood welled from the pit the curse had dug into her arm. The pain lingered, and with it fury and fear.

Ma. Gods and demons, Ma had been right there at the heart of it. There she was. Shaking her hands where they'd touched Dawn's skin, not with the panic of a cold burn, just the instinctive recoil of a woman whose shower had, without warning, forgotten hot water was a thing.

Dawn was laughing, crying, both. She looked up at Tara with a victor's wild disbelief.

Behind her stood the crowd. Staring. Afraid. Tara heard that fear bloom into anger. Edgemont gathered away from Tara, away from Dawn, the blind god taking shape.

Tara knew these people. She had grown up beside them.

She knew what they could do when they were angry.

Sand whipped through the air. Behind her, storm clouds charged the wall. She heard bowstrings, and the first cries of pain. The attack had begun.

Gods, her arm hurt. Her wound throbbed as if it was alive. Not a good sign.

She forced herself to her feet. Blood dripped down her arm, stained her shirt and jacket, fell from her fingertips to spot the soil. She marched through ash and the dead man's body to Dawn's side, and helped her up. Tara's moonlight and silver work knife burned in her grip, and in its light she saw her blood-streaked hand veined with black. The pain could wait. She boxed it up for later. She had to be an icon now, image more than flesh, implacable, furious, and pure. "Dawn is my student," she told the town. "She just saved your lives. Show some gratitude."

She did not face the crowd. She faced Mrs. Leary first, then Nell Ott, then grizzled John Thibodault, then Vaughan Braxton. She could have shouted into the echoing silence to no effect and never touched the heartless god they'd formed between them. But not one of them could stand alone against her.

She was done pretending to be weak, to be like them, to be anything other than what she was. Her wound burned and bled. She wanted to make something suffer, and if she wasn't careful, it would be these people she'd grown up beside. Fortunately, there were other options to hand.

She pulled Dawn to her feet. "Come on," she said. And, to the Pastor, still staring at Dawn and the skeleton and the ash on Tara's shoes: "You, too. All of you. We're going to the wall."

13

Anger drove her to the wall, a hammering engine in her heart like the enormous steam contraptions Abelard built to drive the trains of Alt Coulumb. Anger drew the village behind her, Dawn and Pastor Merrott and Ma and the rest. It would have pulled others too: the dead of Blake's Rest, sure, and why not add more, pile all the bodies from Alikand and Alt Coulumb in her wake, shovel Denovo's victims and all the God Wars corpses in a sledge with cold iron wheels to bear the weight. She would drag them. Anger was the only fuel she'd need, and anger was endless.

"I told you," she said, her voice tight as her grip on Dawn's wrist, "to be careful. I told you to keep yourself under control."

"He was hurting you! He would have killed them all if we weren't there."

"And they might have killed us."

"You would have stopped them."

"I did stop them. Without scaring anyone, or hurting anyone. Because I kept control."

"You shouldn't have to."

"They're scared, Dawn."

"They're idiots. We saved their lives. They should thank us. It's not fair."

"Of course it's not fair. What single thing ever is? But we have a job to do."

"What job?"

She pointed up.

Lightning-lit storm clouds towered over the wall and pressed down against the blue lacework of Edgemont's wards. The wind smelled of ozone and desert. From the wall, she heard the bow-strings' twang and the answering report of cursethrowers. Those were the outward signs of the struggle, its traces in the physical world. But they were not the truth.

"Think of this as a work-study session. Lesson three. Close your eyes."

Dawn did, and gasped. Tara felt a surge of pride, under her fury. The girl had the sight already. She was a good student.

"I see it. In the storm. Like . . . threads."

"The curse," Tara said, "is a crude thing. Back in the God Wars, the Craft was young, and its workers were not so subtle yet. It's hard to build a careful weapon, but it is easy to build a hungry one. The curse is a slightly smarter slime mold. It converts everything it comes across into a tool to feed itself." She blinked, and saw what Dawn saw: the storm as a circling, howling thicket of thin black thorns and worming white thread, trailing a pus-laden umbilical from the Badlands: a link to the Raiders' hive, a conduit for their power and their hunger. "If those roots get past the wall, they'll eat the town's soul, and its people. So that's our job: stop it." She cracked her neck. "Think of it as your first pro bono case."

"How can we fight that?"

"Do you see that thin curving wall? Off-blue color? Those are the town wards. Edgemont tells a story by existing: we are a place. We are here, and here is us. All beings tell themselves the same kind of lie."

"What lie?"

"That they exist."

"Don't they?"

"Not for long. Not on any timescale that matters. Not like a number exists, unchanging and integral. People die. Towns die. Nations, gods, worlds. The curse argues against Edgemont—by pressing through, by claiming territory. If the Raiders work past our walls, they'll claim this land belongs to them, and drink it dry."

"That's . . ."

"Facile logic. But it works, out here, far from the Courts of Craft. If we hold those wards, we'll win. If not, we'll see."

Guards fought on the wall: they shot bows and crossbows, and took cover as curse bolts tore the rampart. A heavier blast cracked the wall itself. Packed soil sloughed down into the village and a glowing body tumbled through the air. She could not see who it was. She almost let the guard fall, then thought of Connor, and slowed his plunge with a wave and with a hundred thaums she knew she'd miss later.

The guard landed safe. He wasn't Connor, but the younger man, the farmer who'd hit on her at the wake. Gasping, dazed, a hole torn in his thick neck by a splinter of wood. She didn't know his name. He should survive, with care. If they stopped the attack.

Tara marched toward the breach.

Ma caught her wrist.

Tara turned back. What Ma saw when Tara looked at her, Tara could only guess, but it was not what she had expected. When she met Tara's eyes she only said, "Come back to me." As if she were talking to someone else, saying words she wished she'd said some other time.

"I will." Flashes of curse and guard-light washed the town. Storm winds howled. Ma let her go.

Tara turned to Dawn, and to Pastor Merrott. "Follow me." Her arm ached. She woke a long-dormant glyph to stem the blood flow and keep her tissues animate. She glared at the others behind her. "Since I came home, you've all watched me from the corners of your eyes, waiting for me to grow horns and raise the dead. You want a show? Here it is."

She marched up air toward the gap in the wall.

"Um," Pastor Merrott said. "We're. That is."

"Flying." That was Dawn, in wonder.

When they settled atop the wall, Tara said to Dawn, "Never do this. Anger is a bad foundation for Craftwork. What you work when mad, you will work wrong. When you've gathered power, even a moment's rage can do great harm. And if you forgive yourself the harm you do when you're angry, you'll train yourself to work still greater evil calm."

The fury-engine pounding inside her lent its force to her voice. She was briefly conscious of the irony before the irony, too, burned.

"But you're doing it anyway," Dawn said.

Tara shrugged, and turned to the battlefield.

Beyond the wall, darkness. Raiders galloped half-seen through the sandstorm, impaled upon their bone steeds, two beings made one by the writhing curse. They trailed the storm like a banner. At a word from Cavanaugh the guards loosed arrows, but the storm caught them and turned most aside. One thudded into the rib cage of a Raider who had only half a face, and when he cackled at the pain, lightning bridged the gap between his teeth. The curses they threw from their arms were corkscrews of black that glanced off armor or sank into flesh. The blast that shattered the wall had come from the storm itself, and another built there as the Raiders circled, circled, nearer.

"Tara!" Connor slid to meet them in the breach, bow at the ready, face bright with guard-light. She was fiercely glad to see him, but there was no time. Another blast like the first would split the wall. She imagined Connor's neck opened like the neck of the farmer boy below, his body pierced through, or missing from the ribs down.

The guards were tiring. Their light dimmed. Cracks spread through the lattice shield.

"Pastor," Tara said. "I need you to let me run the village wards. The alarms, the guard-light, all of it." He drew back from her outstretched bloody hand. "You can't stop them. I will."

He was a good pastor, which was to say that he was a man not made for war. But he was strong enough to trust her. He took her hand, and the wards poured into her. She felt those knotted cords of village faith, Edgemont straining to exist against the storm. Paltry, ill-woven work. Surely the town that had scared her for so long was more than this?

In the dark beyond her closed eyes Tara saw the real world, the bare world, all accidents of skin and meat rubbed away. The wards of Edgemont in her hands were a web of blue thread, spread through the community, binding its fields and buildings and people. She held them all, the guards' light and strength, the minor turnings-aside of ill fate, and that stupid, stupid alarm. They pulsed in her grip, something larger than a rabbit's heart, smaller than a deer's.

She sorted the alarm from the other wards: a ragged loop of light. She needed it: not for the construct itself, clanging uselessly now, but for the boundary it represented, the insistence that the invading force should not be here.

Gods, but it was poorly wrought. She'd expected its triggering line to be anchored to some conceptual geometry or demarcation—the town limits, say. A surveyor's map. No luck. It wasn't even a circle. They'd just sent some kids out with sticks and told them to draw a line. Stupid theology. If you work the Craft with things that only represent themselves, the knife a knife, the bowl a bowl, the corpse a corpse, you have no symbolic leverage, no room to maneuver.

No sense whining about it. She could work with this. But she needed power, more than she held in her own soul, more than she could gather from starlight with that storm bearing down. She held Edgemont's wards. She could drain the whole town if need be—no. Bad idea. She was trying to stop the Raiders, not do their job for them.

She needed power to fight back. So she'd have to find some.

Edgemont's guards shone on the wall beside her, radiant with the Pastor's blessing. The guard-light kept them whole, strong, and safe. It was their last line of defense against the darkness, but it wasn't enough to win. And she could make better use of that power.

She snapped the guard-light. All along the wall, the guards lost their strength. The faith that powered them rushed into her—and now she turned her attention to that line around the village, the little trench they'd dug to make their alarm, which was, if Cavanaugh or Pastor Merrott or anyone out here had the skill and wit to use it, a better wall than any mass of pounded dirt.

Tara's recent experience of priesthood hadn't left her with much of an appetite for intercessory prayer, but she offered one now: *Seril, Lady of Light, save me from amateurs.*

Edgemont had few ties to the Craft. It could not draw on the power of the Courts to protect itself, the weight of so many million Craftworkers' faith that the world worked a certain way. But Tara could. And, with the power of the guard-light, she could make a claim. There was a history of continuous occupation here, a claim to identity and integrity in the half-made wards she held. And if the Craft understood anything, it understood property.

Great engines built to take the place of gods surged now in answer to her call, staking Edgemont's claim to these fields, this patch of rock.

Blue-white fire erupted from the ragged alarm-line in the dirt, and towered to the sky. She raised her hands, shadow-clad and clawed. Flames lanced into the storm.

And the storm screamed.

The pus-white strings and black thorns of curse withered like the petals of Dawn's flowers. The curse was a dumb and hungry mind, built to feed by scared people in a hurry. Modern Craft was a mechanism more subtle and vast, and so much hungrier. What remained of the curse fled those flames, back through the umbilical to its hive, howling in fear across the desert.

And then the storm was only wind.

Dawn shuddered beside her, rapt.

Tara opened her eyes.

The Raiders were running, those left alive. The storm settled. She sagged against the wall, and handed what was left of Edgemont's wards back to Pastor Merrott. He fumbled the catch, but did not let them fall.

Exhaustion took her then.

When she exhaled, her breath froze water in the air. She turned to say something to the girl beside her, or to the man whose presence made her heart beat faster, but she could not remember their names, or what order she had to tense the muscles in her leg and lower back to keep from falling. She began to fold.

The others caught her and held her up. They helped her from the wall. Without meaning to, she drew life from them. Color came back, and names. Merrott, Dawn. Connor said, "You saved us."

But Grafton Cavanaugh—another name—was marching toward her. "What did you do?" Furious.

Connor, simple and dear: "She stopped them, Dad."

"The guard-light's broken!" He advanced on Tara with his finger out—but by now she'd worked out which muscles raised her head, and when he met her eyes he shuddered. Maybe he saw the shadows in them. "The wall's breached. There are more Raiders in the desert, and you've left us defenseless. They'll come back, and they'll come to kill. And you'll be gone. In your whole selfish life you never spared one thought for the folk who raised you, for your father or mother or your town. You wanted to punish us. Fine. You have. Now get out of here. Run away and leave those of us with roots to tend them."

No one spoke. Many watched. His voice echoed. There was blood on his face, and blood on his hands.

Hers, too.

Tara said, "No."

She shook off Connor's arm, and stood on her own. Grafton Cavanaugh took a step back. She saw herself reflected in his eyes—furious, licked with shadow and flame. She had wasted too much time being careful. Dawn was right. They did not understand. So it was her job to make them understand. Lightning danced between her fingers, and her glyphs burned. Out of the corner of her eye, she saw Dawn grinning fiercely.

"Your wards," she said, "were patchwork hedge witchery. A stiff wind could have broken them. That's not your fault. You were weak. You did the best you could.

"But I can do better. I will. I will build you new defenses. I will remake your guard-light, stronger. And we will stand against the Raiders when they come.

"What I just did was a challenge. They know I'm here. They want revenge, and they want my strength. They will come for me in a host, with their Seer at the head. At the death of the moon, when their power is great. And I will break them. I am the Chief Craftswoman to Kos Everburning and Seril the Lady of Light of Alt Coulumb. I have wrestled gods, and I will not abandon you." She breathed out the last of her rage and said, softer now, "My father would have wanted me to stay."

That was a lie. She knew it, and so did Grafton Cavanaugh. But he could not argue.

Neither could Connor, for all the horror on his face—or was that awe? In the canyons he'd told her he wanted to stop running. But she had thrown a gauntlet. He would ask her later, in private, if there was another way. Later, too, Tara's mother would hug her fiercely and Tara would remember her saying "He did not want to worry you," and wonder for whom her pa had been afraid, and why.

———

That night while the others slept, Tara stripped to her bra on the back porch in front of the whispering corn, and tried to clean her wound. She'd left her shirt in cold water to soak. Little hope for the jacket, but it was black and with luck the stain would not show. She swabbed blood from her skin with a sponge; the back of her neck prickled, and her arms were gooseflesh. If there were any justice in the world she would have been asleep for hours now.

If there were any justice in the world, that wasn't the only thing that would be different.

Welts climbed her left arm where the curse had struck her— raised lines that would scab and crack over the next few days. Those didn't worry her.

There was a shallow hole in her arm. Her glyphs were trying to knit the tissue closed, but when she set her knife above the wound and squinted by its light, she saw something black and slick and squirming inside her. She might have thought it was a shadow, if she had been an idiot. When her knife drew nearer to her flesh, the slick thing twitched against her muscle, burrowing.

She pinched her knife's blade fine and sharp with the fingers of her left hand, and scratched a circle around the puncture in her biceps, just in case. She folded her tie into a wad of silk, tested it between her teeth.

She pressed the blade into her arm. Her jaw clamped down. Her teeth bit hand-painted silk. A tight noise escaped her throat.

Kos and Seril, the cut was just a few millimeters deep, but she felt as if she'd shoved a hot poker through her arm. The curse wriggled. That was worse than the pain—almost worse—feeling something that was not her moving in her flesh. She would have turned off the nerves in her arm, but if she did that she'd have no way of tracking it, if it tried to run.

Just a little deeper. Her blade's tip found something that was not *her*. The blade parted like a pair of tweezers, and she caught it. She bit down on the tie in her mouth, and pulled.

The curse fought back. Tiny barbs sank into her muscles; it spread roots toward her nerves. She felt like she was trying to pull herself inside out through that wound. She almost threw up into her tie. Of all things it was the thought of the conversation she'd have to have with her dry cleaner back home that saved her that indignity. She heard a low long agonized sound and mistook it for someone nearby doing something horrible to livestock, before she realized it came from her own throat.

The curse withered as she pulled, but a small piece dug deep, down into the meat of her arm, a dense hard knot inside her flesh. It wrapped around her bone and drank the strength she used to pull against it.

She could do this. Just a bit more. It had to break sometime. It had to—

She felt it scrape her bones.

The world went away for a while, except for the parts that hurt.

When the heaving pain passed, she found herself awake, lying on her side. A trail of spit connected her mouth and the wadded tie. Her knife had vanished when she passed out.

She did not want to lift her arm and hold it to the stars, to the moonlight. Did not want to see what was left of her. But there were many things Tara Abernathy had not wanted to do in life, and she'd done most of them already.

Where the hole in her arm had been, she saw a glossy black circle shot through with white threads. The containment glyph on her biceps burned silver and pale against the black. She felt the curse bunched up hard and hot inside, as those white threads tested the cage she'd built for them—snakelike, vicious, hissing. The glyph would hold for now. But she was cursed.

In frustration, in fury, she tried to pray. Seril might be able to heal Tara, if she could reach her with a prayer. But when she tried to open her mind the curse in her arm lurched hungrily. The spiritual vulnerability a priestess assumed in communion with the divine was, to put it mildly, contraindicated when you had a monster nestled in your arm.

So Tara lay on her back, breathing hard. Far above, the stars laughed at her.

What a godsforsaken mess.

She needed medical attention. She couldn't save herself, and the Pastor couldn't beat this. Two nights' walk would take her to a rail station, and she could hitch from there to Addington where the small airfield would flare for a dragon to Chikal, or all the way back to Alt Coulumb. Surgery, two days to recover, three at the outside, then a red-eye back—she could make the round trip in a week, leaving one week to prepare Edgemont for the Raiders' counterattack. Which wasn't enough time.

She had looked Grafton Cavanaugh in the eye, promised to save this town, and dared him to call her a liar.

The curse pressed cold against her glyphs, but they would hold, for now—if she was careful, if she didn't push herself. Two weeks. She could make it that long. And if the curse claimed a little more of her arm, well, she could live with the consequences. There would be time to recover, later.

So long as it didn't reach her heart.

She made a fist and felt a coal of pain inside her arm, but the muscle kept its strength. When she relaxed, she thought the curse looked no larger than before.

14

After the battle came a day of rawness and rest. Families saw to their wounded, counted their losses. The farm boy whose neck had been torn open turned out to be a Braxton cousin by the name of Tomas. Tara came to their house to offer help, but Esther Braxton met her grim and quiet on her porch and would not let Tara inside. Tara gave her antibiotic salve and told her how to use it, and tried to let the matter go.

You could only dictate so much even with a normal client, and Edgemont was not a normal client. Nor did they see her as their Craftswoman. What then? A prodigal daughter? A cuckoo chick in the nest?

Tara was too tired to be angry. Esther Braxton and the others had reasons for their fear. Stupid reasons, provincial ones. Dawn had killed a man and turned a patch of the village green to ash. Now there was a smooth divot of soil six feet across and three feet deep carved out of the grass. It would always be cold to the touch. They'd shoveled out the ash, so they did not have to ask themselves which bits of the drifting white dust had been soil and which bone. They had seen Tara, uncloaked, break a Raider attack single-handed. They did not understand and so they were afraid.

Hands that did such things were not healer's hands. And, to be fair, Tara had wanted to scare the shit out of them.

She slept most of the first day.

She carried some reserves of soul in case of emergency: a stash of coins; a six-armed statue of a fanged and skull-necklaced Dhistran goddess Raz had given her, which Tara liked because the goddess always seemed to be winking and giving her the thumbs-up; a thin volume of poems from Centervale, which Shale had found in a used-book shop dockside; a piece of demonglass from Alt Coulumb's arch. Bits of your soul leak into things you love. She arrayed them around her as she slept. Her dreams were tossed with memory and fever, and when she woke the coins meant no more to her than bare metal, and the other talismans were just things again, as if she'd picked them off a shelf in a store. But she was herself, her soul replenished, the world bright with color. The statue and the book and the demonglass would gather new echoes of her over time.

She had never been comfortable with idleness. Awake and bored with her own exhaustion, she lurched to the edge of her bed. The black folder stood monolithic and undisturbed on the dresser where she'd left it, three feet and several subjective miles away. Dizziness ate the corners of the room, but with a groan and a lunge, she snagged the folder, and sank back onto her quilts, breathing heavily.

Sure, she was worn out. But she could read. Maybe a plan would suggest itself. Some new angle of approach. She undid the cord that held the folder closed and drew out a sheaf of papers. Light reading. Had to keep her toes in the water.

The typeface would have been knee-high on an ant. The letters swam before her eyes.

Just a few lines.

She started awake to find her body strewn with papers, and Dawn standing over her with a cup of tea. The sun was setting outside.

She scrambled up, shoved papers back into the black folder. "You should have knocked." She tied the folder shut. Its glyphs crackled as the security wards reset.

"I did." She looked as if she wanted to ask a question, and thought better of it. "Your mom made this. She told me to bring it to you. Says there's soup when you're ready."

She checked her arm before she went down to dinner. Worm-like tendrils spread from that hard bolus of curse in her arm, but her glyphs held. Perhaps the bolus had grown by the width of a pinhead. Perhaps not. Her skin near the wound felt hot to the touch.

Downstairs, she found Ma waiting with soup and good brown bread. She ate more than she planned. Ma joked with Dawn about the cornfield, about how Tara used to pester hedge witches who passed through town for lessons. When the meal was done, she lurched back upstairs, collapsed face-first in bed, and dreamed of being eaten, and not in a good way.

The next morning before first light Dawn was sitting on the couch, fully dressed, waiting.

Tara let her wait a minute longer as she poured herself a cup of coffee.

"You don't have to do this for them," Dawn said.

"I broke the wards."

"To save the town."

She shrugged. "They can't afford to hire anyone on my level to fix them. Hells, most of my classmates couldn't manage it. Not enough practical experience." She finished her cup and went back to the washbasin to clean it out. After a few years away from home, you really started to get used to indoor plumbing. "Come on. You'll learn best by doing."

Connor was waiting for them when they reached the fields.

Behind them the village was still waking. Vaughan Braxton stumbled out to deal with his chickens, renowned in Edgemont as the noisiest, most obstinate, and least pleasant of a noisy, obstinate, unpleasant species. The Braxton birds didn't all hail from the same stock, so village consensus held that the problem was cultural. The kindest hen dropped into that coop would turn bloody-minded in a week. The joke ran that they took their cue from Vaughan Braxton himself, or from his sons, who'd been known, when drunk, to take swings at log piles they thought were looking at them funny.

All through Edgemont cows were milked, butter churned, cisterns and irrigation trenches worried over. This was a normal day, people told themselves. They wrapped the blanket of normal around themselves, and still they shivered.

"I don't understand why he's here," Dawn said, with a frown at Connor. To her he must look like any number of farm boys she had known, everything she wanted to escape. "He doesn't have any power at all."

"*He* has ears, though." Connor smiled easily. He knelt to run his hand through ripening grain.

Her eyes were sharp and suspicious. "Are you a priest?"

His laugh belonged in the Badlands, where it could echo off rock and desert flats and canyon walls. He seemed cramped in town. He plucked a piece of long stiff grass and bent it between his hands.

"He has what we need," Tara said. "Knowledge." As Dawn opened her mouth to ask another question, she raised her hand. "Remember your principles: the Craft is a way of knowing. The specific outweighs the general. To name a thing is to control it. Time for another lesson."

"Lesson five?"

"I lost track of the numbers. To guard this land against the Raiders we have to know it better than they can, every border and boundary, every hill and well and field. I left when I was just a kid, and even if I'd stayed I never would have learned it as deeply as Connor has. Most people drawn to the Craft have minds bent for abstraction, like yours, like mine: we seek out patterns more than particularity. We'll see a funeral and ask why there are speeches, why there are songs, we'll ask why the priest raises her hands at certain times. We'll compare it to other funerals we've seen." The example twisted in her mouth. She'd chosen it out of masochism. "We ask these questions before we ask who's dead. It's a habit of seeing, or unseeing, that lets us do . . ." Shadow trailed her fingers as she drew them through the air. "What we do. To see beyond that habit, we need Connor's help."

"I know these fields." He was weaving the grass into a ring. "And what's past them. I've been walking through here and out into the Badlands ever since I could shimmy past my Mom's ankles."

"But why do we need that?" Dawn wasn't quite looking at Connor, who wasn't quite looking at her. "You said we used geometry. Circles and lines. Why not just make a big circle centered on the village green?"

Tara must have been this dense herself at some point. Likely worse. In a way Connor's presence made it easier—when she'd asked him for help she'd said, "I'll be teaching her while we work, it might bore you," and he'd answered, "No. I want to listen. Maybe I'll finally learn to tell one emperor from the next." He'd sounded eager at the thought, as if she'd promised to show him a new canyon or a fat black snake with scales in a pattern she'd never seen before. He wandered this new territory, feeling sand shift underfoot, and drew no conclusions. He would never be a Craftsman, but he was an easy audience. She was not used to that.

Dawn was different. She wanted to understand, and in that desire she attacked each explanation, sifted what she knew for contradictions, tested statement against statement. Dawn in Blake's Rest, Tara in Edgemont: perhaps to grow in the Craft you had to distrust the world you were given. Hate it, even. But there she was abstracting again. "The Craft has many tools for defending property, but we can only invoke them if we precisely identify what we want to defend. Edgemont is not a circle, so any circle we draw would either enclose territory we cannot claim, or leave out land that belongs to us. Either way, that leaves us open to attack. If we claim some ground as Edgemont that isn't Edgemont, perhaps all our claims are equally baseless. If our claims are disproven, our protection fails. If we don't claim territory that does belong to us—if we leave off an outbuilding or the corner of a field—there's a hole in our defenses, and if they can prove one hole exists, they can argue others into being."

She drew a book from her purse. Glue cracked and stitches in the spine strained when she opened it. The spidery handwriting on its yellowed pages looked shriveled and alien. "This is the town's original land registry. It's a hundred fifty years out of date at least." On a span of bare soil she spread a cloth that, once it was unfolded completely, became a square of slate dark as the space between the stars. She set the book atop the slate, chalked a silver circle around it, added a few pieces of cursory accounting, and, finally, uncapped a pen and placed it tip down in the air above the book. The pen stuck in empty space and hovered there when she withdrew her hand. The curse twinged in her arm, but she ignored it. "We have to update the record—to match our Craft to the land. So we have to learn the land." She looked up to Connor. "Ready?"

He hesitated. There was a difference between seeing a black snake with unfamiliar scales glimmering before you and offering that snake your arm to circle, crush, or bite. Still, he held the grass ring out to her. She accepted it and stood. He smiled. To her surprise, so did she.

"Watch," she told Dawn. "It will be your turn next." And to Connor: "Start here."

He told her the field's story as they walked. It belonged to the Leary family, though they'd had it on loan from Great-grandfather Cavanaugh at first, until in his grandfather's day they traded it for good pasture nearer to the quarry. They rotated crops through here season by season, and next season they'd leave it fallow for grazing. And those stones down the slope? Grandpa thought they were Quechal, and the carvings look much the same as those out by Blake's Rest. The soil around them's too hungry for honest work—only weeds grow there, and livestock shy away. "Ann Leary used to bring us out to drink there when we were fourteen, fifteen. We thought we'd discovered the place for ourselves. I bet our parents thought the same. You know all this already, Tara."

"I still need to hear you say it." She hadn't been invited to those sorts of parties. But he was. She imagined him sitting there, quiet, drinking little, his wide eyes open to the dark. What had the kids done out here after the fire died, in the place their parents let them think they did not know? She imagined moonlight slicked over his chest, along the curves of his body, the ridges of muscle. She forced her mind back to the path, to the chill of Craftwork in her feet, to the sun. The curse throbbed in her arm.

They held the grass ring between them. As she walked, she trailed Craft: a boundary, defining and naming this space, setting it apart from any other. She took his story and boiled it down into an abstraction she could use. The pen twitched over the land registry, annotating in silver, its pages turning by magic.

When she closed the border around the field, she felt it lock in her mind, in the ledger, in the Craft, and she felt at once the thrill of success and an artist's failure. She could not have drawn the border without him, but there was so much it did not contain—his voice or the pressure of his hand through the grass ring or his story about the time Ann Leary, drunk, had tried to cast a spell to drive the Cavanaugh goats mad, not understanding what a spell was or how one might be cast. She liked his voice. It was smooth, from lack of use.

Dawn had been watching, and by the end of this first part she was tense and eager and flushed, as if she'd been the one at work. Of course, watching was a kind of work, watching deep like that. "Let me try!"

Golden-eager. Connor laughed, unbowed out here, unfolded. Tara liked this moment. She would fix it in amber, wrap it in Craft to preserve it against time, if the Craft would not mar it in the wrapping.

"Go ahead."

The next field was also Leary land, older, with grimmer stories. It had seen a threshing accident back a hundred years before—Tara knew this tale—a farmhand who bled out in minutes while his friends ran for help. Everyone in Edgemont who traced family back to that time claimed the farmhand was a relation, except the Learys. In some tellings he was not a farmhand at all, but a traveling singer knifed by some lover over his affair with her husband, or her affair with her wife, or . . . There were many versions. On one fact all agreed: even in drought, ever since that death this Leary field grew green and straight and lush. Old gods? Spirits in the earth? The singer's curse, or his blessing? The teller chose the tale.

Eyes closed, Tara watched Dawn work. The girl understood the project: she walked the land into being with each step. She was cold, tense, her technique marred by a profound need to get this right. She wreaked her knowledge on the land. Color seeped from plants where she walked, and frost rimed her footprints.

That was not a problem yet, but it might be soon. Tara rose to walk beside her. Connor glanced a question at Tara—*Should I stop?*—and she shook her head. How to do this? Dawn needed ease, and ease was not Tara's strength.

She spoke gently, but Dawn still jumped. "You're pressing too hard. Just touch the space. Know it. Hold it. Let it go. Move on."

Through clenched teeth: "I want it."

Tara knew how that felt, to know the strength of your own grip and think, I could squeeze this world until it stopped thrashing, raise it to my mouth, crush it between my teeth and gulp the juice. "You can have it—once you learn control. The world's a willow tree made of fine glass. You want to touch that willow, to sway its branches and watch them break the light. But the Craft is a metal fist. It takes time to move it with the grace that lets you shape without shattering. Practice now, while you're weak. The greater your strength, the harder it is to learn delicacy."

Dawn tried. Her will bore down, and grass withered at her feet. But her brow eased, and the withering stopped. Connor looked from the green grass to her, silent: *wow*.

Tara shared his thrill, at first, but when she closed her eyes, she saw her own Craft woven threadlike through Dawn's, guiding, steadying, shoring. She hadn't realized what she was doing—but she recognized the technique, and the memory rose like acid in her throat.

Start with an image, and from that image build a story to guide the mind and heart. Use a steady voice, a calm hand. When the student opens to you, apply that same sensitivity, that grace you mean to teach, to climb through their work and bend it to your purposes. Enter through their trust. Once inside, you can shape them.

That was how she'd learned at the Hidden Schools, from many teachers. That was how Professor Denovo prepared students for his collection.

So: was this how you taught the Craft, in fact? Or was this only how you bent people, how you hollowed out a space inside them for your will to nest?

Her heart raced and her breath came short. She should not be here, she should not be doing this. She should not be anywhere.

You're losing control, she told herself. Stop.

The sun shines. Feel its heat on your skin. Follow that back. Let your lungs fill, let blood do its job.

Scaring Dawn would not help her. Faking calm, Tara unwound the threads of her own will from the girl's mind, stepped back, and waited for Dawn's structure to collapse, for the grass to die and the field as well, and why not all Edgemont and the world?

But Dawn did not seem to notice. The grass stayed green beneath her feet. Her steps were steady, her forehead smooth, her shoulders loose. She followed Connor, and listened. The pen darted over the register and the pages turned and the breeze blew and she was doing it. She moved through the willow made of glass.

When Dawn finished the field, she laughed and jumped and hugged Tara, and almost knocked them both over. She was wild with joy. "I want to do the next one, too!"

She was tired, but she did not lose the knack as she worked the next field. Tara's nudge had settled her into the right frame of mind. It wasn't that bad, surely. A technique was only a technique. A bad man could use a good tool, and a good woman could use a bad one.

Tara watched her work in silence, and brooded.

They walked the rest of the Leary fields that day. After dinner she lay in bed and pondered the ceiling of her childhood room until a stone struck the wall outside. When she looked out, she saw Connor, waving.

She pulled on a skirt and blouse and boots, and snuck down to meet him on the porch. She was only sneaking as a courtesy, because she did not want to wake Ma, who slept early, or Dawn crashed on the couch, but still she felt a rush of being thirteen again, as if her whole life since had been a feverishly vivid dream.

He waited for her, a dark familiar shape beneath the stars. "I thought you might like to take a walk."

She started walking and he fell into step beside her, his pace and presence calm. She wondered where he was leading her, then realized he was not leading at all. They wandered the edge of the fields. Moonlight silvered tips of grain that bowed and rose like waves.

He had never seen the ocean.

"I brought a lamp."

"I can see in the dark," she said, which was not quite true. But she needed less light than most. "Plus, it's peaceful like this."

"This is the first time you've worn normal clothes since you got home."

"Normal clothes?" She raised an eyebrow, and he hissed as if realizing he'd set a checker wrong.

"I mean, like I remember you. You used to dress like this all the time."

"Well. I'm home now." She turned "home" in her mouth like she might have turned a smooth rock, tasting it, careful not to chip her teeth. "If I thought I'd stay this long I would have brought more suits." She gathered the skirt with one hand and swirled it around her ankles. Memories drifted out like dust, from old days in Edgemont and all the time since. How you dressed changed how you felt. She could almost melt into the outfit and become, not herself as a teenager again, but some other kid, a kid who liked it here, who'd never dream to leave. But clothes could not change the curse in her arm or the glyphs on her skin. "I'm surprised this still fits."

"It fits just fine." He sounded—gods, was he embarrassed? He was looking at her, and when she glanced back he looked away, and ran his hand through his close-cropped fuzz of hair to cup the back of his skull. The movement did nice things to the muscles of his shoulders and neck and his long lean arms. His clothes fit just fine, too. "You wear suits every day in the city? Must feel you're always heading to a funeral."

"Or a holiday."

"Which happens more?"

She shrugged. "Did you ask me out to talk clothes? Not that I mind the company." Or the clothes. His, specifically. Gods.

"You just seemed quiet toward the end of work. Not so Dawn could tell, she was so happy I don't think she'd have minded if you came at her with a knife. But—well, I wanted to ask if there was anything I could do. Anything you wanted to talk about."

She'd been wondering if he would ask, and hoping not. She did not want to tell the story. She hated gaining practice. She hated having to talk about all this as if it mattered to her, as if it defined her. Pain was like grease: handling it worked it into you. She wanted to rub her hands together until a layer of skin burned off.

Professor Denovo was dead. She had his skull for a paperweight on her desk, for all the gods' sakes. Years had passed. If you believed the scholars, every cell inside her had died, sloughed off, and been replaced. Her body was different, and her mind. She prayed sometimes—her! She wasn't the same woman anymore.

She had been silent for a long time. And she was holding Connor's hand. Somewhere in that silence she'd reached for it.

This isn't about him. "I had a bad teacher at the Schools. He snuck inside his students' minds, to teach them. And for other reasons."

"That doesn't sound good."

"No. And . . . I did the same thing with Dawn today—just a little, to set her work right."

"You're afraid that makes you like your teacher." He shook his head. "That's not fair to you."

"He's not the only one who did it. Most of my teachers worked their Craft through the students, to guide us. He just went further. A lot further."

"So this thing, this trick—" He waved his free hand, and the look on his face was so frankly puzzled, so far beyond its depth, that she felt a pulse of affection for him, this pretty, gangly man, alien to the waters where she drowned. "It's a tool, isn't it? Like a chisel. You can use it to carve wood, or to stab people. If he used it wrong—"

"I don't think he did. I think he . . . found a chisel people had been using to open letters, and used it to carve wood instead. He carved me so that I'd reach for the chisel, too, without realizing. And when I'm done training Dawn, maybe she'll do the same."

"People aren't blocks of wood, Tara."

"I know some sages in the Shining Empire who'd disagree."

"See, there you go again. I don't know the Shining Empire, but I know we have choices. Free will."

She squeezed his hand tight. Free will. What a goof. She wanted to climb in his head and live there. "What does 'choice' mean?

Other people carved us with tools handed down to them, and they gave us those tools in turn, and the chain goes back to the first apes and farther. There are scholars in the Hidden Schools who flay minds open and lay them out on tables to watch them work. If you put a person in front of two balls, green and blue, and tell them to grab one, it doesn't matter which—and you're watching their brain closely—you can see which ball they're going to grab before they know they've decided. We think we know our mind. But we're just riding on a raft on an ocean in a storm, arguing which way the waves should take us."

Her words had rushed out, gaining speed as her voice rose in what she realized was a kind of panic. He did not talk for a while, but he didn't let go of her hand, even though she realized she was holding him hard enough to hurt.

She eased her grip. "I'm sorry."

"I don't know how to answer any of that," he said. "I don't guess you do either. When I find myself hung up on big questions without answers, sometimes I realize I'm using them to cover for small questions I can answer, but don't want to ask."

"She's smart, Connor. She's smart and she's good and she doesn't know how scared she should be."

"She's been scared before." His voice was gentle. "I don't know what her life was like, out there on the Rest. But you don't have to look at her long to see she's had cause to fear. I don't think people hurting other people to control them started with the Hidden Schools. Every big god and small town in the world has shaped people. Even Emperor Someone the Fourth."

"Second." But she laughed—at herself, at him.

"You're a good person, Tara Abernathy. Whatever carved you, it left more than scars. Maybe you'll mess Dawn up by teaching her. You can't control what she'll take from you, or what she'll become. Knowing you, that's got you tied in knots, because you never liked things that didn't stay just the way you wanted them. You can help her, and you can help us. And you're trying. Even if you're afraid."

"Are you afraid? Of me?"

It was a dangerous question, because Tara asked people questions for a living, and she'd learned to see through lies. Truth might be beauty and beauty truth and so on, but sometimes in the course of human events you found yourself standing on the edge of a grain field under the moon, asking a specific sort of person a specific sort of question—the sort of question you asked not because you wanted to know the truth, but because you needed to hear a certain answer, and believe it, whether or not it was true. If Tara had realized this was one of those times, she would not have asked at all.

But he said, "No," and she believed him.

After he'd gone, she knocked on the Braxtons' door.

Vaughan called for someone to open it, and Esther did. Her face was hard. She had not slept well the last few nights. Tomas's wound needed care.

Tara stood outside in the dark, in skirt and blouse and boots, her hands folded.

"I can help your son," she said. "Will you let me try?"

Esther Braxton frowned, first, then took her arm and ushered her inside.

15

Day by day, Edgemont came to join them in the fields.

The kids were the first, as they were the most curious and had the least work to do at home. They watched in silence with large dark eyes. They were not judging, Tara tried to convince herself. Or, at any rate, they were not judgmental. Kids just watched like that: they took each new thing and held it to light and turned it against the other small pieces of the world that they had gathered, working the puzzle. Once in a while they asked questions. "Why silver?"

"It's clean" was the easy answer, and almost true. The kids nodded to her and to each other and fell silent, and an hour later, one would ask what she meant by "clean."

The sun climbed and the day grew hot and Tara sweated through her blouse. Even then she did not remove the loose jacket she wore, which covered her bandage and the curse in her arm. It was still growing. She checked each night. Once she thought she heard it whisper. Sometimes, even when the sun was high, she felt it wiggle.

When she called halt for lunch the kids ran back to the village with the full bolting speed that grown-up legs forgot. Tara unpacked the lunch Ma had made and spread it on a heavy blanket on the grass, only for the kids to come back, bearing a pitcher of tea and stoneware cups. A young boy with a scar beneath his eye gravely offered Tara tea. It tasted sweet and chill. "Thank you." Cold tea wasn't something you could just buy at the corner store in these parts—you needed ice, and ice did not come cheap in Edgemont. "Did you steal this?"

His answering grin was large and quiet.

So, the kids were all right.

She knew why they'd come. Anyone who scared their parents was worth a look. But she didn't know why they stayed. Her work with Dawn and Connor was painstaking and slow, without any flash save for the dance of pen on paper. It was every bit as rote as planting. You just had to walk in a line and listen to the ground and do your best not to kill everything around you.

Okay, maybe in that respect it was not quite like planting.

There was one other difference: Tara liked this, and she'd never liked to work with growing things. John Abernathy had loved farming, even after his back soured on him. He'd tried to teach his daughter the joy of fields and fresh-turned soil, of pressing a tiny seed down into the dark and asking it to return to you a hundredfold. But for Tara, planting meant interminable hours sweating in the hot sun when she could be studying or reading adventure novels about griffins. The closest she ever came to sharing her father's joy was an adolescent phase during which she found solace weeding: she was carrying a lot of anger, and that layered pop and give when she pulled up pokeweed by the root felt—like something, like anything at all.

As she worked she remembered Pa and wondered what he'd think to see her here.

Press a seed down into the dark and it will return a hundredfold. The dead thing goes in, the living comes out, remade. She traced the glyphs on her forearm and wondered what else Pa had passed down to her with an unintended slant.

She went to the cemetery every day. She took care to visit only when the sun was up, always stood with her hands at her sides, and brought flowers, and yet the village's eyes still followed her to the graveyard gates. Esther Braxton had been publicly, effusively grateful after Tara healed her son, and Tomas showed off his scar to all the pretty girls and boys at every opportunity, though he hadn't repeated his good-natured approaches to Tara since. (A certain sort of man never could quite get past the memory of your hand several fingers deep in his neck.) They were less scared of her now.

But they still watched her when she went to her father's grave. "What do they think I'll do?" she asked the gravestone and the drying flowers and the inscription she still couldn't bear to read. "Just pop you back up out of the ground? As if it was that easy." At first she thought she was laughing. "It's fine, Pa. I'm fine."

He never spoke to her again. Not that he'd spoken to her that night on the road. That had been a hallucination. It must have been. But no matter how she tried to shake off that waking dream, she remembered his hand on her shoulder and missed it. Everything she'd learned at school insisted he was gone, as gone as anything ever was. Her father had been a temporary association of long-running causes and effects, just like everyone else. Those effects had not terminated with his life, but their intersection was over.

He hadn't come to speak with her that night. He couldn't hear her now.

But still she spoke to his grave. And listened.

Dawn learned fast and hungrily. Each morning before sunrise, Tara slumped downstairs, gray as the land outside her window, to find her student fresh as if from a feather bed rather than a night on Ma's couch. Dawn had already eaten breakfast and cleaned her plate. Dawn had already swept the floors. And Dawn waited at the breakfast table with her scrounged-up tools: basin, knife, training slate, silver chalk, notebook, pen. Ready.

At the Hidden Schools most students learned skills and tricks and, ugh, sure, why not call them "spells," the way casual cooks learned recipes, adding ingredients by rote, never asking why you salt here, why vinegar there, why this type of vinegar and not some other. You could ace exams that way. The girl everyone agreed was on track to come first in Tara's class, a frizzy-haired and freckled kid with big round glasses, had an encyclopedia's memory and a golem's eidetic recall, but so far as Tara could tell she had never given the first thought to how her charms were made, why she held her hand one way and not the other, what was true about words and locks that let one open the other—no thought, that is, to the questions of true Craft.

Dawn got it. Observation, directed. Knowledge and pattern. The interconvertibility of soul and matter. Beings tended to see minds only in beings like themselves—rocks, naturally, think only rocks can talk, and they're right, at timescales meaningful to rock. Structure and complexity beget responsiveness, adaptability, and at high levels, consciousness—you can bargain with just about anything if you are patient and understand the language.

So you learn the language. And you learn patience.

Dawn treated each lesson as if it might be her last—as if she expected a great hand to pluck her up someday soon and carry her two hundred miles into the Badlands, leaving her to reconstruct the Craft from the principles she'd mastered so far. Which made a certain amount of sense, given what little Tara knew of the girl's history. Few details were forthcoming. Dawn seemed to treat the past like a dead bird on a sidewalk: there was nothing to be done, other than to weep if she had to and move on. She had grown up on the road, a season here, a season there, sometimes in day-laborers' camps and caravans, sometimes just her and her dad. Dusty work. Blake's Rest had felt like stability at first, and comfort. Maybe it would have stayed that way if her father hadn't died. She could see that Dawn wanted to think so.

When the first glimmers of talent for or inclination toward the Craft rose within her, Dawn had sought what help there was. She learned what she could from the old women in the camps, absorbing their tangled and half-remembered hedge witchery, traditions ten thousand times older than the Craft but far less consistent, far less powerful. Most of the heirs to the old ways were gone now, their lineage confused and broken. In the God Wars, too many scared people had found comfort in painting the local old wise woman on the edge of town as an agent of the great and terrible Enemy. One mob could wipe out millennia of weird transmission from grandmother to granddaughter. True workers of the Craft could melt your fields to glass, wither your country, and impale you on spears of lightning, while the local hedge witch could at worst, in a fit of pique, lame a goat or curdle some milk. Humans were the same everywhere. The best fights to pick were the kind where the other guy couldn't fight back.

"So when do we get to the good stuff?" Dawn asked one morning, after she'd made a mouse skull gnash its teeth on cue.

"The good stuff?"

"I saw you beat the Raiders. And I've seen what's left of God Wars battlefields. Broken mountains and twisted land. Skeleton machines. How do I learn to do that?"

Tara examined the blackness of her coffee and pondered the many things she could say next. "You are."

"I'm learning geometry and theory. Rule after rule." And she *was* learning them. Tara had tutored many junior students back at the Hidden Schools, and she had never seen one improve so quickly. But Dawn was never satisfied with her own progress. That was one reason it came so fast. "But I want to help."

"You are helping. I wouldn't be able to work up the field wards so quickly on my own."

"I mean, against them."

And there it was: the cold edge to Dawn's voice, which worried her. "Against the Raiders? Or against Edgemont?"

If Tara had been asked that question, at Dawn's age, she would have played dumb. She'd have claimed she did not understand, because one of the ways she tried to protect herself from people was to pretend they would not really harm her. Their threats were jokes, that was all. Camouflage and deception were defenses she could deploy even against herself. But Dawn did not have the luxury of that illusion. "Either."

"I am getting you ready to fight the Raiders. That's what the wards are for. The Craft is particular when it comes to property. Once we can name Edgemont, we can call the Craft's power to defend it. And when you stand on that wall beside me, you'll know this place and its defenses well enough to help."

"The Raiders aren't the only threat."

"Grafton Cavanaugh is a blowhard, but he's not dangerous. The rest of this town is harmless enough."

"You thought they might try to kill us on the village green, the night of the raid. And they still watch you when you go to talk to your father."

"That doesn't make them a threat."

"Seems like a threat to me."

She sighed. "They are afraid. And in a way they are right to be afraid: not of us, because we mean them no harm, but of our power, because if we did want to hurt them, they would fall. But we don't want to walk that path. Once they're afraid of us and we're afraid of them, everyone starts looking for a bigger stick than the other guy, just in case. Wouldn't it be better if nobody was afraid in the first place?"

Dawn looked skeptical. "I'd still want a stick."

She finished her coffee and considered the girl: cold, and brilliant, and not wrong. She lifted a rake from the porch. "I suppose we should cover rudimentary self-defense. Follow me."

The hill out back between the two trees was burnished red with the sunrise. Dawn stood, windswept and ready, more ready for this than she had been ready to be born. Tara hefted the rake, testing its balance. "All the 'good stuff' flows from boring fundamentals. Seeing, knowing, naming. It's dangerous to get flashy before you're ready. That way you end up all reflex and technique, no wisdom, no cleverness, no ability to improvise. You might as well be a priest at that point. Here." She passed Dawn the rake.

"What do you want me to do with it?"

"What do you think?"

Dawn looked from Tara, to the rake. She seemed to be convincing herself of something. Then she gripped the handle in both hands, and, with extreme care, tried to poke Tara in the stomach.

Tara guided the rake handle away with the back of her hand. She couldn't suppress a roll of her eyes. Students. "Do you want to learn, or not?"

Dawn's eyes hardened. The rake handle flashed around, quicker than sight—and bounced off a curved wall of shadow two feet from Tara's skin. Dawn was off-balance, and the unexpected rebound sent her tumbling. Tara reached to catch her—but at her touch Dawn recoiled, teeth bared, animal and angry. The rake swept around again, metal tines toward Tara's face.

Tara caught it. Her glyphs burned silver. Her hand was a claw-tipped shadow. The rake handle rotted through in her grip. Its tines fell rusted to the grass. Then Tara realized what she'd done, what had happened, and stopped. That was not a teaching moment.

Dawn's eyes widened and she slumped to the ground, like someone had cut her strings. "I'm sorry, I'm sorry, I'm sorry."

Tara reached for her—but stopped herself before she touched her. Dawn settled on the hillside in a heap, chest rising and falling fast, her gaze fixed on a point far away. "It's okay, Dawn. I'm fine. So are you."

Tara waited for the girl's breath to settle. She didn't want to ask what had happened. She suspected, and she did not want to make Dawn go through it again.

"I just," Dawn said, at last. "I need to be. Ready."

"Take your time."

"You made a circle," Dawn said, eventually. Tara was not inside her mind, but she thought she understood its course. Principles and logic were easier to process than the memories that had overtaken her in the moment she felt Tara's unexpected touch. She had lived hard on the road and harder still at Blake's Rest. "You made a boundary with your mind. Like with the wards. Circles." She pointed. The grass at Tara's feet looked like it had been dead a long time. Great. Ma would kill her. "You know the space."

"It's my space," she said. "I can assert my right over it, against your intrusion. I told you, a circle is an easy shape. Geometry lets you work fast."

"But that's not what you did. The second time."

As if Tara's means of defense was the most significant difference between the two exchanges. Well, if that was the difference Dawn wanted to focus on, let her. "The second time I used these." She lit the glyphs in her arm, let shadow flow from them. "It's like referencing a point you've made before, rather than making the point again. Faster. More efficient. Once you've been glyphed, I mean. It hurts a lot, even before they work the silver in. Glyphwork relies on Craftwork precedent, so it obeys the same principles."

"Why?"

"You're asking, why does the Craft work?"

"Yes."

They shouldn't be talking about this. Tara should be taking her own inventory—and caring for her student. But Dawn leaned toward her, and in this moment her fear was gone, and she seemed to have a different history altogether than her own—the history of a clock, perhaps, a precision instrument assembled from gleaming metal. She was, after all, becoming a Craftswoman. Few people came to the Craft if the becoming was not, for them, easier than being human.

"There are different theories," Tara said. "Some people think the principles of the Craft are part of natural law—that they're inherent to any social environment, like mathematics is inherent to human cognition. And some people think that first group is full of shit." Dawn looked blank. "Let's start one layer up. Do you know where gods come from?"

"In the beginning," she said, tentatively, "was the Cosmic Egg. And then it split, and the two halves were called, um, something and . . . Wait, no, that's not how it goes. There was, wasn't there a woman who fell from the sky? And she had . . . seeds?"

Okay. She breathed deep. Take it from first principles. "Gods grow from groups of people. Like a town, or a city, or a country. It's like how a tree has one trunk, but many tiny roots. You're made of cells, right? Just like a plant is. So, you think you're *you*, but you're also . . . a lot of tiny things moving together. Gods are like that, only the tiny things are people. Gods emerge from the interaction of soulstuff in a community, so long as there's a kind of space for them, made by individuals' imaginative surrender to something greater. That space is what we call faith." The comparisons weren't quite apt—gods were emergent network phenomena, and like any network they could be implemented on, or ported to, substrates of different complexity. Humans were just their native habitat. But it would serve.

"Sometimes gods are good. Sometimes they're hungry. Vicious. Evil or just cruel. Sometimes one group in a community turns their gods against others. You get religious schisms, apocalyptic civil wars. Crimes were committed by gods, and the Craft was an experiment in justice. What if there were rules prior to gods, rules even gods had to follow? What if we tried to have faith in those rules, rather than in the local cloud spirit and her anointed king? Maestre Gerhardt and his fellow scholars went looking, and found those laws. Or perhaps they made them, wrote them so deeply into the world that even gods were bound. Every argument in every Court and Library, every claim of property by right rather than force, every piece of soulstuff exchanged on the planet, it all gives strength to the Craft. And that is why you can't hit me with your stick."

She watched the girl and tried not to look like she was watching. This was not a line of conversation to make anyone feel better—but it could make one stop feeling, for a while. A stillness spread through Dawn as she listened, a clerical calm Tara had seen when Abelard or the gargoyles knelt to pray. As if Tara was reciting a liturgy or promising an afterlife.

"Okay," Dawn said. "I want to try."

On their last day working on the Braxton property, Esther Braxton herself came out into the fields, prim and round in her gray dress, bearing a cloth-covered basket.

Tara didn't notice at first. She was walking a stretch of field and listening to Connor, who told her how this particular field was kept fallow because of Vaughan Braxton's grandfather's superstition, like how a host might set out an extra cup at a feast. She worked that story into the world, and her eyes rested on his face, on his soft mouth, on the lines of muscle down his shoulders through his arms. His quiet rolling voice washed away curses, ghosts, and Raiders.

They finished the field, sweating, tired. Thank gods she was good at her job. Thank gods this ward-walking was routine work she'd have shucked off onto an associate at any decent firm. Otherwise the knife of her power might have cut the world deep while the rest of her was distracted by that voice, that jaw, that mouth.

She jumped when she saw Esther Braxton. (Why? Embarrassment? She'd been working. Listening to him. That was all. Right.) "Mrs. Braxton." She adjusted her shirtfront. "How's Tomas?"

"Well, thank you." Formal, considered. "Is that what you're doing out here? Gathering stories?"

She had stared down gods, but she still did not quite feel like a grown woman when faced with people who had minded her when she was young. "The stories help us name the land, and guard it. Connor's been helping."

"He's a good boy. But would it hurt your work if his story's wrong?"

"Wrong?" Connor looked confused. "Everyone knows that story."

Esther Braxton looked satisfied by that. As they spoke, the kids had drawn close to her basket. But they scattered like dandelion seeds when Esther Braxton looked at them. Her reputation didn't seem to have softened since Tara was a girl. She repeated, "Does it hurt your work if the story's wrong?"

"It might," Tara admitted.

Esther's weighing expression conjured bad memories for Tara, but this time she wasn't trying to explain away a fire she'd set while playing conjurer (lessons learned from that experiment: don't use tippy candles for a summoning circle, and always tie up the sacrifice in case he gets cold feet). Esther Braxton handed off the basket without looking—one of the kids ran up to take it— and advanced on Tara. "Eat the first pie," she told the children. "Leave the second for them that's working. I need to speak with Ms. Abernathy alone."

Tara had never been Ms. Abernathy in Edgemont before.

She followed Esther into the field, away from the kids and Connor and even Dawn—who moved to join them before Tara waved her back. When they were out of earshot, Esther turned her back to their audience. "Between us," she said, "Shep Braxton's ma was born in Regis, but her family was from the Shining Empire. They were in debt to criminals out there. Now, Shep's pa met her while he was out in Regis mining, and she came back home with him when her parents died. The man they owed chased her down. They fought here, and she killed him and buried him in this field. I don't know if this was her family's tradition or if it's Imperial magic, but it went like this: if you kill a man on your own soil, you leave that land fallow four generations to honor the death. So we did, and we still do. But we don't speak of it." The story came out crisp and in a rush. She'd never told it to an audience before.

Tara reeled. She ran over her work in her mind, adjusting its basis, shifting a glyph to the left, to the right, claiming the corpse belowground, the blood shed on the field. "Thank you. I'll keep the secret."

The other woman nodded once, and when she looked up she wore that bright smiling mask that every kid in Edgemont knew was the sign Mrs. Braxton had stood down from battle stations. "Now, let's see if those children left us pie." Dawn waved to them from the circle of kids, smiling, her lips and fingertips red.

Others came after that. The field's owner, or her husband, or a cousin or daughter or son or grandfather, whoever in the family kept the secrets, wandered out as if they'd just so happened to be passing by. They brought gifts, pies or tarts, a loaf of bread, a bottle of cider, and stood apart, listening to Connor. And once in a while, when Connor was done, they took Tara aside and told her the real story.

Others came, too, folks with nothing better to do—or who could pass their work along to children or younger siblings. She expected them to leave soon. Her Craft wasn't much to look at. But they stayed to watch, and in the end, like the kids, they asked questions.

Tara was halfway through walking a field on a particularly bright hot day when she heard Dawn say, "—anything can power the Craft, since there's soulstuff everywhere. That's why you have to be careful when you work. If you get distracted, or if you're in trouble, you can draw more than you mean to."

"So it is dangerous." But not so dangerous as the edge to that voice, which belonged to a hard-faced young woman in slacks who stood in a tight cluster of spooked men. No one was passing tea now. The background conversation ebbed.

Dawn didn't notice the hush, or else she decided the best way out was through. She no doubt told herself she would not be intimidated. Which looked, to them, like she was the one trying to intimidate. "Of course it's dangerous. Everything is, if you're bad at it."

Even Connor stopped talking and turned to watch. Tara slid up beside Dawn and resisted the urge to set a hand on her student's shoulder. She smiled to disarm the situation, or tried. Her smile had too many armaments of its own. "The Craft can be danger-ous," she said, emphasizing "can." "But we're not doing any new Craft here. Just surveying the ground so we can defend it later. The danger is," she almost said "minuscule," and substituted "tiny." Then she realized that any audience that could under-stand the rest of the sentence wouldn't be thrown by the word "minuscule." She'd trained in necromancy, not marketing and communications. "Dawn, why don't you help Connor? Are there any other questions?"

She expected silence from the crowd, a nonplussed shuffling of feet. But the kid with the scar under his eye raised his hand, as if they were in a schoolroom. Tara indicated him with her out-stretched hand, palm up, and realized after the fact that this was how her mother called on kids she taught. "But if you're not mak-ing anything new," he asked, "where does the magic come from?"

So, with a glance back over her shoulder at Dawn, she drew a breath and tried to tell him.

———

Ma had not been part of the crowd, but Tara detected a slight self-satisfied edge to her quiet that night as they set the table for dinner. "What?"

"You told me once that you'd never be a teacher."

That had been an argument and a half, not long before she ran away. "Dawn's just an apprentice, Ma."

"And you're lecturing the village, now."

"That's not teaching. I'm just . . . explaining Craft. Half this stuff they could have picked up from any library that passes through. Hells, you and Pa taught them most of it."

Ma's eyes flicked up, and Tara realized she'd cursed. After a panicked moment, she decided that once one had been out of one's parents' house for the best part of a decade, and saved a few cities (one of them twice), one was entitled to a certain license with re-gard to vocabulary. She also decided not to curse in Ma's presence again, there being no sense pushing one's luck.

"Your father and I never practiced sorcery." Ma was getting

better talking about him. Was that something to be grateful for? They had not talked much since the funeral, beyond the small necessary words required between two people who shared a house, a kitchen, blood, and they rarely mentioned Pa. They stood on a bridge made of thin woven straw above a pit, and no matter how gently they placed their feet, with each step a new strand gave way. And then, as she set the bread board on the table: "He'd have liked to see this."

The bridge broke. Tara fell, and Ma reached for her, falling, too. Hand found hand in the dark.

───────

The rest of the week passed slowly, under a bright sky. There were more questions every day. At first they staggered her—didn't these people have anything better to do? But then, they were her clients. Of course they wanted to learn how she meant to help. Even the priests of Kos Everburning in Alt Coulumb understood the basic elements of her work more than these people she'd grown up beside.

Dawn and Connor walked the fields while Tara taught. She missed the simple work (and not at all, thank you very much, the rather more complex sensations she felt while walking with Connor Cavanaugh), but the arrangement had its benefits. These days, when she worked her Craft, she felt the curse stir inside her. Growing.

That night she had to bite a leather strop as she peeled her shirt from her skin. She saw tendrils spreading down her arm, like the fingers of a splayed hand, the central bolus palm-sized now and seeping tacky gray fluid. It was large enough that she could see fine white threads writhing within the black. She cut new wards into her skin, as deep as she could bear, and laced those carvings with silver salt; the pain eased, but not the pressure. When she slept she heard a surf-wash of fishhook voices out of sight.

There was, to be perfectly honest, a part of her that panicked, that wanted to run. She talked herself down. You're cursed. Deal with it for one more week. You'll live.

She focused on Edgemont's questions, and on their secrets.

She heard tales of bodies buried, of dead children and scattered ashes. *This was where my great-grandfather had his heart attack. This was where my grandmother hid a young man who fought for the Craftsmen in the Wars and turned up on her back steps one night bleeding, barely conscious. This is the field where my great-grandmother turned back into a bird and flew away.*

"It feels wrong," she told Pastor Merrott one late night on the church steps, sipping tea. "I shouldn't know who killed who on the Braxtons' back forty. Whose great-grandmother was a crane. Last week they almost killed Dawn and chased me out. And now they're telling me things they can't bear to tell each other."

She'd paused in her work for the drink. Not all the Craft they needed could be done by daylight, for an audience. After dark, in the church undercroft, in privacy, they carved the inscriptions and glyphs that would let them invoke the Craft to defend against the Raiders.

Here they were alone. Only Pastor Merrott knew this work was being done. Tara guided Dawn through the grand curves, taught her the glyphwork alphabets and sacred geometry, which words she could speak out loud and which would draw the wrong sort of attention. Candle wax burned their fingers; in the circles' light Dawn's face had a strange luminous quality. The small creases that formed beside her eyes when she squinted seemed deeper than canyons. The girl drank it all in as if she were dying of thirst, and after each gulp she gasped, wiped her mouth, and asked for more. The analogy made Tara nervous: people near dead of thirst had to drink slowly, or else their guts would burst. But Dawn, learning, looked so happy that Tara could not bear to hold her back.

Pastor Merrott sat beside her, hands clasped in his lap. "There are goats—" He stopped himself, laughed into the hollow of his chest. "I don't know how to talk to you, Tara."

"I'm sorry?"

"I don't mean that in a bad way. I just tend to tell stories. That's much of what a sermon is, a story that binds people in one image, one thought. People come to me for guidance, so they expect to be, well, guided a little. But you've seen things, done things I can barely imagine. I worry you might think I'm condescending, or trying to teach you something you already know."

"It's fine, Pastor. We're on the same team here." Which featured on the great long list of sentences she never thought she'd say. But she liked him for that hesitation, then realized that she was meant to like him for it. His concern and vulnerability, however genuine, were also tactics he'd chosen to deploy—and she liked him more, realizing that, because she respected him.

"You've heard of sin goats, I suppose."

She laughed at the bleakness of the image. "You think that's what they'll do to me after all this? Once they've told me their dirty laundry, they'll drive me out into the wilderness? They tried that once already. It didn't take."

"I don't mean it like that," he said, too quickly. "It's been a long time since you lived in a small town. When you want to be alone in Alt Coulumb, you walk out your front door and turn left. When Connor wants the same, he has to head two days into the Badlands. But not many people know the Badlands like Connor does. For them, the pressure builds. They hold their secrets, and with good reason. There's a level of honesty few of us can bear. Some of these people have been carrying sins for generations. And you come along, with your promise to save this place and to leave. Of course they tell you what they can."

"And who, I wonder, is encouraging them to confide in me, Pastor?"

He smiled for all the world like an innocent man, and eased himself to his feet like an old one. "Good night, Tara. Please do lock the undercroft when you're done. I don't think either of us wants to explain your work down there."

She toasted his retreating back with her cup of tea. "Good night, Pastor."

She crossed the fields off one by one on her map, and the days off on her calendar. Before bed she checked her curse and saluted the moon outside her window. She did not pray again. One night she tried to seek the nightmare telegraph, but its corridors were full of skeleton mouths and white, writhing threads.

Unable to get back to sleep, she untied the black folder and read. Its contents hovered around her like bad planets, the etchings and lithographs, the glossy pictures, and of course the memory crystal she had brought home from Alikand two years before.

The pictures, the legends, the descriptions of vanished artifacts, those might mean anything, taken alone. Every culture dreamed of the end of the world. It was only natural. Cultures were made of people, and people were self-centered, and people died. Gone one day, just like that. It didn't take much. A few atoms changing position. A blood clot in the brain. A necromancer could bring your body back, but your body wasn't you. Everything you saw, everything you loved, snuffed out in an instant. And it happened every day, to millions of people, good and bad, each a universe gone forever.

So of course human beings told stories, about how there had been worlds before this one, and those worlds were gone now, and how one day this world, too, would end. They told those stories again and again, carved them into stone and painted them on cave walls and passed them down generations, because people needed help to make sense of the strange and brutal planet they found themselves upon. No reason to take those stories literally.

But then there was the crystal, glowing with ghostlight in midair. When she touched it, she heard the sound, which had not been a sound when it was recorded. It had been captured out in the void beyond the sky, where there was no air. But things out there in the dark made waves of a sort, propagating through nightmares and light. When she touched the crystal, Craftwork translated those to sound, and she heard footsteps, massive, slow, and drawing nearer.

She had work to do back home. She was running out of time. She had a curse in her arm. She had grown up dreaming of the day she could leave Edgemont. And yet she stayed.

Why was she still here? She owed the town a debt, yes, but there were other ways to pay it. She could have left, found help, sent gargoyles back. Shale's people would enjoy the fight. And she could have got back to work on the black folder. On the footsteps.

They were far away, she told herself. She didn't even know who *they* were. She had seen shadows. Cave paintings. Half-melted reliefs in Quechal temples.

There were so many things happening at once. A week more or less would not hurt.

She'd get no more done tonight. Let it go, for now, she told herself. Sleep. She gathered breath, and let it out slowly, and with it she released her fears. There were more of those than she expected.

"Tara?"

She froze.

Dawn stood pale as a banshee in the doorway, her nightdress drifting around her ankles. "I couldn't sleep. I saw Craftwork. What is this stuff?"

"Nothing." She didn't want to explain. "A long-term project."

Dawn plucked one of the lithographs from midair: a cave painting, in ochre and crushed beetle shells, of a tiny marble with brown continents and blue oceans, in the grip of an immense clawed shape like a spider or a hand, vast as suns. "I don't understand."

"It's fine." She took the lithograph from her. She meant to be gentle. She meant to be reassuring. Dawn's expression suggested that she had failed. "Get some rest. We have work in the morning."

———

The next day Dawn was waiting, bright and composed as always, for their lesson and the practice afterward, her slow education in the principles of Craftwork self-defense. Their encounter the night before seemed to have fallen into her like a stone into a still pool, the ripples already settled. They walked in silence from the breakfast table to the hillside. Tara had quietly replaced Ma's rake and borrowed a walking stick from Connor to use instead, in case of further accidents.

"Come at me as hard as you can," Dawn said. "I'm ready."

"Are you sure?"

She shook her head. "Do it anyway."

Tara hefted the walking stick and locked eyes with Dawn. Tightened her grip. She chose her target—the upper arm. The worst she'd leave was a bruise.

The stick swept whip-fast through the cool air and bounced off a shell of darkness, inches from Dawn. "Faster."

She tried again. This time the shell was closer to Dawn's skin, but no more permeable. A third hit, a fourth. On the first strike, Dawn had flinched and given ground, but she handled each blow more easily than the last. Dawn was smiling. So, Tara realized, was she.

Her next swing was fast as she could manage, full force, full power—and she saw, too late to stop the swing, a flash of cleverness in Dawn's eyes. She felt Dawn's argument shift. *This is my space, inviolate* became *force directed toward me is given to me, becomes mine, and I can guide it as I choose.*

A cold fist punched Tara in the chest. She landed in the patch of dead grass, blinking away stars. "Good hit." She gathered herself, brushed off her jacket, and without thinking, reached out. Dawn helped her up.

Tara saw the surprise on her student's face as she rose, and felt a mirrored surprise in herself: Dawn shocked that she had taken Tara's hand, and Tara shocked that, rather than rising under her own power, she had reached for someone else. For Dawn. Without feeling she was making some grand Decision, either. There had been no sense of forcing herself through an ice field. She had just reached out, without thinking, and the girl accepted.

Dawn stepped back. Tara thought she might have been about to ask a question, and if she had, Tara thought she might have answered it. But the sun was rising, and they had work, and Dawn remembered, then, what she had just done—her triumph obscured the rest.

They walked together, smiling, to the fields.

The crowds were there, larger than ever, and Connor. Even he had changed, she thought, in the last two weeks—he was tired, but he looked happier, less like a picture cut from a magazine illustration, less alone. The air was cool crystal and the sky's dry blue its most perfect shade, and the sunlight rolled golden down.

She realized then that she was happy.

She tried to tell Connor how she felt. She'd taken to joining him as he tended his goats in the late afternoon. The critters gathered when he came, climbed walls and wells and rocks, and returned even the most sidelong glance with their own challenging glare. Ancient geometers had thought spirits hopped from body to body at the brink of death. They were wrong—souls were pretty fungible when you got down to it—but if they weren't, Tara wouldn't mind coming back as a goat. "It's not that I like being the center of attention."

"Though you do." He shooed a goat off the well.

She laughed. "It's a sort of control. When everyone's watching you, you know they're not sneaking up behind you." A goat rammed her leg with his forehead. She bent to pick him up but he scrambled away. "The last time I lived here, after the Schools . . . people didn't know what I was, or why I'd left. I couldn't tell them. I was sure they wouldn't understand. But also no one asked."

The well chain rattled. She walked around to help him with the crank, set her hands between his on the shaft. As she let her muscles work she remembered another well in another city a continent and an ocean away, a fierce and quiet priestess watching her draw water. Connor reminded her of Kai—they had the same quiet consideration, all their knives directed inward.

Work sweat smelled so unlike the city sweat she was used to, the sweat of systems under strain. His smell was clean salt.

When she looked up his large eyes were looking down. "What?"

"I should have asked you for the whole story. I wanted to."

She remembered that night on the hill after the dance the first time she'd come home, the stars bright and tempting overhead and this boy beside her. Not a boy anymore. She stopped the crank. "Why didn't you?"

He looked down at her hands, then back. "Gods, Tara. Have you met yourself? It's not just the Craft or the gods or the glyphs.

It's . . . listen, I go into the Badlands for weeks at a time, and I love the desert. But every time, I come back. You, you just kept going. You always knew who you were. When you were around, the world felt so big, like anything was possible. Back then . . . if I had asked you what was wrong, and you'd answered, and I'd seen cracks in you like I could see in me, there would be a crack in that feeling, too. I'd know you didn't have it figured out. I know that's not a fair weight to hang on you, but—"

She kissed him.

She hadn't meant to. She hadn't meant *not* to. She was leaning close and a current ran from her mouth through her chest down to her hips, and the same magnetism that had, these last few nights when the house was dark and still, drawn her hand down between her legs while she clenched her teeth to keep from crying out, drew her across those few inches, settled her lips on his. She stayed close. She breathed him.

It had been a long time since she kissed someone, and a long time was worse in some ways than forever. She tried to be calm, to wait for him, to hold herself teetering on that edge and give him room to decide.

His large eyes were dark and bright, and his lips found hers. There were so many reasons not to do this, and she was sure if she stopped to think she'd come up with one. Instead she kissed him again, tasted him this time as her hands found his ribs and back and his hands her sides. The crank handle, let go, struck her thighs as she pulled him to her, and that sharp sweet pain curled her fingers and she drew him closer. Her cursed arm ached and throbbed and even that didn't break the mood. Her hands dug into his back beneath his shirt. Her chest pressed against him, and her shirt and bra felt tight as if a drawn breath would burst their seams. Nothing could contain her. She filled the world. She wanted to be inside him, to have him inside her. His heartbeat was firm, his body swelled into her when he breathed. He was ready, and from his eyes she could see he wanted her and feared what was happening between them, and she liked the wanting and the fear, and she showed him the white of her teeth.

It might have lasted a thousand years. She could do that—stop their hearts and hold them in that moment's strain as their pan-icked brains came unmoored from time—they'd done it in the Hidden Schools once they learned the trick, deadly dangerous and sweet. There was no Craft here, though, just the moment thicken-ing around her by her mind's own magic, until the bucket hit the water.

They stood beside the well. There were goats all around. Be-yond the goats, a fence, and beyond the fence, fields, and in the fields, folk coming home from work, houses silhouetted against twilight, and nothing between them and Edgemont.

He pulled away and she let him. Someone might have seen. They all might have seen.

She was not afraid. But this was hers, and his. Edgemont did not deserve it.

"Tonight," she said, and before he could say anything else, she left. The goats did not offer her a path.

Dinner conversation was light and sharp. She laughed too loud and told jokes that landed askew. She felt feverish and famished and she wanted to swallow the world. Lying awake in bed later, she wondered whether Ma or Dawn had noticed. She lay, wonder-ing at ceilings. The sheets were soft but her skin was so sensitive they rasped over her like sandpaper.

How slowly could seconds pass, how could stars linger in their courses, how deep was the night in which she waited, hungry, in a bed too small for her, as her thoughts spiraled out to fill the room and the village and the Badlands, too, only to gather the universe back in and fill her with space and time and doubt. Could he have misheard? Had she pressed him beyond his limits? Had she fucked this up, too?

A pebble bounced off the wall beside her window.

She dropped from the second floor, cushioned her fall and landed beside him without sound, took his hand and let him lead her, to make him think that he was safe. Sometimes she stopped him, to keep his foot from a root or a hole that might have turned his an-kle, a twig that might break and make their passing known. They walked in silence. And in the hollow of a hill that faced the Badlands, she took him.

He was timid as he undid his clothes, as if afraid of the hunger they'd shared beside the well. His body was hard with work and wandering, and with need. They'd lost their names somewhere on the way. She left hers in that bed, and his never fit him completely. Her hands slipped on laces, hooks, the simplest movements so fumblingly complex. She didn't have to get naked for this but the cold did not bother her and she wanted to lie empty and bare beneath the stars. She had never let herself *want* while she grew up here, not out where anyone could see, because the things she wanted set people running, made them light torches, grab pitchforks. But want was in her breath and blood and she was full of it as she caught his chin and guided him to her lips.

She drew him into her first, and when he propped himself on his hands she cuffed her fingers around his wrists and caught him with her thighs, wanting mastery and the strain, the certainty she was there and so was he; it built and built with aching slowness, a torture to them both. When she wanted more, she took more—she bucked him off, and, sensing what she needed and half smiling, he pushed against her arms as she pressed him beneath her to the blanket. The night was cold but so was she. Her hunger blighted grass, killed insects that flew near. She was a great pit like they said stars dug in the sky when they died and they both tumbled into her together. She held the whole world and him. Dimensions fell away, time first, then roundness, until they were shadows on a wall, then a long thin wire without end, and then just that single point, nowhere and everywhere at once, straining—he made a sound, she clapped her hand over his mouth, not because she was afraid of the noise but because she wanted to hold it, to hold him, this, rightnow/forever, but to grasp was to strangle, and though this one point was all that bound her to the world, she curled her fingers and toes and let go.

The world cracked, unfolded, and was gone.

Pain brought her back—the dull coal-throb in her arm, in time with her heartbeat—and in that gentle aftermath she did not even mind.

After, while they recovered, she trailed her fingers over his chest, her glyph-rings glowing. His hairs rose toward her touch.

"That was . . . ," he said, and trailed off, wondering, unable to say what it was exactly.

"Yes," she answered, unable to say either.

It was a start.

He eased her to the grass, sat up, and watched her, eyes wide. She felt a stab of terror, lying naked before a gaze that frank—an urge to collapse around the cursed arm and hide it from him—but his eyes tracked uncomprehending past the wound. Of course. Naked, she was an unfamiliar landscape, arms and legs and chest and belly inscribed with glyphlines glittering in moonlight, that quicksilver scar on her neck from Alikand. She was proud of her scars and glyphs, of the survival and work they represented—except, of course, for the curse. What did he think, as he puzzled over a body so different from the bodies of other girls he'd known?

To lie still and let him look felt like jumping off a ledge into the ocean, without checking to see how far down the water was or whether there were rocks.

He looked, half-awed, and then he bent to kiss her.

She did not ponder futures. She lacked agenda, plan, or scheme. If any were needed she'd make them up on the fly. She'd done as much before. Back in Alt Coulumb, and for that matter all her life, Tara never gave in to anything, even sleep, without a fight. But sleep for once found her unresisting, and even the voices of her curse kept their murmurs low.

Connor blushed a little when they met the next morning, and she might have blushed, too, even though she met his eyes and smiled, bright and easy with nothing to hide; regardless Dawn seemed to sense something had changed between them. She didn't ask, though, only walked beside them to the last fields on their list.

The sky was perfect blue and the ground received her feet and the breeze was light and gentle from the east. Every day should be the first day after a long drought. She felt easy and open. On the walk they traded jokes; Dawn picked dandelions and blew their seeds out over the hills. She shouldn't, they were weeds, but Tara was in no mood to tell her that.

No children joined them on the way. No idlers left their chores. She'd grown used to a gathering, but they walked on alone. She knew where they were bound, of course, and so did Connor—there were only so many farms and in the end they'd reach this one—but still she'd told herself it would be fine. She would hear Connor's stories, do the work, and let that be all. No need for argument, confession, reconciliation.

When they reached the Cavanaugh land, Grafton was there, waiting.

16

Connor, sweet and, in this moment, kind of dumb, stepped between them—as if whatever his dad might try before witnesses in daylight was anything he could save her from. Dawn joined him, her eyes narrow and her mouth set. More worrying to Tara were the shadows that gathered around her student's fist.

"We don't need you here," Dawn said.

Sweet, and unnecessary. At Pa's funeral, Tara had been vulnerable—to Grafton, to the world. She was not anymore.

Tara stepped forward. "You don't have to do this, Grafton."

Dawn turned to her, angry and questioning. Tara put her hand out, palm down. *You're here, now, not in Blake's Rest back then.* And: *I can handle this.*

"No one knows these fields like I do," Cavanaugh said. "I'm here for the village, not for you. The Pastor asked me to come."

Tara thought about the sin goat. She did not want to know this man's secrets. She did not want to understand him. He was small and angry and he hurt those close to him. But he was still a client. She held out her hand for the grass ring, and when Connor did not pass it to her she turned to him with a look meant to reassure; it didn't seem to work, but still he surrendered the ring. Dawn held the book and pen tight to her chest. Her eyes were scalpels. She saw someone else where Cavanaugh stood. "Dawn." The girl passed Tara her tools, like she might have given a duelist a sword.

And Tara walked with Grafton Cavanaugh.

He could not settle into a pace. When Tara slowed to match him, he'd speed up. When she quickened her step, he eased. The grass ring frayed between them, and a few strands popped. She tried harder. "We rotate corn with barley and pasture here," he said. "My eldest cares for the cattle. We're thinking about peanuts, but their draw on the soil is considerable. The cows help, but I don't know how much rain we can count on what with the unruly weather." The grass ring strained between them. "What?"

"You need to tell me what makes the field special. What makes it yours."

"I am telling you."

"A crop rotation. A farmer contemplating peanuts. I've seen plenty of those."

The old man sucked his teeth. And Grafton Cavanaugh was old, though she had not thought so before: old as her own father. Shocks of gray ran through the curls of his hair. His hands bore scars of work and his limbs were thick. The Grafton Cavanaugh of her memory, her father's lumbering friend, Connor's terror, had eclipsed the man beside her, aging and alone.

He said, "My great-grandfather had the planting of this field, and my father, rest him, did not care for it well. He was always off, wandering. When I was a boy this soil was farmed out, all but sand. Your pa and his pa helped me work it when my dad wasn't around—your Grandpa Abernathy gave me the notion of rotating, which my old man didn't like, seeing as he didn't like change much, or thinking about the farm at all. Each new task he had to mind back home was one more nail through his feet into the floor. My brother and my sisters helped me turn the crops. When the fields turned green he called it a miracle." Tara remembered Connor's stories, his grandfather playing his flute in the Badlands. Her heart made unexpected motions in her throat.

They did not talk as they walked to the next field. It was pasture for the season, all grass and cows and the smell of grass and cows. She could not see the Cavanaugh house from here, or the village, or the well or the goats, or Dawn and Connor, who'd lingered behind.

This wasn't so bad, so far.

"Your father came to see me here, you know. The night you left."

Fuck you.

"Not when that witch spirited you away. The first time, when you were a girl."

She'd known which time he meant.

"Now, you'll remember that John Abernathy crossed the country in the middle of the Wars, barely sixteen, fighting what horrors who can say. Despite what he must have seen, he was glib and light, always ready with a trick, and he loved his daughter. When you left he chased you. Followed the caravans for miles."

She'd known he would. That's why she was clever about it—rather than joining a caravan in Edgemont she'd walked cross-country to the rails, hopped a westbound freight, jumped off, and met with the caravan at the watering hole she'd arranged with the witch who promised to teach her the basics. She'd brought a small knife and a large knife and a map and dried meat and several poisons she'd brewed according to such recipes as she judged accurate—you never could tell when you'd need a good poison. She knew the rudiments of Craft already, but all the same she was surprised how easy it was when she began to learn, as if she'd settled into her proper groove. At the time, she thought it was destiny. Much later, she'd wondered over the difference between destiny and a predator's lure.

"He cried in my arms, out here. He was so afraid for you. He was furious—with himself. He knew you would go, because he had gone when he was your age. But you were their only girl, and you never belonged here. When you left, it felt like he'd never made it home from the Wars. The only way I could talk him down was by making a promise I couldn't keep. 'She'll come back,' I said. 'She knows you love her. She'll come home.'"

"That's it," she said, fast, sharp, as soon as she could. She didn't want to hear more. "Next field."

Barley, this, growing green. Past the edge of the plot stood a ring of tree stumps, the bare earth between them dotted with pipe ash. "We used to play music out here. It's one thing to play on the green or at the pub, quite another to play for your own self." He wavered then. "He trusted me for six months, that you'd come home. When you didn't, he started to hate me. That passed, in the end. Or he learned to hide it. It was my own fault, for giving my word on a thing I could not control. But if I had not told him you would come back, he might have chased you all around the world."

"Or he might have accepted that this was what I wanted, and let me go." She did not like this story. She did not want it to be true, did not want it to become a fact she knew, to settle it into the world through Craft.

"You should have given him a chance."

"I gave them every chance. What the hells was I supposed to do? Hang here and rot like a fruit on the vine?"

"Is that how you see all of us? You tell my boy that's how you see him?"

She curled around that hit, too deep and physical for anger. The curse bunched and knotted in her arm. "He's not rotting. But he can't leave, even if it would save his life. He loves this town."

"And you don't."

"I owe it." She growled the words. "I couldn't have come from any other place. But if I stayed here I would not have lived. I'm trying to learn how to love this place now, hard, and fast. Because he would have wanted me to. Because that's the only way you all survive."

"You don't owe this town shit, Tara Abernathy. You left it and never looked over your shoulder once. You swept your trail so you couldn't follow your footsteps back."

"That's not true."

"You want to talk about what you owe? You owe your pa, and what you owe him you'll never repay."

"Then what the hells am I doing here?"

"Trying." He made that word a sneer. "You want to save us so bad you'll break us all to bits to salve your guilt. This place is a trap for you. You've been learning every secret but the one you don't want to know. You hurt your old man deep. He sat there, hating me while he played his fiddle, hating me while he passed the whiskey, because I robbed him of a chance to save his girl."

"I wasn't his to save." The whole world pulsed—no, that was her. "I didn't belong to him."

He grinned toothily and looked down at his feet. "Field's done, I guess. On we go. This won't take as long as I thought."

Sweet corn, next. She said nothing.

"I was fourteen and working this acreage when he came to tell me he was leaving. John was barely more than a boy and dreaming boy dreams—big city lights and fortunes, a world that was changing every day. He was going to save some rich man's life, fall for his daughter and work his way up by smarts and his own hands, just like in those books he read, and if that didn't happen at least he'd see the sights, get knocked on the jaw a couple times and come back one split lip richer. I wanted to stop him. I didn't want to see him go. I didn't want him to leave me here alone. But no one ever could tell him the time of day. So we sat with arms around each other as the sun went down. He asked me to go with him. I could imagine him on the streets of Alt Selene, I could see him bright and ready anywhere in the godsdamn world, but I could not imagine leaving.

"There was a storm that night. He left, and then the whole world went mad and Alt Selene fell and I gave him up, but the world gave him back to me. He always did come back. So when I saw him crying so many years later, I took a chance and bet you were made the same."

She could see the lure, smell the bait. She matched her pace to his.

They reached the last field, which lay fallow.

She did not offer him the ring.

"What?" His voice was sly and sidelong. "I thought we were here to tell stories."

"Whatever there was between you and my father—or wasn't—it's not my business. I loved him. I know he loved me. That's what matters."

"None of this is your business. You loved each other, sure. There's love all over and it trades for pennies a bushel. But he knew you'd not be coming home again. He read your letters to me, when you sent them. He was so proud of you, and so scared. The demon in Alt Coulumb, whatever the hells you got up to across the World Sea, and all the adventures in between, each time you'd send some chipper note back and he'd remember the day he ran away from Alt Selene. He always told me he made it out because he was small. Nobody noticed he was gone, nobody cared. And since he was smart he sussed out how to fold your ma up small, too, and sneak her out with him and save her, before the Wars got her like they got the rest of her family. But there you were, getting bigger and bigger out east. He knew just like everyone knows that this peace can't last, that it's breaking year by year. And when it goes you'll be right in the middle. Why do you think he went out into the canyons chasing my boy? He had to save someone, and he couldn't save you."

She couldn't speak.

"After all that you have the gall to come back and lie to this village, and lie to my boy, and to that girl, and to yourself even, that you belong here. That you're one of us. You're not here to help us, or her. You just want to be better-than. You want to be big. That's all you ever wanted. That's all any Craftswoman wants. You like it when Esther Braxton comes to tell you her secrets, but you'll never tell Esther yours. You'll teach that girl, but not enough to make her strong. You are what they made you in that fancy school and no more. And you left us, and you left your pa, and that killed him."

She stood heavy as a raised axe, each breath straining with the anger Connor did not let himself feel, and a special electric fury all her own, crackling behind her eyes. The curse echoed her rage. Its wave-whispers merged with the pulse of blood in her ears, promising, tempting—let me out. Let me hurt him. Grafton swelled in her vision, not just ready but hungry for what he thought would come next. For her to smite him with her power and justify his scorn and fear.

Once, she would have done it. But she was older now.

She curbed her power and her rage. She shrank, and as she did so did he, until they were small figures in a large world, and she had to laugh—at her, at him, at the roles they played for each other. Not happy, not scornful. For the most part, sad.

He swayed as if a hard wind had struck him from an unexpected angle.

"Sure," she said. "I killed him. Why not? And he killed himself. And you killed him. You coaxed him into joining the guard, and shamed your son so he couldn't share his plans with you, and he went to my pa instead. We're all killing each other, all the time.

You want his death to be Connor's fault, Dawn's, mine, everyone's but yours and his, but I'm done playing that game. Own your shit. The Seer's coming, and the Raiders with him, and whatever you think of me, I will fight them and I will end them. If you're sad and angry and you want to hurt someone, join me on the line. But I have better things to do with my time than to listen to you one more godsdamn minute."

She threw the grass ring to the ground between them. She held out her left hand, relishing the ache of the curse in her arm. The book closed itself and flew to her grip, and the pen. She caught them without looking.

"Tara," he called after her as she walked away. "We're not done here."

"I am," she said. "I know you well enough."

17

Tara woke sometime after three o'clock in the morning, from hard hot dreams of bones and hooks and sex and fire and a storm out on the Badlands, dreams of spiders the size of stars, dreams in which she hung like a marionette from a web of silver wire as a monster in a tweed jacket broke her ribs with pliers and pulled her open. Panting, sweat-slick, she lit the ghostlamp on her bedside table and pushed up her nightshirt's sleeve.

A slim tendril of curse had slipped past her ward to climb the inside of her arm, reaching for her heart.

She cut it back as best she could and added new layers of ward. Out past her window, fields ran to the road, and beyond the road lay the Badlands. The Raiders were out there, boiling nearer. Like called to like.

Two more days.

A cold light glimmered on the hill, between the trees.

She found Dawn near the circle of dead grass, playing mazes with a rat.

She had covered her slate with neat circles and glyphs, picked a flower from the yard, set it in the center, and wilted its petals to fuel the maze. Watching her, Tara felt a stab of pride. The girl hadn't built her maze from light or cold fire or wind coaxed to stand at attention. Nor had she whispered to the rat, ordering it to respect her lines. Her lines could not be crossed because that was the nature of a line: a border, a boundary, a wall. She had drawn the maze into the world.

The rat wriggled through the turns, bent itself near double to round a tight corner, snaked down a jagged run, seeking the crumble of cheese Dawn had left in the center. But the cheese lay inside a perfect closed circle. Dawn nibbled on more of that same cheese as she watched the rat.

"You couldn't sleep either."

Dawn shook her head.

Tara closed her eyes. The chalk walls were printed in lightning on the black, and the rat's curled soul ran through them. Soothing to watch someone else run a maze for once. She sat beside Dawn and passed her the black folder.

"Open it."

"Tara." She did not know what to say, so she stopped.

"Open it."

Dawn unwound the string and tipped the files out. She paged through them in silence, lingering over etchings and lithographs. Her brow furrowed as she teased meaning from densely typeset articles in obscure journals. The crystal hovered between them, throbbing with inner light. "What is this?"

She sighed. "The end of the world, maybe. One of them."

Dawn looked at her. It wasn't a shocked sort of look. Tara was indifferently good at chess, and once she'd played a game with Abelard, who was still working out how the little horsey moved. He spent half an hour struggling over his moves, scheming the best possible outcome of every play, and losing piece by piece. When she revealed checkmate at last, he'd looked like that: he had not been able to see where it was coming from, but he had known it was coming. "One of them?"

"There have always been ends waiting. High-energy Craft strains reality. The more we work with it, the greater the risk someone will get something important wrong, and our world will rip open and a new one will pop out, like a fungus from an ant's head. Or demons will pour through the rift and eat us. Or else the Craft will simply eat the planet, like you ate Blake's Rest— Craftwork makes wasteland from fertile fields, burns forests to ash, melts the roofs off cathedrals. Everything has a cost. The Craft demands more soulstuff than we can safely take from the stars, so we take it out of the world. And then there's politics. The God Wars ended in a truce, but peace sits uneasily between

Gods and Deathless Kings. The world's dry tinder. There are plenty of sparks."

"I didn't know. But . . ."

"But you're not surprised. No. People feel it, even if they don't have words for what they feel. Something has to give. But people are trying. And things change. I've seen them. Maybe they'll change enough in time." The rat turned down a blind alley. "Wrong move, sport."

"No," Dawn said. "The crossing path's a bridge, see? The lines arch over."

The rat reached the end of its alley, bent its head, and slunk under the chalk bridge and out the other side. Tara golf-clapped. The rat circled the center. "Nice. I didn't notice the third dimension." She passed her the crystal. "And then there's this."

Dawn took it, and listened. "Footsteps."

"I heard a rumor, and went looking. I had to send someone beyond the sky to get this. Out past the air, where it's all black and deep except for the stars. You can hear—not sound, but vibrations in nightmare, patterns in light. And we heard footsteps, far away, drawing closer. So that's what I have. That, and a bunch of old nightmares scrawled on cave walls." She fanned the pictures out between them. Dawn picked one up, turned it over.

"What are they?"

"I don't know."

"They look like demons."

"Quechal myths call them *skazzerai*. Not a Quechal word, by the way. We translate it as demon, but High Quechal has a different term for what we call demons now. In myth, they tried to eat the sun at the dawn of time. When you look, you find them all around the world, in cave paintings, nightmares. Hardly reliable testimony, but . . . we know something's coming. As if we weren't killing ourselves fast enough."

"Why are you showing me this?"

You'll teach that girl, he'd said, *but not enough to make her strong.*

"I'm showing you," Tara said, "because you have to know the truth. The world is bigger than Blake's Rest, bigger than the Raiders, bigger than Edgemont. And it needs us. That's what you're getting yourself into. When I started to learn the Craft, I wanted freedom, and understanding, and power. I wanted to get away. I thought I could carve out a niche raising the dead and defying gods from some corner office, where I'd work until my flesh dried off and flaked away in the cold breeze, until all that was left would be a skeleton in a very nice suit. I don't want that anymore. But even if you do, I don't think you can expect to have the option. Learning the Craft, today, isn't about the job, the lifestyle, the undying power, the tradition, the office. It's about charting a course through the end of the world. And what comes after."

"Then what are we doing here? Why are you helping them?"

Her challenge was frank, her gaze level. Tara could tell she'd been working up to this question for a while. "You wouldn't?"

"Would I help Grafton Cavanaugh?"

"He's not the only one who lives here."

"But this whole place is so small. You're talking about the world, Tara."

"And Edgemont is part of the world. For them, this is the big picture."

"But you don't have to be here. You don't have to help them."

She could lie about this. But she'd told herself she wouldn't do that. "We've failed each other a lot, this town and me. Someone has to suck it up and do the work. And they're trying. Even Cavanaugh. He's afraid, and he's angry, and he's a small man so he can't think of any way to deal with his fear and anger that doesn't involve hurting people."

"They're not worth you."

Tara looked up, sharply. "Don't talk like that."

"It's true, though." Dawn sounded surprised when she said it—surprised and far away, as if she'd turned back to a familiar memory and found something new there. She held her hand out at the maze, the frantic rat inches from cheese and unable to cross the line. "They're stuck here. They can't see what's coming. Even if they could, they don't have the power to do anything about it."

"I'm not sure anyone does."

Dawn drew her hand back, clenched it into a fist, and closed her other hand over it. "Should you be risking your life here? For them?"

"That's a bad line of thought."

Again, surprise. "Can a thought be bad?"

"Yes," she said, less certain than she sounded.

"That," Dawn replied, "sounds like something the people with pitchforks would say."

"That's fair." Tara slowed and felt her way through the concept. "All lines of thought open doors, and that one opens doors that should stay closed. If we measure worth by capacity, then what's to stop the world's strongest hundred Craftsfolk from sacrificing its billions to live forever, omnipotent, among the stars? What's to stop the strongest one from sacrificing the other hundred? Eternity is a long time. Our work revolves around contracts and property. What do we become, when we see people as things to be owned or traded?"

"I used the flowers."

"Flowers grow back."

"So do people."

She laughed at that. "You've got the right sense of humor for this line of work. I'll give you that." She watched the rat search. "Why didn't you give her a way to win?"

"Sometimes there isn't one."

Tara pointed. "Maybe you should tell her."

The rat reached the circle at the center of the maze: a curved end line, like the bridge. She sniffed, and wriggled under it, just like she'd wriggled under the bridge earlier. Before Dawn could grab her she'd snagged the cheese and scampered off.

Tara couldn't help but laugh, at the rat, at the night, at Dawn's confusion. "There's something to learn from everyone, I guess." She gathered the papers where they'd fallen and slid them back into the folder. "Let's get some rest," she said. "If we can. We'll need to be fresh for the investiture."

———

On the village green, Pastor Merrott took the cup Tara offered him, lifted it high, and drank.

Edgemont's guards watched him. The silence drew them forward, their faith bright against the black-and-silver of Tara's closed eyes. She stood calm and hoped the Pastor would hold it together. She'd warned him, as they finished their work beneath the chapel, "You're the keeper of the village wards, so you have to be the point of contact between what we've done and the larger structures of Craft. But the joining process hurts. Everyone already thinks I'm half a witch. I don't want to compromise their morale by making them watch you suffer at my hands. We should do this in private."

"On the contrary," he'd assured her, "it has to be public. Secrets scare people. We will celebrate the joining in daylight, on the village green."

"When you collapse, they'll have the pitchforks out before you can recover."

"They know you're on our side. Even Grafton—"

"We," she had said as she corked the bottle of swirled silver-and-purple distillate she'd mixed for him to drink, "are not discussing Grafton Cavanaugh."

"He's a decent man. He wants what's best for us."

"Good for him. Let's go."

And now she stood on the green in daylight and watched Pastor Merrott sway, his eyes screwed shut and his teeth clenched so tight she could pick out individual striations in the muscles of his jaw, while the Craft burned inside him. She wished she'd not been too angry about Grafton Cavanaugh to walk him through the stages of suffering he'd feel when he drank the potion down. *I was pissed* would be cold comfort if the mob came for her.

She was nervous, and hoped Dawn could not tell. She didn't need to look to know that hope was false.

He shivered first: that was the chill of subjection, as the potion identified him to the Craft. Then he began to twitch, as if insects crawled under his clothes: distant machines traced the wards he carried, and read the plans they'd drawn up of the village. Most people weren't used to such careful, mechanical regard.

And once the pieces were sorted out, the bond took hold.

His lips peeled back from his teeth. His eyes went wide. His body jerked. A high noise escaped the prison of his mouth. The Edgemont guards drew nearer. Tara didn't see any pitchforks yet, but she was glad she hadn't restored the guard-light.

Pastor Merrott fell into her, his arms around her shoulders. Without meaning to, he grabbed her wound, and she hissed in pain. Under the robes he was a slight man. She had braced to catch him thinking he was heavier, and staggered now from the weight that wasn't there. A moan rose from the audience. Tara almost told Dawn, *run.*

But it was over. Pastor Merrott drew a shaky breath. Leaning on her, he turned to the crowd, smiled weakly, waved. They cheered—for him, and, as he raised her hand, for Tara. Doubt was gone. The Braxtons and Learys and the Cavanaugh cousins cheered as if she was one of their own.

Pastor Merrott, still waving, leaned close and said, so fast that afterward she wondered if she'd imagined his words, "People like to see a little weakness. It helps them relate."

Before she could ask what he meant, he stepped forth, and called the guards to receive their investiture.

One by one he gave them the talismans they'd prepared— round shields on leather thongs, with Craft sigils for identification and tracking, simple enough that Dawn could do most of the work. And one by one, Tara activated them. Each guard bent before her and she touched brow and breastbone and shield, ignoring her curse's hunger for the souls they laid bare. She woke the sigils. The gold light and armor of their office was webbed now with silver blue. They were stronger, faster, more integrated, and easier to control. When Tomas Braxton, fresh-grown skin livid on his throat, reached the front of the line, she expected him to hit on her again or at least grin slantwise, flirting, but he bent his head in respect. She felt uncomfortably ceremonial, almost priestly. She wanted to stop, but there was a line.

Connor shuffled up next, his shoulders and his mouth soft. Whatever she was feeling, she must not have hid it well, because he smiled and sank to one knee with a theatrical sweep of his arms, like a knight in a picture book.

When he stood, glowing, she whispered, "goof," in his ear and he whispered back, "priestess," with that same mild accusation, and grinned when she scuffed him on the side of the head.

At the end, Grafton Cavanaugh shouldered through the crowd, and walked to Pastor Merrott like thunderclouds used to, to bend his head and receive the shield.

Pastor Merrott said, "Thank you." Grafton stood before Tara then, and she couldn't tell how much of the charge in the air between them was her and how much him, and how much was her memory. Was that mockery on his face, or scorn, or, even, regret?

Someone has to suck it up and do the work.

She gave him his shield, and he turned from her, shining.

———

She sat awake on the front porch long after dark and stared up at the moon she'd watched die one sliver at a time. Shadow always advanced. Tension gave the silence its own sound, clear and high and everywhere at once, between the crickets and the wind. Tomorrow the Raiders would come. She felt them nearing, felt the curse inside her call out to the great sick web that bound them. She wanted them, wanted the fight and what came after, though she feared the changes it would bring.

She could not stay here, she told herself. This was not her place, no matter how much she had learned it and loved it in the last two weeks. She missed her friends and her work. And she needed to go back.

But she was telling herself all this, which meant she needed to hear it. She had meant to walk out of Edgemont after the funeral and never return. So why was she here on this porch two weeks later, reminding herself of all the reasons to leave?

Gods, she had hated this place growing up. Hadn't she? She still did—didn't she? The stares, the fear. Less of that back in Alt Coulumb. But then, no one back in Alt Coulumb knew this part of her—knew Pa, Ma, Pastor Merrott, any of the others. Connor.

Could she, possibly, stay? What would that even mean?

She recoiled from that question and settled her mind on more comfortable prospects, like the monsters crossing the Badlands on the sandstorm's wings.

Tomorrow it would be over, one way or the other. She couldn't punch Grafton Cavanaugh, but there were no rules about Raiders.

The screen door opened. Porch boards creaked. A weight settled in the rocking chair beside her.

"With all the early rising you've done the last two weeks, I thought at least you might learn to sleep at a reasonable hour."

"Hi, Ma." She looked up at her and avoided the thought of age. Stupid thing to duck: of course people you love grow old, and someday they will die. That's the nature of the world without the Craft. Not like you to deny the truth.

Well, yes. Certainly time did march on. But if she had found the prospect copacetic, she would not have become a necromancer. "I don't need much sleep anymore," she said. "I'll be fine." Her body chose that moment to betray her by forcing a yawn.

"You'll burn us out of candles and lamp oil."

"I don't need much light, either. And I can make my own." Three weeks ago, she would have manifested a tiny flame above her fingers, to show off. She satisfied herself with the gesture now, and a smile Ma did not return.

Ma sat grim and erect and still in the rocking chair. After her sojourn in Alikand Tara had traveled east around the Shield Sea to Apophis, and there in a drowned temple, dedicated to some cat goddess long since gone, or else waiting somewhere in ambush—it was hard to tell with cat goddesses—she'd found a statue that looked just like her mother, staring at her from the wall, across six thousand years of history. Slowly and smoothly as that statue might have moved, Ma reached out and set her hand on Tara's arm. Her touch was soft and sure, and she had no way to know she'd set her hand right over Tara's curse. Tara tried to ease into the touch, to calm herself, to sit there, godsdamn it all, and be assured.

Then Ma squeezed.

Tara's flinch took her up and out of the rocking chair and halfway over the porch railing. Ma just sat, arms crossed, one eyebrow up. Her black eyes reflected the light of the glyphs Tara had woken by reflex in her pain.

Tara breathed, at bay, unable to find words.

"Show me," Ma said.

"I didn't think I was that obvious."

"I am your mother."

Tara rolled up her sleeve. It was a sign of how she'd grown used to the sight over the last two weeks that her first reaction to her mother's hiss of breath was to say, "It's not as bad as it looks. I'll last until I get to a decent hospital."

Ma's eyes were narrow. "It's the Raider's curse, then."

She was too tired to dance around the point. That wouldn't work with Ma anyway. She let herself nod.

"Gods, Tara."

"It's under control." That eyebrow didn't go down. She tried again. "Once the village is safe, any good doctor can fix me right up. If I lose a little of the arm, it's worth it."

"Can you fight with that thing inside you?

"Sure."

Tara's mother was a master of silence.

"I have to be there." Tara heard more iron in her voice than she'd ever dared show when her mother looked at her like this. "Pastor Merrott hasn't worked with the Craft before. The guards aren't used to their new strength. Someone has to face the Seer."

"And that has to be you."

"It makes sense for it to be me." Sense was only half of it. She wanted to end the Seer before all Edgemont—to pay him back for her father, for this rotten pustule in her arm. She wanted to drink his life and break his will and tell him before he died that she was her father's daughter. And then snap his neck before all Edgemont, so they'd know what it looked like when she really wanted to hurt someone. "I want it to be me."

For a long time no one spoke but the wind in the corn.

"Your father." Ma stopped after those words, leaving Tara space to object to this line of conversation, though even Tara could see that this opening was a trap. "John Abernathy never knew how to give up. There was a Shining Empire story he loved—I don't know where he learned it. A certain farmer lives in a certain valley. When he brings his crops to market he has to cart them up a mountain, and back down again. He hates this mountain. So one

morning he takes his shovel and goes to dig a few shovelfuls of
soil off the mountain, and he does this the next day, too, and the
next. A neighbor asks what he's on about, and he says, I mean to
move that mountain. One shovel at a time? asks the neighbor.
One shovel at a time, says the man. It's too big, says the neighbor.
Maybe I won't move it, says the man, but my children will dig,
and their children, and some way down the line, the mountain
will be moved." She breathed, weathered a storm beneath her
skin, opened her eyes. "He loved that story. Sometimes I wonder
if he understood it."

"This isn't about revenge," she said. She didn't believe herself
either. The curse turned in her arm.

"Connor told me what happened in the canyon. That's John to
the heart: he can't run. He set himself a task and worked until the
task broke or he did." Tara heard her father move from present
tense to past in her mother's voice, and everything she'd meant to
say shriveled in her throat. "You're his daughter. If you fight the
Seer, you will not stop until the fight's done, or you are. You'll
forget Edgemont and me and your own safety, because of John.
I have lost you too many times to lose you in my own home. Do
you understand me?"

"I'm here to help the town."

"To all the hells with this town." Thunder from the clear night
sky could not have shaken Tara so much as that whipcrack whisper. "This town has been kinder to me than it has to you, though
never quite so kind as it likes to think. I have friends here. I have
raised their children and taught them of the world. But you are my
blood and his, and we were glorious together. We were the kind
of heroes each age sees once or twice before it goes, not because
we won kingdoms or made our rivals weep, but because the whole
world set out to kill us and we did not die. After that, all we wanted
was a small life, a place to live and raise our girl, and they came for
you with fire, they hated you not understanding what you were.
After they chased you off, it was only by your father's grace and
his good arguments that I did not walk out into the night with my
sharpest knife and kill them all where they slept. They are not
worth you. You want to save this town—I cannot stop you. But

stay safe. Come home to me. Or my soul will find yours in the afterworld, and it will go poorly for you."

Tara held her breath. Ma sat still, and she was Tara's mother and also Valentine Ngoye of high family in Alt Selene, child of queens beyond the waves, and though she'd fit herself to this country night she belonged to it no more than Tara. Less, even, in a way. Tara had been born here, though she left and defined herself by leaving. But though her mother nested in Edgemont, Edgemont never was her place.

In that flash she remembered Esther Braxton and all the rest crowding close after the funeral, and at the wake, remembered flowers and casseroles, their desperate attempt to knit Tara's mother to the town—because she was not theirs, and would never be.

Tara knelt and took her mother's firm and heavy hand. "I have to fight, Ma. But I will come back." Those were the words she said when she meant *I love you*.

"You better." Ma's hand clutched hers.

She kissed her mother and hugged her, and hid her unease, and looked into the house to seek guidance from the shadows. But she saw only Dawn watching, quiet, cold, a look on her face like she was trying to work out a problem of high Craft.

18

The sun was a long slow explosion far away, burning to death under its own weight. As night came to Edgemont on the evening of the battle, that was just how it looked.

"That's the stormfront," Tara explained to Connor, pointing with her cursed arm out to the crimson and orange and pink that claimed half the sky. The storm called to her, tugging at the white threads under her skin. "We'll have one hell of a fight on our hands." She squinted, judged. "Maybe more than one."

"Well, I think it's pretty."

She glared at him, and he grinned. Around them, guards hustled to their places. Some remained atop the wall. Others patrolled the town line. A few rode, though she warned them against it. Horses did not like the kind of war that was coming. That's why Craftsfolk rode machines, or the dead.

Connor knew the Raiders were out there, but he could set that aside and see the beauty. Through him, she could almost see it, too: fountains of warm light that revealed the gold in the ground, the blue in the shadows, the curve and shape of land.

She shivered. The night would be cool, but she didn't feel cold like she used to. Her shiver had nothing to do with the temperature.

That first night in the fields had not been their last. But while they'd never exactly had a conversation about it, they'd kept a certain distance in public. People knew, of course, Edgemont being Edgemont. In small towns no one has to be told anything. She wondered when the village believed they'd started sleeping together, how far behind the various aunts' and uncles' schedules she was running. She had considered not kissing him, just to spoil their betting pool.

But small-town life, like Craftwork, required a kind of doubled thought: you sometimes had to not know things, to find a legitimate source for information learned through channels you could not disclose. The people of Edgemont knew, but they didn't know they knew. Not yet.

What was going on between her and Connor? Nothing, was the easy answer. (She'd read once that in old Camlaander plays when they said "nothing" they meant sex, which made her wonder what it meant when they said "sex.") Nothing at all. Nothing much. They both desperately needed to get laid. They were alone in ways that made them close and different, and they were afraid and brave in a complementary pattern, hollows fitting around protrusions, curves into caves. She liked his face. But she was leaving once she'd seen this thing through—she really was—and he could not. He needed the Badlands like she needed the Craft. So she could not have him, and she wanted what she could not have.

And—he was not afraid of her. The masks she'd worn in the Hidden Schools and throughout her life in Alt Coulumb, and even now with Dawn, did not quite work on him.

He could look at this sunset and see the colors.

"Stay behind the line," she told him.

"I will."

"Don't let yourself get drawn away from the group. Don't try to face the Seer one-on-one."

"I won't."

"Trust the wards."

"I do." He smiled, not quite hiding his nerves. "I've done this before, you know."

"Not like this."

"And you'll be . . ."

"I'll be fine," she said. "Get out of here. We both have work."

He turned to obey. Before she could think better of it, she caught his wrist, pulled him toward her, grabbed the back of his neck, drew him down, and kissed him.

"Be careful," she said, instead of all the words mystery plays and romance novels wanted her to say next. There were some things she did not want to say by reflex.

"I," he said after the kiss, and there was a pause as he found his breath. "You, too." The smile showed before he ran.

"Thank you for waiting," she told Dawn when she turned back to face her. "And thank you for the chicken." The girl held a black bag over her shoulder; its contents were not happy about the situation. Whatever one might say about the effectiveness of haruspicy for precise divination—and Tara could say quite a bit—chickens did possess some minor practical foresight. Fortunately they couldn't use it to cause much trouble, because they were chickens. "Do you remember the plan?"

"We've gone over it a dozen times."

"And it is?"

"I maintain the wards, and protect the Pastor."

"He's crucial, the keystone of our network. Our defenses should take care of most threats, but I'll be busy with the curse."

"I'll watch him." She followed Tara to the wall. "Are you sure there's no one else you'd like me to keep track of?"

The sly tone of voice conveyed enough meaning. She didn't need to follow Dawn's gaze to Connor, stringing his bow among the other archers, but she did anyway. "You don't approve?"

"He's not . . . you," Dawn said.

"If I was what I wanted, I'd be more than capable of satisfying myself."

"I just don't see it. You grew up here—it's not like you have any, I don't know, city-dweller romantic misconceptions of how pure and noble and green these people are." Tara asked her a question with her eyebrows. "Tourists came through on the caravans sometimes. They had odd notions about farm life. You're avoiding the question."

"Which is?"

"What does he have to offer you?"

She looked back at the sunset and the oncoming storm. "I like his point of view. Now, hurry up with that chicken."

Pastor Merrott and Grafton Cavanaugh came to the line together, walking slow, deep in conversation. Tara tried to busy herself with circle and blood and bowl at the station she and Dawn had set up atop the wall, but she saw them embrace. The Pastor leaned toward Grafton Cavanaugh's cheek for a whisper or a kiss. Not her business which: her business was the battlefield.

The last few weeks of work had led her here. She knew Edgemont, and she could define its boundaries. She could protect the fields and the town from an encircling attack, and focus her attention on the storm, and the Seer.

The Raiders would test her borders by insinuation, by argument, by main force. If they broke through the line of battle, they would claim Edgemont by right of conquest. If the storm shattered her shields, the curse would drink the town dry. They would try to beat her wards in other ways: to claim she had no right to draw them, to attack small failures in their definitions.

The archers on the wall would break the Raiders' physical advance. If and when they failed, the infantry would hold the line. And she would stand against the storm.

From the wall she had a clean view west. The road she'd walked to get here ran back north to the ashblow that had been Blake's Rest, and away south again. Between the wall and the road lay the bare flat ground where her troops—who would not appreciate Tara calling them "hers," but, what the hells, they couldn't hear her inside her head—gathered with their spears and axes. They clustered behind boulders and beneath the crest of a low rise near the road, mostly hidden from the Raiders' likely angle of approach.

Beyond the road, the ground sloped down west to the glass-canyon maze. The canyons were half cover, half choke point. She hoped the second half would work in her favor. The Raiders wanted revenge, and they had come in force, dragging a storm across the desert. They weren't playing clever. She could feel their fury through her curse. They wouldn't march around the canyons, they wouldn't take the road. They meant to overwhelm. They'd rush straight through. She could use that.

At least, that was the plan.

Pastor Merrott climbed the wall. Dawn didn't look up from the town register. "You're late," she said. Tara saw him blush.

"Last-minute consultation. Grafton's worried about—"

Tara shook blood from her fingers. The curse inside her whispered, tempted. Its sickness obeyed other rhythms than her heartbeat: footsteps, drawing near. The Raiders were so close now. "We can talk about this later."

"I know you don't like Cavanaugh."

"He doesn't like me, Pastor."

"He's trying."

"He's welcome to try as hard as he wants, so long as he doesn't get someone else killed."

"I won't let that happen."

She compared the color of the blood in the bowl with the color of the dying sky. "Leave the fighting to the guards. You're a conduit, now, between Edgemont and the Courts of Craft. That makes you our weak point. All my wards anchor through you. You don't have to fight. Just be a riverbed: let power flow through, to the rest of us." He seemed unsure and earnest, and reminded her in that moment of Abelard. She punched him lightly on the shoulder. "You'll be fine. It's like any other blessing, just bigger. I'll be right here if you need help."

"Fine." He echoed her. "Okay. Yes. Good." He looked down at his parishioners below the wall, testing their weapons, buckling homemade armor on, passing pipes. The Pastor's real fear looked softer, more human, than the fear he showed on stage. He was closer to her world than anyone else in Edgemont except Ma, but sometimes she forgot how far apart they were. Dawn rolled her eyes. Tara waited for the priest to work through his doubts. He did at last, with a shake of his head, like a dog who'd run through dirty water. He had no idea how dirty the water was about to get. "How do we start?"

"We already have." A stiff gust of wind threw sand against her suit. The last red light gave way. Stars burned over Edgemont, but out in the Badlands the storm towered against the sky, rotten clouds twisted through with maggoty white threads. "Take my hand."

The Raiders came through the canyons.

Their sandstorm rushed across the desert, gathering speed,

bridging ground and sky. The curse whirled in that towering black cloud, and lightning flashes sculpted the boiling dark into gods and dragons and Deathless Kings. The Raiders' curse remembered the God Wars well. It was born there, and now it was coming home.

The pulse in Tara's arm was hot and sharp and hungry. She heard voices on the wind, no words, just that echoing surf-scream choral wash. Her grip tightened on Pastor Merrott's hand, and in that moment it didn't bother her that he might realize she was afraid.

The curse battered her, and she bore it.

Tomas Braxton cried out; Vaughan shushed him. The guards crouched in their shelter. She felt their prayers—their words, their fear, their need burned through Pastor Merrott into her. She felt his power, the village's faith, like a warm body on the other side of a thin sheet.

Set beside that faith the Raiders were an inferno.

She had expected them to come in strength. She sent their last force running into the night, tails between legs, whimpering back across the Badlands to their hive. They had come to pay her back for their humiliation, to break this town and humble her. Good. The greater their force, the greater her victory.

If the guards held.

They would hold. She was sure of it.

Bows wavered. Beneath the wailing wind, she heard human screams.

Absolutely, 100 percent sure.

The Pastor was holding her hand very tightly. Poor guy. No, wait. That was her, holding him.

The curse scrabbled against her wards, like a rat against the walls of a glass cage. If it got free, it would eat her.

The physical world was a distraction. She closed her eyes and saw as a Craftswoman.

Her guards were starlight sparks against the night, linked in a network of gold wire that bound them to Pastor Merrott. Edgemont lay behind them, a quilt of light, wrapped in her wards, feeding them. And from the desert came the Raiders, so many of them, nodes in the pus-white curse-web of the storm.

At the storm's heart, there walked a man. She saw him with eyes of Craft: a hole in the world, a walking wound. The curse-threads spun and buckled around him, through him. He called to her.

The Seer had come.

Hold, she whispered through the prayer web to Edgemont's guards. The Raiders advanced through the glass canyons. Howling wind bore their burned stench. Dawn chanted words Tara had taught her, maintaining the link to the Courts of Craft. Good girl. She learned fast.

That's the trick. Don't think about the Seer, about what comes next. Think about Dawn: teaching her, working with her. Think about Connor, and what you'll do together after this. Think about leaving Edgemont and going home.

Think of that, and wait for Raiders to hit their marks. Almost there. Five. Four. Three. Two. One.

The Raiders charged through the canyon.

She triggered the glyphs she'd carved into the canyon walls.

She heard the explosions, even through the howling storm. Shaped blasts struck the canyon walls like chisels hammered by a goddess. Connor had helped her find the choke points, and she'd done the math herself. Ten-story blades of glass a hundred meters long sheared off the walls and fell. The curse twisted to defend itself, but pus-lights winked out all along the canyon, and severed threads snarled in the storm. The glass, too, was a product of the God Wars, and everything made in that long bloody century could kill.

Ten Raiders fell at once, crushed under the glass, another ten as the glass shattered and storm wind drove its splinters through flesh, through eyes. She saw them die, felt the pain in her arm ease as each death weakened the curse. Dawn grinned, fierce, joyful.

But the Seer marched on.

A cheer rose from the ranks. She opened her eyes and saw stars over the Badlands again. The storm knelt above the canyons, viscous and thick as a shield. She triggered a second wave of traps, and more flashes of blue light burst skyward, but only five Raiders fell this time. The curse learned fast.

She'd carved the Raiders down. Edgemont's guards were not outnumbered anymore. The next part would be harder.

The storm rushed from the canyons and the Raiders with it. She could see their melted faces and the bones of their skeletal mounts. Ribs jutting from their flesh like teeth from diseased gums, extra arms and legs grafted on, lank thin hair streaming in the wind.

They threw curses at the wall, not yet seeing the guards she'd hidden below the ridge; the curse volley corkscrewed through the air and spent its hatred in the soil or the sky, leaving a sharp used-fireworks smell behind. Teeth gnashed and blades flashed in the dust storm. Hooves kicked up sand that the wind caught and swept like razors through the air.

This was no ordinary raid. They would not devour what they could grab and retreat into the Badlands. Tara had shamed them. They had come for war. And they had come for her.

She lit her glyphs, and revealed herself.

Come on. Show me what you've got.

The charge swept toward her, skeletal almost-horses and Raiders dragging the viscous roil of the storm. They bared fangs and let curses fly, and rode as if they meant to hammer Edgemont's wall down with their hooves.

And now—yes, she checked with her eyes closed—*now*, they were trespassing.

She spoke a word.

Her glyphs lit with blue fire, and the chicken's blood in the bowl at her feet began to burn. The circle glowed. Far away and very near, great Craftwork machines revolved. This place where she stood was real, and the Raiders and the guards below, the storm and the stars, only shadows. The world was an ocean in a storm, but she had given herself a firm place to stand.

Edgemont's fields, its road, its land, lay behind her in patchwork blue. In the heart of the storm, still hidden among the canyons, the Seer burned red and white, awhirl with streams of curse. Curse-threads sank into the ground where the Raiders' hooves fell and drained it, tore it. But the Craft was, to put it mildly, particular on the subject of property rights.

Power from the distant engines of the Courts of Craft surged into Pastor Merrott's body. His eyes and mouth opened but his muscles locked and he could not even moan. He became a conduit. The might of the Craft rolled from him into the guards and to the fields. To Tara's eyes, Edgemont's land glowed; the guards would see it green and real and sharp and oh-so-very theirs.

And Pastor Merrott was torn between them—this town to which he'd come as a humble outsider, this place he'd made his home, with all its people rising up to offer him their faith, and the cold alien hook of the Craft in his spine, enforcing their claim. Sweat steamed off his forehead. Judges trained and studied and poisoned themselves for years to bear this weight, and Pastor Merrott could not match them. But he had the training and conscience of a priest. He could serve. And meanwhile, Tara was free to fight.

Her argument was simple. She had named Edgemont with the Craft, named its every field and boundary and resident, each cow and horse and goat, she had named its birds and their nests. The Raiders were not welcome. They did not belong. They had no claim to this land, and no power here. Let them draw back to the desert and lick their wounds. This place was not theirs. She framed her argument in glyphs and alien tongues, with gestures and flame and triplicate paperwork, and the Craft made it so.

I abjure you.

The Raiders' curses skittered off the soil. Their storm-wind slowed. Mounts reared and pawed the air, snorted lightning, recoiling from the wards. The curse inside her quailed and screeched. She raised her arm for the archers and let it fall. *Now.*

Arrows flew—one flight, a second, a third. Raiders tumbled, Raiders collapsed, burning where they were pierced. As each one fell, the curse-storm lost another node, and power.

It thrashed in the sky, losing complexity, losing vision, for an instant no more than a panicked beast. It gathered itself, howling, lower to the ground, bunched and corkscrewed around the remaining Raiders. They pressed on toward the road, staking a claim step by step, though her wards burned them—and across the road, to the crest of the ridge, where the guards waited.

Spears flashed. Axes fell. Raiders, too.

This was the hard part. Even winnowed, the Raiders were prac-ticed killers, and Edgemont's guards tilled soil for a living. The guards' armor glistened blue-gold. Where curses fell it smoked and buckled, and where the Raiders' pale blades slashed it broke. A Raider fell, and two guards. Blood rained down, and chips of bone. People died. Vaughan Braxton was on the ground, bleed-ing; Tomas dragged him off. Pastor Merrott's breath caught in his throat. He wept. He felt each blade go in.

Not Tara. She could not feel and fight at once. There would be time for mourning after. Shove fear and compassion, sorrow and shock aside. Down a well, if necessary. Pull yourself out of the mud and guts, the groans of horror and pain. Don't be human. Let all this be math.

Six down on our side so far, two dead, four heavily injured. Four on theirs. Another two on theirs, and, yes, one more, each casualty marked by a pulse of spitting thwarted fury in her cursed arm. The land turns their feet, blades of grass gain cutting edges. She redirected the blessings of the fallen guards back to those still standing, to make them stronger, faster, and sent runners to drag the wounded to safety.

White lines writhed in the shredded storm. A clutch of Raiders fell, and she felt a stab of triumph—until she realized the curse had not retreated, just shifted its power across the battlefield to other Raiders, granting them greater speed for the instant they needed to slide past a block or parry.

Guards fell, and fell back. The lines wavered.

The Seer's counterargument hit her then, like a blade between her ribs. You stake your claim with arms—retreat is surrender, a ceding of territory. *What you lose belongs to me.* The Pastor screamed.

A gap opened in her defenses. The curse-lines shifted lightning-fast. The Seer was the curse—its heart, its fittest servant. Com-pared to him, Tara was playing piano in thick gloves. The Raiders' names and minds had been eaten. They were not separate beings anymore. The curse could direct, abandon, adjust them with re-flex speed. And through the storm the Seer marched, a towering flame to Craftwork sight, though unseen yet to mortal gaze. Each footstep was an ice pick in her arm.

The guards began to retreat. *No*, she told them. *Get closer.*

The curse could outpace her because all its Raiders were, fundamentally, the same. Interchangeable targets. She didn't have that advantage. She had to know the people she was sending into danger. It was easier to think of them as numbers—but when was the Craft ever easy?

Tomas Braxton had returned to the fight. She couldn't see Vaughan anywhere. Cooper fell with a spear in his gut. Thibodault hacked at the Raider who held the spear, tearing away flesh and chipping bone, but the Raider lurched on. Cooper and Braxton and Thibodault were part of Edgemont, part of its wards and protections. The Raiders did not have names, but she could find each one through the guards they fought—so long as the guards kept fighting.

It was all close murder now, hackwork with axes and point-blank cursethrowers and sawing blades. The bowstrings fell silent. Archers could not loose on foes without hitting friends.

But Tara's Craft knew no such limits.

She drew her work knife from the glyph above her heart, raised it to the sky, and spoke to the power bound through Pastor Merrott. Shadows swirled at her knife tip, drinking starlight and moonlight and refactoring its power into a glistening vortex.

The sky over Edgemont changed.

It did not so much appear as turn into view: a rainbow, if rainbows were thorn trees. It rippled like sunlight seen from underwater. The aurora was built in the God Wars, for greater battlefields than this. Summoning it here was overkill, and she did not care.

She swept her knife down toward the plain, spoke a word in a dead tongue, and lightning answered. The impact hammered through her. Seconds did not follow seconds. Heartbeats fled heartbeats. She drifted on a sea of fire, writhing before her eyes, open and closed. Her ears rang. No, the *world* rang, and it pressed against her ears.

The battlefield returned in pieces.

Raiders sprawled on melted sand. She saw an arm wheel through the air, fall and bounce. She felt sick. She had never worked Craft like this before. The aurora was an old weapon, a weapon from the Wars. She knew people who had fought back then. Elayne Kevarian never talked about it much. Tara had met the King in Red one time, and he must have liked the Wars, because he'd been very very good at them. What would it make you, to grow used to handling such power? To see a battlefield and think of it not as a horror but a puzzle, a knot of bodies you might untie, or simply cut?

They were winning. The Raiders fell back, those who could. Most were broken, or breaking.

And out of the storm, the monster came.

She saw him with her eyes open and closed: the Seer. She felt him in her arm, in her blood. He drew the rags of storm behind him like a cloak. In flesh he was tall and gaunt and pale in the way desert life should not allow, with a cloth across his sickly glowing eyes, and a wide thin mouth too pleased with the carnage through which he walked. He wore a long black torn and tattered coat that billowed in his wake. His left hand held a spear of bone and his right was a long-taloned bloody mass of curse. His shirt was loose and eaten, as was the flesh below. He writhed with white, and his feet did not touch the ground. Like a Craftswoman gone to war, he seemed larger than a mortal frame could grow: eight feet tall, taller. He was not physically larger—he simply stood closer than the rest of the world. The fact of him mattered more.

This was the man her father had fought with nothing to protect him but a sword and the toy wards Pastor Merrott made. And now he had come for her.

She called the aurora down against him but the curse was faster—white threads writhed thick above his head and the light dispersed, reflected a thousandfold into the storm. Where he set his foot, curse-threads wormed to rot the soil. Guards fell back, and the rot spread.

The wards in Tara's arm shivered and cracked. She groaned and sank to one knee as the curse burrowed into her meat.

He watched her across the battlefield, as he came on. Just her. She could not see his eyes, but she felt them like a blade tip against her chest. He raised his spear, and threads lanced from the storm toward her. She roared up off her knees, forgetting pain, forgetting the curse swelling free inside her, and she broke his threads, one by one; the last hungry seeking line shriveled a few meters from the wall.

And he drew closer.

She was afraid. She had been afraid for weeks: of the curse, of the Raider's hollow eyes at Blake's Rest, of that slithering voice. But she had also been afraid of Edgemont, of people she had known since birth. Afraid of Esther Braxton and Grafton Cavanaugh. Afraid of what they would say, what they would do.

She was done with fear. She was ready to be mad.

Anger bloomed from the mulch of her fear, fire-hot and sweet. She held a power that was built to war on gods, and she would use it. She had promised Ma on the porch that she would not let the Seer draw her out. But here he was. She would make him kneel and bleed and suffer and then she would make him die.

She let go of Pastor Merrott's hand, gathered shadows to her, and stepped off the rampart.

She swept through the air, a streak of silver light, haloed with shadows and aurora flame, and landed before the Seer. Curses wreathed him and power filled her, chilled her heart, drained colors from the battlefield.

She raised her hand. Golden vines burst from the soil beneath his feet and lashed his limbs, climbed into the hollows of his body. He was an intruder here, a monster, an echo of a long-ago war, and she cast him out, stilled the winds of his storm, blinded those eyes that only saw the corruption he might spread. She banished him to the Badlands, where he might wander with the other broken things. He had no place here.

He shuddered and slowed. The writhing threads in his eyes faded to a shabby bone-gray, and for an instant she let herself believe it might be this easy.

Then the rot in Tara's arm began to bubble and grow.

It wriggled toward her elbow and pushed cold past her shoulder joint, forcing muscle fibers apart, climbing fascia, shredding the glyphs she'd used to bind it. If she had been altogether human, the curse would have claimed her then—shot through her blood and heart, drinking her soul to fuel its growth. But she was a Crafts-woman. Her soul was glyphed and warded three times three, and no wild outsider could breach that protection.

She bit down a scream.

At least, no wild outsider could breach it easily.

She fought him on two fronts now. Her Craft bore down with power he could not resist, weakened as he was, his force in ruins, his storm shredded. *I abjure you.* But he had a hook inside her and worked his curse toward her heart.

I belong here, the curse whispered. *You say I am not of Edge-mont. But you are part of this place. You have made yourself its heart—the bond between Edgemont and the world of Craft. And I am part of you. I wriggle through your veins. I gnaw your meat and drink your soul. If you are of Edgemont, then so are we, together.*

The logic pressed against her Craft as the curse wormed in her flesh. But she bared her teeth, and bore down on him again. He was wrong. She was not the heart of the village, not its link. That was Pastor Merrott, up on the wall. She was not of this place. She was a hireling. Paid to fix broken wards. She was an outsider here, as she had always been.

Lies, the curse hissed back. It buckled her knees, it ground her bones. *This soil, you were bred upon it. In your bed in that city so far away you dream its midnight sounds. You grew here. You learned here. You love, here.*

She gasped for breath. The world around them fell away. She was on the hillside again, with Connor, beneath the stars. She was dying, always, dying.

I do not, she replied, with knives of light and aurora fire. More vines hooked him, and lightning lashed down. He flailed with his spear to block it, but the spear cracked. *I do not belong.* It was true. Her will made it so. *I ran from this place the moment I had power. I left my parents and I left my friends. I gave myself to the Craft so fully that in their hour of greatest need these people did not call me back. I know them, I am bound to them. But I am not of them. And no tie of faith or blood or sex will hold me here.*

The argument cut her, burned her. She felt a piece of herself die as she made it. But the Craft would not bind in falsehood.

Blood ran down her arms. She caught his spear and pressed him back and down. His ragged worm-eaten features twisted in panic. His power sought some flaw in the grave-sure wall of her argument, scrabbling over her like fingernails over safety glass. And then: he grinned.

Then you do not belong here either. You cast me out, and so cast out yourself. Come with me. Into the desert. Into the heat that melts flesh, the cold that comforts bone. Come to the truth. Join us.

She stumbled. Her vines dulled and snapped, and her grip on the aurora dimmed. The curse pulsed toward her heart. She fell to one knee. Desperate, pain-raw, she caught the curse and clad it in knowledge of her body—this was not part of her, this corruption, infiltration—she named each muscle fiber, each bone and organ, made her anatomy real and fierce and above all hers, immutable. She built herself into a wall but still she felt those blindly groping tendrils reach down and in, down and through—

He tore his spear from her grip and raised it, sharp and wet.

Pain-blind, she drew power from stars and soil to defend herself. Too late, too late.

The Seer howled. But not with triumph.

A golden arrow pierced his shirt. Its light dimmed as he looked down, and the feathered shaft rotted as his curse stitched up the wound. His writhing gaze turned from Tara to the archer who had shot him, who should be on the wall, who she'd godsdamned *ordered* to keep out of this—

Connor nocked a second arrow, loosed, and then a third.

The Seer's smile turned cruel.

His threads blocked the second arrow, but Tara shifted strength and speed to the third and it buried in his chest, where it rotted, too. The Seer glared at her and the curse set hooks into her lungs, and as she gagged he turned his spear on Connor.

But Grafton Cavanaugh got there first.

The big man threw his body between Connor and the curse, and though his armor cracked and dimmed he marched against the curse's weight toward the Seer, shouting words Tara could not hear, a pitchfork raised in his meaty hands. Grafton's armor dimmed, his light faded. He ran on and in, until with a crack his armor failed.

His left arm withered, like a towel wrung out. He roared in pain. But he had given her an instant's space, and she would not waste it. Tara found her breath, and spun the village's blessing into Cavanaugh, to shield him. He still held the pitchfork with his right, and struck one-handed toward the Seer's neck.

The Seer parried Grafton's blow, but he took a step back. And—gods. There was Grafton's goon squad, following the leader. Tomas Braxton and Jon Darien and Kip Dailey and that whole stupid angry crew, running into the breach with whatever arms they had to hand.

Tara gaped. They were doing it.

An axe took the Seer in his side, though its blade rusted to scrap as it pierced that long black ragged coat. A blow of his claw tossed Tomas Braxton back ten feet, and Jon Darien's leg broke beneath the butt of that spear. But inch by inch, the Seer withdrew.

With each retreating step Tara's pain eased. She named her body into being and threw the sky against him, lances of light and fire. She fed the guards strength. The storm shuddered. Connor loosed arrow after arrow until his quiver was empty. Braxton and Darien and Dailey and Cavanaugh all flailed against the Seer. They were angry and they were fighting back. Turning him away. Driving him from their land, with their own strength.

Away from Edgemont and its wards.

She realized what was happening too late. *Stop,* she prayed to them, but they were too lost to the fight to heed her, pressing their advantage into the Badlands.

She reached for them with Craft, but the Seer was faster. The ragged shreds of storm quickened and congealed. Curse-threads swept out and caught them, noosed them, drew them up and out past the wards.

Connor screamed. So did his father.

The curse netted Grafton Cavanaugh. He struggled, even as

his bonds rotted him. The Seer's thin lips split in a grin. He raised curse-dripping talons toward Cavanaugh's bare throat.

Tara saw her own father, alone in that canyon made of glass.

This was her fault. She had exposed herself. She had collapsed the whole battle to a duel, made it all about her. If she had stayed on the wall, the others would not have run out to help her. And now she was just going to make things worse.

But she would not let anyone else die. And she would not let the Seer win.

I'm sorry, Mom.

She ran toward them, blade in hand, wreathed in shadow, past the wards. But before she could close the gap, a shuddering impact knocked her off her feet, and a wash of light blinded her.

Pastor Merrott fell like a comet to the field.

The Pastor was only half a man now: all the Craft she had invoked to guard the town burned through him. He was Edgemont, as the Seer was the storm.

He landed with a force that cracked the dry ground. The Seer flew back. Curse-threads shriveled in the light that streamed from Pastor Merrott. Connor and Tomas and Jon Darien fell, ragged but alive, mostly. Cavanaugh gasped, curled around his ruined arm, but he was still breathing.

The Seer stood and raised his spear. But Pastor Merrott was there to meet him.

He battered the Seer with the wheeling haymaker fury of a man who had never fought once in his life. The Seer drew back and Pastor Merrott pressed on, weeping diamond tears. Tara ran into the storm, reaching, reaching, her blade the only light in the viscous whirl of sand and curse, her skin cut by dust and bits of flying glass.

Out and out the Pastor drove his foe. Tara cried his name, wove Craft to catch him, but the storm thrust her back.

The Seer had his prey.

Curse-lines tensed and coiled. The storm furled, mud-dense, around Pastor Merrott, and gathered him up like a giant hand. Tara ran and ran, feeding starlight to her legs, her lungs aflame, heart pounding, her legs molten at first then cold as she surrendered her fragile human metabolism to the Craft. But the Raiders were swift as a mistake.

The night was clear. The Seer was gone. And he had taken Pastor Merrott with him.

19

They carried her home past the untouched houses and the church and the village green. The wards had worked. The village was safe. Only its people hurt. Braxton girls ran to the wall carrying hot water and bandages and thread.

Dawn and Ma laid Tara on her bed and she chased them off, told them to go help people who needed it. She'd be down in a minute. She just had to catch her breath. Then, alone, she peeled off her coat and shirt and hissed—not so much at the pain, which was manageable if exquisite, as at what she saw.

Black threads spiderwebbed her arm, through the shoulder, and in—corkscrewing toward her heart. In bright light the threads pulsed; when she pressed her skin, they moved. She felt them strain against her glyphs, trying to grow, to feed. There was still time—if she left tomorrow, or the next day, she'd lay good odds against bad gamblers that she could make it to a doctor.

From this distance, even with her window open, she could not hear the weeping or the screams from the wall.

She buttoned her shirt, grabbed her bag, and went back down to help.

They laid the wounded on the green. Tara and Dawn walked among them, numb, passing judgment. She knew bodies better than anyone in Edgemont, and curses.

Triage was a sorting problem. Head injury, head injury, head injury. Cut, deep cut, deeper cut. Bruised, bleeding, broken.

The kids followed, the same ones who had come to watch them pace the fields, led by the boy with the scar on his face. The younger Braxton women joined them, and Nell Leary. Tara set playing cards at each casualty's feet, red for those who would recover on their own, black for those who needed care, Major Arcana for the cursed. There were not so many wounded as she'd feared, not compared to the Raiders they had killed. And there were not so many dead.

One was too many.

She was aware, as if through water or a dream, of Ma and Esther Braxton in a whirl of villagers, issuing orders. They tended the merely injured with bandages, needles, thread, painkiller tonics. Ma set Tomas Braxton's arm, while Esther and the others held him still. If Ma was the wheel's hub then Connor was its rim, building fires, fetching water and supplies, always moving.

Tara and Dawn dealt with the cursed. Nell Leary and Stephanie Braxton carried the victims to the church's undercroft, on improvised stretchers. Tara led them down, remembering how hard she'd tried to keep anyone in Edgemont from seeing the work she and Dawn had wrought here, the layered circles and inscriptions in the technical languages of the Craft, the palpable darkness the undying candles pierced but did not relieve. All those precautions seemed foolish now. But still, when she crossed the threshold of the church, she felt a moment's guilt, and looked around for Pastor Merrott, to ask his permission for what she was about to do.

The laugh did not make it to her throat.

She operated on them in the dark. She could see here as clearly as by day. Light's absence had an illumination all its own. Dawn passed the tools: the bracelets to glove her hands in dark, the lance, the pentacle, the bowl, the wand. She made her own knife.

The curse in Jon Darien could tell she was coming, and burrowed into his flesh to hide from her. When she offered to take his pain he nodded; she stopped his nerves below his neck, and one by one she dug the curses out. They were small and barbed, and came free with a pop. They writhed on her forceps and hissed when she dropped them into the silver bowl. The tendrils of her own curse cringed in sympathy. *Serves you right.*

It was easier if she saw her patients not as people but as the sort of problems a teacher might pose on a Remedies final: given a curse wrapped around the brachial artery in a helical pattern like so, eliminate propagation risk with minimal blood-flow interruption, using at most three interventions.

Back in the Hidden Schools, when she'd been asked that very question on her Remedies final, she had provided the proper answer, then pointed out that propagation risk could be eliminated entirely with one intervention to the artery. Kill the host and the parasite follows. She passed Remedies with distinction.

They brought Grafton Cavanaugh in next and laid him on the slab. Jon Darien had screwed his eyes up tight against the pain, but Cavanaugh's were open, his pupils wide and shining black. His withered hand curled against his chest and curse-threads writhed beneath the skin. He made no sound.

He had saved his son, and Pastor Merrott tried to save him. People saving people saving people in a great chain that wound around their necks and dragged them all down together into this dark place. This man could not forgive her, blamed her for her father's death, was a monster in his son's mind. But when Connor fell, Grafton Cavanaugh had charged the Seer. And here he was, on her operating table.

Later she would look back at this moment and sift the mixed and multicolored sand of her own thoughts for—nothing so developed as temptation. Unless temptation was the mere awareness of possibility. Cavanaugh's arm was far gone, and curse extraction was not without risk. He might die. And here she stood in a dark room, nearly alone. Dawn watched her from the shadows, but she lacked the experience to question Tara's decisions.

No one was perfect. Anything could happen on an operating table.

She drew her knife and reached for his arm, but before she could begin to cut, he grabbed her with his good hand. The effort hurt him, and his grip hurt her. His voice was a rasp. "Save."

"The curse is rooted deep. You might lose the arm, no matter what I do." He didn't have her glyphs. A competent surgeon could still reclaim her tissues, draw the curse. She was reasonably sure of this. If she left tonight.

"Not me," he said. "Merrott."

She set her hand over his and peeled his fingers from her sleeve.

"Lie back." She let him feel the first cut. She told herself it was kindness: he would want to think he was brave under the knife. She wondered, later, why she had to tell herself that.

She had wanted a good fight and a clean ending. She had wanted to go home. And now she was here.

When it was through, he kept the arm.

She worked swiftly after that.

When the girls helped Kip Dailey limping from the undercroft, Dawn asked Tara, "Are you okay?"

Anger stopped up her mouth, and Tara waited for it to fade before she spoke. "You should have stopped the Pastor from entering the fight."

"I tried."

"You tried." She heard the word crack like a whip in the dark, and felt ashamed. Ms. Kevarian had never been so short with her. Then again, they'd never failed like this together.

"He didn't listen. I reached for him and my hand slipped off and he was moving so fast. I screamed. He didn't look back."

"And they have him now," she said. "The Raiders' loss tonight would have broken them for years even if the Seer escaped. But the Pastor holds the keys to Edgemont, and they have him. When they take him apart, they'll drink this town dry."

"What should I have done?" Her voice sounded far away, as if she was speaking from the bottom of a well, and Tara realized that Dawn was scared. At Blake's Rest she'd learned to bury her fear, to stand very still to wait for storms to pass. Now Tara was the storm.

Tara felt sick. She took a breath in the dark and made herself calm.

"Whatever you had to," Tara said. The words surprised her, the flat weight of them. "That's what I can teach you, and compared to that the Craft is just a set of conjurer's tricks. You could have stabbed him or tripped him or cut him off or hit him. Sometimes there's no good way to do what's needed, so you do what you can instead. You see your chance and make it good. No one will prompt you to do that. No one will tell you *now's the time*. There are men in this world, and more than a few women, who will crush you and collar you while you're waiting for their permission to fight back. And as long as that's true, we can't afford to wring our hands and think, ah, if only we could find the right way to talk to them, the right argument to make, if only we knew the one perfect winning move that didn't break any of the rules we've set ourselves. We have to act. I know you have the knack of it. You grew up harder than I ever did. But you're afraid. Maybe of what I'll think. Maybe of what the world will do if you try and lose."

"Yes." The edges of the word were raw, and Tara bled inside, hearing them.

She looked into Dawn's eyes and saw the animal there. "You can fight. You can stop them. You are a Craftswoman. And if you lack a single charm, a single thaum of soul, you can fight until death and beyond so that even if you fail the bones of the world will bear your mark. Because you will fail. And sometimes you will win, and bad things will happen anyway. I've lost friends. I've almost died many times, and someday I will. I've made horrible mistakes. But I will not let anyone tell me when it's time to fight."

"They tell themselves the same thing, though," Dawn said. "The ones with the collars and chains."

"Yes."

"So how do we know we're not them?"

"We are," she said. "We are the same animal. There's no line built into us, no governor that will stop us from turning into them. The best we can do is find friends who are better than us, and keep them close, and trust them to stop us before it's too late."

Dawn listened to the silence when she was done speaking. "You're not being fair."

"No," she admitted. "I'm not."

"You went down to fight. If you stayed, you could have stopped him. So you're part of this, too."

"I am."

Tara thought about her curse, and the playing cards, red and black. She felt very tired—physically tired, yes, but tired also of pretending, of lying. She folded her jacket and set it on the table beside the surgical instruments. Then she unbuttoned her shirt and rolled up the sleeve, and showed Dawn her arm. The girl reached out, trembling. Her touch was cool, but it still hurt.

Tara said, "You asked if I was okay."

"How long?"

"Since the first attack. It wasn't this bad, before tonight." She pulled away from the girl's touch, with a hiss. "Sorry. I'm not being a good teacher at the moment."

Dawn's gaze dropped to the table with the surgical instruments. Bracelets. Lance. Pentacle. Wand. "Maybe I can cut it out," she said, desperate. "If you coach me through."

"Won't work. It's spread too far. I couldn't treat this in someone else, now—I need a proper doctor. If I left tomorrow, I would keep the arm. Probably."

"We'll go. I can pack. I'll take care of everything. You rest."

"The Raiders have Pastor Merrott," she said, gently. "And when they break him, they'll have Edgemont."

"So let them!" The flare of Dawn's anger made ghostlights surge and shadows writhe. Tears glinted in her eyes. "This place isn't worth you. They hurt you. They chased you out. Let them rot and wither. You're more than this. You have to be."

Dawn caught her then, in an embrace. Her tears wet Tara's shirt and she clutched her, as if a tide Tara could not feel was tearing them apart. Tara hugged her back, gingerly. She set her hand on that long strange golden hair. "It's okay." It wasn't.

"I won't let you do this for them. I won't let you die."

"Dawn, I'm not going to die." Dawn clutched her harder. "I mean, eventually. I mean I won't, like, *die*, die. But I'll get a lot thinner." The girl laughed, wetly, but she was still shaking. Tara took her by the shoulders, pushed her back, and looked into her damp bright eyes. "Listen to me, Dawn. It's not happening now. It's not happening soon. Not if I have anything to say about it."

She blinked away tears, still not getting it. "But you said."

"The curse will grow, as long as it's alive. You can't cut it out of my arm. I can't do it myself. So I need a doctor. Or."

And there it was. The click behind the eyes. The sudden smile. The Craft was a way of seeing. "Or," she said. "We follow Pastor

Merrott into the Badlands. To the Raider hive, to the source of the curse. We kill it. And we save him."

"Can we? They're so strong."

"They took a big loss tonight," Tara said. "So did we. They won't be ready for a counterattack. But it is risky. That's why—"

"I'm going."

She frowned. "That's why you'll stay here. I'll write you a letter of recommendation to my old teacher, Elayne Kevarian. She'll take care of you. Get you into the Hidden Schools, or somewhere else you can learn. I can't bring you along. It's not safe."

"Since when is the Craft safe?"

She had a point.

"I'm not Elayne Kevarian's student," Dawn said. "I'm yours." She took Tara's jacket from the table and held it out to her. "So. When do we leave?"

20

They rode out before sunrise the next day, through the glass canyons, the pair of them alone. They passed broken bodies and drifting ash, and by dawn they reached the Badlands.

Connor was waiting for them.

He sat perched on a boulder, playing his wooden flute. Tara had hoped those ghostly skirling notes were the music of wind through broken canyon glass. The wide brim of his hat covered his eyes. Two horses waited behind him, one saddled, one piled with gear.

When he saw them he stopped playing and waved and smiled, as if they had agreed to meet here, as if they were going on a hike.

"No," Tara said before he could explain. They had packed fast, left early, been discreet. She had thought that would be enough. She did not like being wrong in general, and neither did she like the errant surge of pleasure she felt to be wrong in this specific case.

"You can't tell me this isn't my fight. Or my fault."

His fault? Because he failed to kill with an arrow something that could not be killed with arrows? Because he stood firm against the Seer, and his father rallied to his defense? But he sat unmoved on his rock. They'd grown close enough that she could tell her arguments would not shake him. Like her, he felt guilt whether or not he had cause, and he could no more let it go than she could. "The town needs you."

"You need me more."

Dawn drew her horse's reins too tight, and as it pranced she glowered. "Tara knows the Badlands. She's walked all the way from the Crack in the World on her own."

"And came through half-dead with sunstroke, did she tell you that? The Raiders won't be waiting in their lair with chicken soup."

"I'm better now," Tara said. "And there's no other way."

"How exactly did you mean to follow them, then? That storm doesn't leave footprints."

She drew from her jacket a stone needle suspended by a thin chain from a leather loop. The needle turned freely as they watched, and came to rest aiming out toward a horizon already twisted with heat. "The stone's from Merrott's altar. It will lead us to him."

He raised his eyebrows. "Nice. But knowing which way to walk won't get you there. The Badlands are full of leaky ordnance from the Wars. The landscape's twisted, and reality shifts out underfoot. Knowing what direction they've gone won't help you pass through a labyrinth trap, or climb out of a pitcher pit, or skirt an edge storm."

"You can't help with any of that either," Dawn said. "You have no power."

"Excuse me? Why are you going? Tara I understand, but you're not even half-trained."

Her eyes narrowed. The boulder's shadow thickened into ropes and snapped out, snaring his neck and waist and arms.

"Dawn," Tara said, sharply, and the shadows vanished, though Dawn kept glaring at Connor. "She insisted. It seems to be a common affliction."

"I didn't think you'd leave me."

That slipped past her guard. "I couldn't ask you to come."

"You're not asking," he said. "I'm offering. I've spent weeks in the Badlands by myself. I've crept past half the monsters in the New World at one time or another. You had a two-hour head start on me and I still beat you here."

"I could have gone faster." Gods, was she feeling defensive? "I didn't want to use Craft so near the village."

"The Craft will draw attention in the Badlands. You know that. What lives out there likes the smell of magic. If you're trusting your powers to pave your way across the desert you'll have to fight every step. You'll be hard-pressed to save yourself, let alone the Pastor."

He had a point. Tara's horse stamped, annoyed on her behalf. She eyed the mountains in the distance and thought about her first time through these wastes, how she survived by drinking the blood of vultures she lured down by playing dead.

"I know you, Tara Abernathy. You're not one to set aside an advantage in time of need. You know I know the Badlands. So the only way I can think you'd sneak off without me is if you wanted me along, but you didn't want to let yourself have nice things."

"And you think you're nice things."

He grinned and in that moment she forgot the battle, the loss. He had not stared down the Seer, and she had not stood above his father with a knife. They were kids, insolent beneath the sky. She liked him for offering that illusion, and he liked her for believing it. "I am."

Her hand tightened on the reins. "Ma put you up to this."

He had the decency to look embarrassed. "She told me last night. I would have come anyway when I learned you'd gone. Might not have caught up till sundown, though."

"I say we leave him," Dawn said. "He'll get in the way."

He just waited, with that smile.

"Saddle up," Tara said.

"She's already saddled. When was the last time you rode a horse, anyway?"

"Whatever. Let's go. Before I change my mind and turn you into a rock."

He smirked. "And Dad said I'd never be a hard man."

She gave her horse rein and left him laughing behind, to catch her.

21

On the second day out, Connor guided them around a patch of flat dry ground several miles across that looked like any other stretch of Badlands. The detour set Dawn grumbling and might have frustrated Tara, too, if she hadn't noticed the rainbows that swirled above that flat expanse when glimpsed out of the corner of her eye.

Human peripheral vision didn't see color, as had been explained to her at length during eyeball dissection at the Hidden Schools. The eye was only a fine-grained instrument at the center of its focus. The high-color world most people thought they saw was an illusion knit by sleight of mind and rapid movements of the eye. And yet: out of the corner of her eye, she saw rainbows.

While they waited at a spring for their canteens to fill, Dawn hefted a stone and contemplated the sand flat. Connor saw what she was thinking and tried to catch her wrist, but before he could reach her, she threw.

The stone sailed, fell, landed, and rolled. Tara watched. She did not see any rainbows. She did, however, see the mouth that opened in the ground beneath the stone, and its layers of gnashing crystal teeth.

Connor glared at Dawn, who gaped at the sand flat where the mouth had been.

Tara's canteen filled. She capped it and added it to her bag. "I hope that's settled." No one spoke. She mopped her sweat away, wet her bandanna in the spring, and tied it across her forehead to cool her. Then she adjusted her hat against the sun and stood. "Let's get moving. I'd like to reach those hills before night."

At the fireside that evening, Dawn chewed dried meat in silence while Connor played his flute soft and lonely. He'd told her the night before that he liked to play faster tunes, but out on the Badlands it was best to be mistaken for wind. Tara paced around the flames, stretching muscles bunched and sore after too long on horseback. The curse ached in her shoulder.

Dawn swallowed. "What was that thing?"

Connor set down his flute. "Nobody knows."

"You mean, *you* don't know." She was looking at Tara instead, with an expression that made Tara wish she had a better answer than:

"He's right. Mostly."

"But how is that possible? It must have been born. It must die. There must be other things related to it, even if that particular sort of monster only, I don't know, grows or hunts or lives out here. Someone must have given them a name."

A dragon had mocked Tara for a similar assumption years ago, and she felt her mouth quirk lizard-wise as she tried to frame the answer in her own words. "Names are not the same as truth, or knowledge. The word 'rhinoceros' just means 'that thing with a horn on its nose.' Most names work like that, even the names we use in Craft: they're labels. They refer. You're making a number of assumptions, among them that this is a member of a class of beings. If I'm not mistaken, it's the only one of its kind. Not the last—the only."

"Then where did it come from?"

Tara sat down. "You tell me."

Dawn's face went through some interesting changes before she spoke next. "You're serious."

"Remember what I said back at Edgemont about gods, and complexity."

"This is mean."

"This is educational."

Dawn frowned into the fire. She spoke one word at a time with breaks between, spinning the fuzz of her thoughts into thread. "So, life is a kind of pattern—all life, gods and humans and whatever that was out there. Small patterns link up to make bigger patterns. Each level . . ." Tara tried to keep her face neutral as she listened to the girl think. "Each level's a base for the next, and guards the ones below."

Tara did not let herself nod or smile. When she first decided to teach Dawn, she'd worried about her own desire to break out slate and chalk and pointer and enter full-on lecture mode. She had underestimated the electric joy of watching the girl piece truth together on her own.

"You called that thing an accident. And gods died out here." Dawn bit her lower lip when she was lost in thought. "If you hurt a god, it might hide in something else. Could gods live in less complicated things? In rocks and stones?"

"Not well," she said. "But when they do, they don't look like that. You're on the right track, though. Keep going. What do you need to have, to make a pattern? Say, if you wanted to make a cat's cradle?" She held her hands apart and spun thin blue lines of Craft around them to demonstrate.

"You'd need string, I guess," Dawn said. "Fingers. Something to weave the pattern in and against. You'd need time, and energy, that you weren't using for something else. I suppose those are sort of related, time and energy. You'd need to know how."

"Generally speaking," Tara said, "if you want a pattern to arise in nature you need a substrate, which is a fancy way of saying you need something to make the pattern in, plus energy, time, and a seed—any asymmetry's enough. Any small difference. The more you have, the less time the process takes."

"And," excited now, eyes glowing with reflected fire as she leaned in, "there was a war here."

"Yes."

"Lots of gods and Craftswomen throwing lots of power around. The desert is the . . . substrate? Lots of energy. And there were gods and Craftsfolk dying everywhere. Blood on the sand. Abandoned munitions. Plenty of, what was that word?"

"Asymmetry."

"Asymmetry. So new patterns would form. Not quite gods, not quite machines. Accidents."

Yes. Exactly. Full marks. Tara tried to take Dawn's success as a given, to disguise her pride—let the kid feed on discovery rather than acclaim. But, damn, was she smart. "That one eats light, I think, but everything's made of light if you hit it hard enough. Craftwork rearranges the world, and makes new patterns. If you're not careful—and we weren't careful back in the Wars, because we didn't know any better and because we didn't have time to be— those patterns take on lives of their own. That's where the curse came from: a weapon we used against gods, or that gods used against us. A parasite that disrupts and absorbs the patterns it finds. These days we split major works of Craft between many Craftworkers to avoid this problem: if you give people simple, knowable work, most of the time it doesn't try to eat them. Plus, there's less of a chance you'll contradict yourself and write a hole into the world."

"You mentioned that before. Does it really happen?"

"It happened to a friend of mine." She poked the fire with a stick and sparks danced up. In the middle of the desert she should have felt alone, but instead all the ages of history clustered around their fire, monsters rubbing shoulders with monsters. "Most of the time when that sort of thing goes wrong, it only makes a tiny hole, enough to kill a careless Craftswoman, not enough to cause lasting damage." She set the stick down. In the sky above Alt Coulumb there rose a shining arch of demonglass with a flaw in the shape of a girl at its heart. Strange how, when you took on a student, all your personal tragedies, your friends' disasters and despair and even their deaths, were transmuted into lessons. "We got very lucky. But she still died."

"I'm sorry," Dawn said, and after a silence that went on too long, her voice tentative, continued: "Is that accident in the sand flat really . . . alive?"

"What do you mean when you say 'alive'? It eats. It defends itself. It's hungry and simple and nasty, but you could say the same about a raccoon. Most accidents don't reproduce, but some can. That's one reason we're reluctant to clean places like this up, even though they're dangerous. The ethics are uncomfortable. Even for us."

Dawn stared back out into the dark. She went very still when her mind worked, as if all the force that animated her body was otherwise occupied. Even her voice had a faraway, dreamlike sound. She was still getting used, Tara thought, to talking about her ideas, rather than brooding over them in midnight silence. "What about the Craft itself?"

"Okay. Run with that."

"You said a pattern takes substrate, energy, and a seed. All the deals and contracts of the Craft, all those wards and bargains overlapping—they must make really complicated patterns. That's a substrate. There's so much energy involved already. And there must be seeds all over the place. Asymmetries. Could there be patterns in the Craft itself? Could it have a mind? Could it grow . . . accidents?"

Tara leaned forward. After the memory of the demonglass arch, the cold thrill of abstract reasoning was a relief. They might have been sitting on leather upholstery in a tutoring room at the Hidden Schools, with a coffee service and sherry a bell pull away. "Craftwork can host minds—that's how Deathless Kings survive: they create frameworks of Craft to host the self-perpetuating patterns of their minds. And I've seen Craftwork constructs that caught sentience from gods—but that was on Kavekana, and those constructs were being treated like gods anyway, with priests and worship and everything. You're not talking about that. You're talking about truly autonomous behavior. The system acting on its own. Self-aware."

Eagerly: "Could it happen?"

"I don't *think* so. The rules of the Craft are rigid—they were made that way. The Craft takes, and it doesn't give back. Gods come out of gaps, of slack, of quiet spaces, and the Craft doesn't have a lot of those. We build contracts and systems to reduce uncertainty—so while there's a lot of energy involved, very little of that energy is free. But we make a lot of transactions, and they bunch up against one another, and that bunching-up sends ripples through the system as it seeks balance, equilibrium. Patterns emerge. Maybe one day those patterns would gain enough complexity to wake up." She shook her head. "I have to admit, I hope not."

That pulled Dawn back from wherever her thoughts had taken her. She landed off-balance in the present moment, surprised by the existence of emotions, of hopes and fears. "Why?"

"If it did, how would we know? It would look like a problem at first: a system behaving in a way we didn't expect. The first step most professionals would take if a contract started to behave weirdly would be to find out what was happening and stop it. When a corpse wakes up, the mortician stabs it through the heart before it can rise. If the Craft was aware, its first experiences would be of waking only to be killed, again and again." She adjusted the coals. "I lost a year that way in Denovo's lab before I could break free. I don't know what was a dream and what was not. I wouldn't wish that on anyone."

"But you did wake up." As if repeating a prayer. "You got out."

"Yes," she said.

Dawn asked the next question tentatively, as if the answer scared her. "How?"

"He hurt a friend of mine. The one I was telling you about, actually—the one who died. Seeing her in pain woke me up. Made me ask questions I hadn't thought to ask before, questions I'd been taught not to ask, about what was happening to us."

"I'm sorry."

"You said that already." She broke the stick she'd used to stir the coals and broke it again until she held four small hot lengths. She tossed them into the fire, and stood. "We should sleep. Long day tomorrow, and after."

Out in the dark away from the fire the stars unfurled and the ground lay in shadow, hidden and unknown. That was the great lie of cities: they told you that the place where people lived was bright and clear and sensible, and the sky a swirling void of melted neon horrorforms occasionally relieved by brave sharp points of light, when in fact that swirling void was a shadow the city cast, a shadow in its own shape. You had to leave to see the truth.

She sighed, hitched up and buttoned her slacks, and wandered back.

Connor stood by her tent, flute in hand, watching stars.

"You sat quiet through all that," she said.

"Don't know much about the topic, is all. I wanted to give the girl space. I don't think she likes me much."

"What gives you that impression?"

"Oh, the glares and the disregard and the distrust and the throwing rocks at monsters. Not to mention the scorpion in my bed last night."

"Did she really?"

"No, I figure that the scorpion was acting on its own initiative. If Dawn wanted me dead she'd be more direct."

"I'll talk to her."

"Don't. I don't know her well, but I expect I stink of what she wants to leave behind. And she's jealous."

"Jealous?"

"Of . . . us. Of my time with you."

She kicked soil. "She's a smart kid. She wants to learn."

"You can't see the way she looks at you. She wants to drink you up."

"I'm glad you're here."

Neither one of them had moved, but the space between them seemed to condense and harden, as if they stood on either side of a glass wall.

Back in Edgemont it had felt so easy to reach for him, like her whole life she'd been playing a favorite game a little wrong and had finally found a page of rules she'd never noticed before. Now, even if he was technically her guide, they played by her rules, the rules she'd taught herself to survive the world of Craft. Be fast, be hard, be clever and ruthless and swift. She had sculpted a self to fit those rules, like a golem shaped out of clay, and baked it and worked it with magic until its skin could shatter steel.

On the island of Kavekana they placed criminals in animated statues that broke them and rebuilt them into model citizens. Resist the statue and it tore you apart, but did not let you die. Work within its bounds and the statue fed you ecstasy. Criminals on Kavekana wept when they were freed. They begged to be imprisoned once more. *Give me that strength again, give me tracks to follow, make me part of something greater than myself.*

The curse was inside her. It would grow until she reached the Raiders and ended this and, if she was lucky, walked away. Her path was dark. Survival was not assured. So why did she feel more free and easy now than she had since she opened her mother's letter back in Alt Coulumb?

Connor had grown close to her in a moment when they could both pretend the self she had sculpted and baked and worked and wore through battle after battle was just an accident, a mask, rather than her true and final form.

She thought of Deathless Kings she'd known, their bodies withered, their bones and appetites immortal, sustained in their power by chains they took for arms. She had thought their transformation occurred on the moment of death, but maybe it began much earlier.

"You're good at waiting," she said with half a smile, rueful.

"Comes from too much time out here."

"I really am glad you're with us. Not just because we need a guide. You're about to see who I am at work—real work, not the small-time stuff I did back at Edgemont. Not the person I've tried to be these last few weeks."

"That person is still you."

"I'm not so soft as she is."

"If you don't like who you are back east," he said with a church-voice quiet, "you could stay."

What a thought: to walk away from Alt Coulumb, to break the life she'd made and find some quiet place out of the way of history to live free of consequence and chains. Abandon duty, friends, and future. Abandon the black folder and those footsteps in the sky, and let them be somebody else's problem.

The possibility introduced a kind of vertigo. He was serious, she could tell, and she could also tell he had a reasonable sense of how likely she was, or was not, to take him up on the offer. She met his eyes and tried to look kind. "You don't get it." Here she was, cursed in the Badlands with an apprentice in tow and a camp full of Raiders ahead of her, on their home turf, as a clock ticked down to zero hour. You know: happy. "I love this."

When they woke, they found the hills had moved around them in their sleep, but the needle still pointed true, and west.

22

Travel makes its own time. In familiar circumstances, at work, at school or play, routine blurs days into years. Time becomes a childhood home, so lived-in that its features vanish under constant touch. Old books and lost gadgets accumulate in corners, unseen because they have been seen too much. But four days on unfamiliar sand build a palace.

When Tara last came this way she had landed far to the north, and as she wandered east she'd shied clear of the damage from the Wars, but the needle led them into the worst of it. When she closed her eyes she saw forms like those of Craft, but of unknown colors and unfamiliar shapes, bubbling and rotting, twisted and furtive, vanishing as soon as they were spotted.

With each mile she grew more grateful for Connor's presence. He hadn't yet said "I told you so," though he'd come close once or twice. When they stumbled into a labyrinth trap, he guided them back out: Tara and Dawn might have spent hours or days lost in the shifting walls of bone, or announced their presence to half the desert breaking free. She might have guessed that she should not look at the glowing faces trapped in the lake of glass, but she would not have known to leave them an offering of fresh-killed game to ensure protection from mirages and heat madness.

They ate well. Tara had packed food that would keep and cook easily if it needed cooking at all: dried meat, nuts, hard cheeses, bread. But Connor knew the edible cactus from the vampiric, the toxic fungus from the tasty, the fragrant night-blossoms from the psychedelic, and more impressively he noticed them, picked them out of the landscape a quarter mile off while carrying on a conversation, the way Tara would notice a wrongly italicized comma or a misnumbered page. He'd brought spices in his pack, and dried lemon peel, and he found hand-sized beetles that, seared, didn't taste altogether different from shrimp.

The days were gold and the nights silver, and the not-quite-silence of the trail curled around them like a mother dog sheltering pups. Even the dull ache of her curse was almost welcome, its pulse and pain a sign they were on the right trail. Tara would have enjoyed the trip—at least, she told herself she would, though she might just have found something else to worry about—she would have enjoyed the trip, anyway, if they were making better time.

Nothing was wrong exactly. The horses kept good pace. Dawn was a solid rider, and Tara was surprised by how easily she herself adjusted to the saddle after a decade of, what was it they called walking in Camlaan, "riding shank's mare"? But the Raiders lived deep in the Badlands, and though Connor guided them through or around each hazard with ease, she felt each night as the fading of a chance.

"The Edgemont wards renew on the full moon," she explained over dinner on the fourth night. "The closer we come to the full moon, the weaker the Pastor gets. The Raiders have to be camped on this side of the Crack in the World; at this rate we'll get there two days before they break his wards."

She tried not to think about what might be happening to him now.

Pastor Merrott was a good man. Good men stepped up and did what was needed, and sometimes suffered for it. But she'd gotten him into this mess, albeit with his help, and she would get him out of it.

They pressed harder, woke earlier, and drove themselves late. The horses tired, and so did they. By dusk Tara was so weary her hand shook as she renewed the wards around her curse. But they could only go so fast. There were mines beneath the sand, and century-old war machines, and accidents, and the corpses of dead and hungry gods. One wrong hasty step would end their journey.

She used her nights to teach Dawn. How to attack, by drawing soulstuff directly from an enemy, by calling cold fire, by making her body stronger and more vicious by analogical description, asserting the integrity of muscles that ought to shred, of bones that ought to break. How to transform others through the same process. How to argue through wards, how to negotiate with existing Concerns. Tara showed her the core glyphs concerned with each skill. "Remember, they're just shorthand," she reminded Dawn as the girl traced the glowing lines and nested geometric shapes on her arm. "They reference long-form agreements on file in the Argent Library at the Hidden Schools, and in the archives of the Courts of Craft. Some people rush to glyph themselves up and forget the underlying architecture. That's a mistake. If you don't know the fundamentals, you'll end up arguing against yourself. A smart practitioner—or goddess—will eat you alive."

The blue lines made mazes in Dawn's wide blue eyes, and the glyphlight shone alien through her pale hand. Tara's skin chilled and goosefleshed up and the centimeter between her and Dawn grew tense and thick. A spark leapt between them. Something like a spark, anyway—but when she yelped and pulled back the spark remained in the air between them, a zigzag crack, burning.

"I'm sorry," Dawn said, sharp and fast, but Tara was looking at the sky.

"That wasn't you."

In the daily business of the Craft, one often assumed the worst and hoped one was wrong. This deep in the Badlands, this close to the Crack in the World, on ground poisoned and made weird by the Wars, there wasn't much room for hope. For an instant the stars hung still above, the moon a sliver, the Badlands dark and changeless. Only that crack remained, a finger's length of light that pulsed with the rhythm of a heart.

Far away, a sound that was not quite thunder rolled.

"Edge storm," she said when they reached their camp, which Connor had already half broken by himself.

"Edge storm," he confirmed as he rolled his tent. "Big one, too. I threw yarrow stalks when I heard that crack, then I threw them again when I didn't like the first answer."

"How bad?"

"Still the better part of a day's ride off."

"It can't be that far. I heard thunder."

"Like I said. It's big."

"How big?"

He lashed the tent to his saddlebag. His horse whinnied and stamped; her eyes were wide, and she only calmed when he rubbed his hand along her neck and fed her a piece of cactus paddle. Tara knew how the horse felt.

"Connor. How big?" She was conscious of Dawn watching her, waiting for her, measuring the situation's urgency from Tara's own bearing. Don't panic, Tara told herself. The kid needs to see everything's solvable with a cool head and a clear heart. Even if what you want to do right now is shout and break things.

"If we ride north all night, we'll be on pace to skirt its edge and come back around as it passes."

"We're talking, what, a day's detour?"

He looked at his saddle, at his horse's gear, rather than at her. "Five."

"We don't have five days."

"That's if the storm keeps on track. If it veers after us we won't escape no matter how we run."

"If we waste five days the Pastor's good as dead."

Connor's hand tightened around his saddle horn. Ridges of muscle stood out on his forearm, as if a great wind blew against him and the horse was all that rooted him to the world. "So we go back, then. Ready the town."

She said nothing. Connor turned to her. She saw his fear, and understood, though she was not afraid herself. Well. She was afraid, but not in the same way.

If Tara were alone, she would not have hesitated. If Tara were alone, she would not have had to explain her plan. She understood the risks she ran and the stakes she wagered, she knew sometimes when there were no good bets you had to make a bad one with upside potential. When she worked with others, they were, well, not exactly equals, but peers—Shale and Abelard and Caleb and even Kai, each an adept in their own way, with their own powers and positions. They had faced Craft before, they could check her judgment. She had marched into a mountain that was a god with a man by her side whom years before she would have called a mortal enemy. They were all different, but they were the same kind of fools. They did not depend on her.

She was a teacher now. She was guiding Dawn and Connor through the world of Craft surely as Connor guided them through the Badlands. They trusted her to keep them safe. But they also trusted her to win.

"We can't go around," she said. "So we go through."

She wished he would have asked a question then, or joked about how he hoped she knew what she was doing, so she could snap back *so do I.* It was worse to be trusted. He untied the tent. "Then we should rest. We have a long day tomorrow."

She nodded and reached to help him.

"What," Dawn asked, "is an edge storm?"

"A problem," Tara answered. "And an opportunity."

She slept uneasily that night, her dreams feverish and vivid and formless, as if she was drowning in paint. Hands dragged her down and if she let them, if she breathed those colors in, she would wake in some other life, some other world altogether, as fit to its chains as to the chains that now she wore. She would wake somewhere else, someone's goddess, someone's wife, not herself at all.

A grip found her arm, more real than her terror, and she sat up in the dark with glyphs aflame and her work knife in the hand whose wrist Dawn held. Knifelight flickered off the girl's strange face.

Tara let the knife fade. She breathed until her heartbeat slowed. "I'm sorry. Did I hurt you?"

"You were talking in your sleep." Talking, Tara knew, was the wrong word, but it was kind. "Do you always have bad dreams?"

"Not most nights. But bad dreams run before an edge storm." She tried to lean back, but Dawn held her wrist firm. The girl's knuckles were white, her eyes taut. "It's okay, Dawn."

Dawn shook herself and looked at her hand as if surprised to find it there on Tara's arm. She let go mechanically. Tara rubbed her wrist. The girl wanted to present a smooth and eager shell to the world, but underneath she churned with fear. She had chosen her teacher well.

A heavy wind blew coarse sand against the tent—but this wind did not howl, and the scraping was too regular for sand. The legs made pinprick patterns, six by six by six. Tara cast a ghostlight outside the tent and overhead, throwing the insects' shadows through the thin fabric onto her body and Dawn's and onto their bedrolls: the silhouette of claws and legs and arching tail.

Inside Tara's heart there was a kid who recoiled from the scorpion shadows, and she held that kid tight, enjoyed this shivering sign of the distance between them. "I had a friend back in the Hidden Schools," she said as the scorpion tide flowed over them, "whose parents moved to Dresediel Lex for work, into a house they didn't know was built on a scorpion migration line. That was the first I heard of scorpions migrating. There's nothing much you can do about them. When the seasons change, they go where they go."

Dawn drew into the center of their small tent, pressing against Tara. "They're running from the storm?"

Tara sat beside her, arm against arm, leg against leg, under the shifting shadows. "Yes."

"Where do they come from? The storms."

"From the Crack in the World. It creates a sort of pressure differential, only with reality, not air. Do you know what that means?"

Dawn shook her head.

"For the most part things—air or water or heat or charge—want to be evenly spread. Storms are a mixing process. They happen when great differences meet—hot and cold, low and high, positive and negative, reality and dream. The Crack is a Wars-wound so deep that other places and times bleed through it. When a change draws near in our world, we end up out of balance with the infinite others. So you get a storm, where futures flash like lightning and crumble like thunder. A storm of destinies."

"Oh." Silence, and scorpion legs like rain upon the tent. "And we're heading into that."

"We can't go around. Once we're inside, we'll have options." She did not say, *if we survive.* "We'll ward ourselves and ride through. Rules are soft in the storm. Distance becomes malleable. We can cover ground fast."

"What will it be like, inside?"

"We'll be surrounded by other times, other worlds. So long as we stay inside our wards they'll be no more real than shadows, but like any story, they'll gain substance if we give ourselves to them. We could get lost out there and wake in other lives. But if this works, we'll make it through in time to save the Pastor."

Dawn sat in skittering silence.

Tara tried to joke. "Some shortcut, right? So long as we don't all die."

She looked at Tara then, solemn and tender. "Is it always like this?"

"No. Hells, it isn't even always like this for me. I know a lot of Craftswomen who went right into private practice after the Schools and stayed there. They work on big multiparty sorceries, the kind of magic that changes the world in ways most people will never understand—which means that maybe it doesn't change the world at all. They kill gods and raise Concerns from the dead, and they can't explain what they do on a day-to-day basis even to themselves. When they die they'll keep going, or retire to some island where they can spend centuries pretending to feel the sun on their faces. They have a place, and power, but they rarely use that power because the place protects them as long as they don't stray. There are many roads a Craftswoman can walk. Most don't lead out here." She felt so heavy as she spoke those words, but she was a good enough liar to turn to Dawn and flash a grin, an edge of teeth in the dark. "That's the trade you make when you learn the Craft, a trade no one in the Hidden Schools will ever tell you about save with whispers about students who strayed too far and fell: you trade compliance for power. You have strength so long as you use that strength to stay inside the lines. But the world's broken, and its lines are cuts through flesh. You know that, and I know that. So we do what we can. We give up what we must, and use what we get to help people. And that leads us out here."

"It's broken," she said, "and it's ending."

The many legs sounded like rain. "Yes."

"What can we do?"

As if that question could have an answer. But there was something golden in the fact that she had thought to ask at all. "I don't know," she said. "I've come up with a dozen plans, but when you squint they're all basically the same: conquer the world. Once you have the world, you order people to fix things. And if they don't agree, that's what undead armies, mind control, and heavy artillery are for. There are, for example, a handful of major market centers, the Chikal Exchange, Dhisthra, Camlaan, some minor ones, each built around the body of a god—if you devoured those bodies, you'd have the world's flow of soulstuff under your control. That would be a good place to start. Eventually you'd have to reckon with the Courts of Craft, lay siege to the Argent Library, which binds all lesser archives, rewrite the foundations of Craft. You'd need a lot of power and skill, but I'm good at what I do, and power is just a question of time and logistics. People would try to stop you, of course—or things that used to be people—and you'd probably die in the process, or worse, but we're talking about the survival of the entire species, forever. That justifies a lot of risk."

"So why don't you?"

"Because that's what monsters do. It's easy to make plans like you're moving toy soldiers around a map or kicking over sandcastles. Real people would die, and there has to be a better way. But I can't see one. At the end of the day, I was trained by a bunch of megalomaniacal necromancers, so all my solutions look like megalomaniacal necromancy."

"You don't trust yourself."

"That's part of it. Sure."

"I trust you."

Tara did not know how to answer that.

The scorpions passed. The tent and the desert lay still under the weight of the coming storm. She shouldn't have said anything. Dawn wanted reassurance. She wanted to know Tara had a plan.

She wanted kindness and a path to follow, words she could cling to. But someday, if Tara succeeded, Dawn would find herself in the dark beside a student of her own. Would Tara want her to remember her own teacher reaching for a mask?

She did not like this doubt that had crept into her, through cracks in the walls of her soul. Nor did she like the breeze-light voice inside, asking if, between the two of them, Dawn was really the one who needed to be reassured.

"We should sleep," Tara said. But Dawn lay a moon-bright hand on her shoulder, a hand that was heavy as a chain and almost kind, and in the shock of that unexpected contact Tara turned to her without a role, no Craftswoman or mentor or protector or even guide. She was just herself, a woman alone on a dangerous night. And she sat beside another woman, younger, who understood.

"Go to him," Dawn said.

She shook her head, not against Dawn but against the ache inside her that answered, that wanted him, that needed a body beside her, beneath her. No—not a body, not any body, that was another swirling scarf, another misdirection. His.

Not forever, not in some way that would shove continents around and rearrange eternities. But there was a tender line between them. And that line scared her, because when she traced the spot near where it was tied, she found others rooted there, and those lines ran across continents to Alt Coulumb and beyond, to people she had left behind because she could not let them help her, because she could not let them see her weak.

This smile felt strange on her face, because it was not a weapon. She did not know what she meant it to accomplish or convey. She had not meant it at all.

She took Dawn's hand from her shoulder and drew her close. Her cheek was cold and her heartbeat even. Then she left, rose, slipped outside barefoot despite the scorpions, and zipped the tent behind her.

The scorpions parted where she stepped. She circled around the small fire's ashes to his tent, unzipped it, entered. Connor lay curled on his side, as still as if the world was at peace.

There was so little room in his tent. She didn't mean to wake him, but she tangled herself in her trousers as she slid them off, and he uncurled languid on his bedroll. His eyes opened and he looked up at her in the dark. She, naked, saw him wonder at her, saw him realize she was not a dream. He reached for her thigh, but she pressed his sheets tight around him, trapped his arms under the cloth and between her legs, felt his torso arch as she bent down, wearing an altogether different smile that rose unbidden from within.

"I hoped you—" he said, but what he hoped of her she did not learn, because she closed his mouth with a kiss and a *yes* and he answered her and after that they were too busy to speak.

23

In the cool gray morning she tied Connor's arm to hers and hers to Dawn's and painted their skin with glyphs. The brush shook in her hand, but a deep breath, an easing of the muscles of the chest and arm, calmed her enough for the detail work.

"The needle will guide us through. You'll hear voices on the wind. You'll see visions through the lightning. Ignore them. But the storm's most dangerous trick is knowledge. You will find yourself knowing things you've never learned, or starting to know them—like the tip of a memory, or a taste that unfolds into your childhood. The knowledge is not always false, but it is always from outside, and if you follow that memory from reference to reference, it will wrap you in the world you're remembering, and you'll never come back." She blew the ink dry on Dawn's skin. "Don't break the thread. Keep to the light. Follow the needle. That's all."

They set off.

Heavy air weighed the horses down. The horizon was a blur at first, then that blur stretched up to embrace the sky. They dismounted, and Tara whispered to each horse in turn, telling them horse stories of good oats and grass and running water. When she was done their souls were in her grip. They saw nothing, heard nothing. She'd considered doing the same with Connor and Dawn. Human minds were not so different from the minds of horses, but a mind once compromised could be compromised again. And an edge storm was, in a way, nothing but compromise.

From far away the storm was a towering mass, clearly separate from the Badlands through which they walked. As they drew near it faded out, became a yellowing and greening of the sky, a burden on the air. But for days the air had been heavy, for days it had tended toward this sickly color. Had they ever been outside the storm? Or was the storm everywhere?

First there was the windblown sand, and thunder rolled in the murk beyond. The horses kept pace, spookily unspooked. The needle pointed straight. The painted glyphs shed a circle of light at their feet, and in that circle the ground held steady.

Lightning crashed behind them. She realized they were deep inside the storm, and had been for a while.

Sand lashed her cheeks. She'd pulled her hat low and her bandanna up to cover her nose and mouth and she held her eyes to slits and looked at the bottom half of the world. She breathed her own air back in.

She followed the needle. With each step she told the world a story, working her Craft. The needle pointed toward Pastor Merrott, through the storm. The storm was a singular entity separate from the Badlands, and as such points within it could be seen as interchangeable. So why wouldn't their next step take them to its farthest border, to the place where the needle led? She would never win such an argument in the Courts of Craft, but the storm was not a firm and self-constant Judge. She felt it stir and start to listen. But they'd have to go farther in for her will to rule.

They walked on.

The lightning did not flash anymore. When it cracked, its trails stuck in the air, spreading and crossing, and between the bright and glass-hard lines she glimpsed cold stars and the curve of something black and glistening and huge.

"What was that?" Dawn, shouting against the wind and the sand and the roll of sound, which Tara realized now was part thunder and part something else.

"Keep walking," Tara said, and tried not to think about the *something else.*

Tried not to think about the scorpions crossing her tent last night, or about the black folder, or about footsteps beyond the sky, like spider legs on a marble floor. She tried not to think about the shapes half seen through the windows the storm opened overhead and all around.

"Tara?" Dawn again.

"Keep walking."

"Tara, you said they would show us different worlds."

"I told you not to look."

"But it's all the same."

She looked up.

Lightning domed the sky and through the spaces in between she saw the world—one singular world, split to many facets. The Badlands stretched beyond, ash gray and frozen, pierced by broken crystal towers taller than mountains: the wrecks of skyspires.

She recognized the buildings. They should have been all across the globe, from Xivai to the Shining Empire to Dresediel Lex. They fled here to make one last stand, too late. Jet-black spears like holes in space pierced them through and sank into the soil, through the soil into bedrock and magma beneath. Look up, and those spears towered into the sky.

There was no wind in the frozen waste beyond the storm. No sand to squint against. The world lay dead. Deeper than dead. In Tara's line of work, *dead* was a place you came back from.

"Tara, I can hear them." Tears froze in the corners of Dawn's eyes. "The footsteps. Tara, it's *them*. This is what happens when they get here."

"Keep walking. Follow the needle." It pointed straight and true. With each step the lightning dome shifted to keep them at its center. This was the storm: the change all through its heart, its singular identity. Use that singularity to reach the other side. Don't ask questions. Don't look up—

to where the black spears join and twist into an iron web, to those great depths where self-assembling many-legged thousand-eyed structures the size of small moons and framed of bone and iron climb and curl and feed and pulse in their cold common dream—

and certainly don't look in—

to those spears, those strands not made from iron after all but from thin spun carbon tubes clasped round with shadow gathered from the star-depths where they walk, and at each spear's heart a hole the shape of a being that once was something not altogether unlike human—

when we cut one down and carved it open we found tissues fossilized, but by machines not minerals, tiny clockworks with hooks and spires and springs, more complex the closer we looked, like a trellis grown through with vines, they were unmistakably organic figures, mouths and gills and hearts and livers and eyes, microstructures all overgrown with nanofilament carbon, all hollow, all screaming—

—survivors claim they heard an offer, a deal. Surrender all. Gain all.—

—carved them out from the induction beds and those who recovered did not appear to register sensory input, but when we showed them the machines the patients clawed for them again. One patient whose left leg was severed during the extraction tried to walk on the stump to get back inside. Attempts to convene through nightmare telegraph—

—of bliss and bliss and bliss forever and don't stop cutting, oh please don't—

—please—

—surrender all, gain—

Remember the needle. Remember your path, remember why you're here. Don't let this dead world's chill draw you in. Don't even ask—

—how? Or who? Or what? Not so different from a god, in fact, though no god could ever evolve this way, gods as a rule being effectively limited in size given the poor state of infrastructure thaumaturgy before the Wars. You must recognize that the Craft's core contribution to human thought was not the power it offered, but the new way of knowing. Controlled experiments permit optimization, and optimization does not accept limits. Gods are an evolutionary process, an emergent phenomenon arising when lesser beings act together. They use souls as a distributed platform to perform grand operations. But evolution is slow, and niche-constrained, and emergence is inefficient. Under Gerhardt we studied how to do what gods did, and then we studied how to fight them, kill them. Why not learn to do what they do, better?

There was a needle before her, yes, and a path, but the lines of lightning drew nearer all around and the thread tied around her wrist was tight, the sigils on her skin aflame. She recognized that last voice and could not let herself believe it—that there would be an echo of Alexander Denovo even here, inside her, the smug assurance of a man more comfortable with being right than anyone she had ever known.

Gods encourage faith by instinct with the tiny endorphin hits you feel at prayer, with the physical hacks of synchronized breath and music, the endocrine joy of belonging. Why settle for such crude tools? Carve into the substrate directly. Make people better. Make them useful. Make them ideal platforms, rapt in that cocktail of bliss and terror and pain that renders nervous systems predictably responsive. Standardize. Optimize. Iterate. And if we can do this, if we can imagine doing it—assume an isomorphic universe. How special are the conditions required for life or something like it? The system we're describing would be a strange attractor, many roads in, no roads out—and once it was in place it would reach beyond—

Was this knowledge coming to her from outside? Or was she remembering it now, some lecture from her smothered years at the Hidden Schools, the man pacing while glassy-eyed students took notes—drawing from their curiosity, anticipating each objection as he explained the secrets of his power?

She wanted to know. She had to know. What she learned here she could use. The footsteps were so near.

But none of this would matter if she fell through. This was another world. Maybe this was all other worlds. Their futures, bleak and certain. Focus on the needle, on the silver thread, on Pastor Merrott, on Edgemont. On Connor, by your side, watching the needle as if there were no monsters overhead. On—

Dawn. Who wanted more than anything to know.

Dawn, who slipped free of her thread to step through the lightning, arms flung wide as if for a lover's embrace.

She burned bright against that ash-gray world, her eyes open, staring up, and the darkness rippled toward her, with its many thin and hooked legs.

Tara caught Connor's arm before he could run for her. She

tried to speak but the air was too dead to carry her voice. His eyes met hers. She shook her head.

And, carefully, she untied the thread around her wrist.

She grabbed its farthest end, the one Dawn had untied, mouthed, "Stay here," and ran.

The lightning passed over her like a waterfall and the world around was cold. Frost formed on her skin. The clouds of her breath were cut by machines too small to see. She did not breathe in, did not look up or out, tried not to think—just reached for Dawn, whose outstretched fingers were already coated in quicksilver fog, who stood rapt beneath the immense many-legged thing that moved against the stars above.

Tara tackled her. She fought, through air heavy with machines. Tara was stronger. The thread bit her palm, but it had been woven for the kind of messes Craftswomen got themselves into, and did not break. Connor somehow kept his footing. Dawn screamed again and again, taking in lungfuls of the quicksilver fog, of the dust in the air that tensed and writhed with the monstrous intent that owned this whole dead world.

Step by step Tara dragged her back, though Dawn's nails clawed her arms and cheeks—back to the lightning dome, smaller now than it had been seconds before and shrinking still. New stars lit the night: eyes in that dead sky, revolving to face her. A mouth opened beneath her feet.

She stumbled through the lightning, and as Dawn collapsed and the stars that were those eyes bore down against the thin barrier between the worlds, Tara threw her will against the storm, certain as a scream, driven by all her soul and all the power she could seize.

The world was rotten, and split.

24

Connor would not wake up.

Tara felt nothing. Feeling was a waste of energy and time, and she was out of both. She bandaged his arm where the silver thread cut in and wrapped gauze tight to keep pressure on. He had cut himself deep as he clutched his horse's neck to anchor Tara while she dragged herself and Dawn back across the gap between the worlds. His crisscrossed wounds missed major veins, and when—*when*—he recovered, he would have a new set of scars to show off when he rolled his sleeves. They could compare, his scars to her glyphs. They could joke about whose hurt more.

When he recovered.

Dawn hugged her knees, stared wide-eyed at the body, saying nothing. Tara wanted to reach inside her, take hold of her guilt and squeeze until she screamed. But she worked instead, and waited for Dawn to speak. In the end, she did. "What can I do?"

"Nothing." She peeled back Connor's eyelid and his eye rolled up into his skull. Stars and the moon watched overhead. This was a surgeon's theater, like the one where Tara had worked through her first dissection practicum. Those cold points of light were her judge, his silence her failure. "You've done enough." Connor's gums were pale, his heartbeat weak and steady, his breath shallow and slow. When she closed her eyes, he was hardly there at all. "His soul's weak and getting weaker. If I touched him directly with the Craft, I'd break what little he has left. He'd go like them." She nodded downslope where they'd left the dead horses, skin taut over their bones. "We need Pastor Merrott. A priest doesn't have to take to give." She was a priestess, still, of Seril—but Seril was not here, walled off behind the curse that twisted toward her heart.

They had come so far in seconds, and her battle with the storm had all but drained her wards. She felt the Raiders' surf-scream chatter, she felt the curse unfurling in her flesh. "When we get him back," not *if*, and don't add *in time*, "he can save Connor. But we have to move fast." They'd passed swiftly through the storm. There was a chance Pastor Merrott had not fallen yet. A chance Tara could pull the shreds of her plan together even now.

"I heard a voice," Dawn said. "Inside my head. When I was on the other side."

"That's how the storm works." She checked his pulse again, at throat and wrists. It was weaker. "I told you so. And still you slipped the line."

"I had to see, Tara. I had to know. They're coming. You said they're coming. I had to try. I had to learn."

"And what if I didn't save you? What if we didn't make it back?"

"We did."

"We did." She turned to her across the body—across Connor. "And here we are."

She reddened. "You're the one who took us in there."

"There wasn't any other way." The sentence started life as a howl, but she clenched her throat and framed it into words, bit each one off between her teeth. She remembered the eyes in place of stars, the lightning closing in as she seized every shred of power she could grasp to throw them headlong through the storm. The horses' souls popped like grapes between her teeth, and too late, too fucking late, she'd felt Connor offer himself as he had back in her bedroom—and her need accepted before her will could hold it back. "There's no godsdamned time to argue." She drew her knife and began to carve a circle around him in the hill's hard side.

"Tara—can we beat those things?"

She'd spent minutes coughing silver dust out of her lungs when they made it through the storm, bent over and hacking bits of herself onto the sand, at last aware enough to hear Dawn coughing, too, and understand she had to pull herself together, to help—and to realize what it meant that Connor hadn't tried to help first. "I don't know." Lies. She'd promised herself she wouldn't do that, when they started. "I'm not sure. Maybe what we saw, it wasn't what I heard in the crystal." She finished the circle and added glyphs.

"You said the storm shows the past and future."

"*The* past. *The* future." She was too tired to hide her scorn. She'd shut down the parts of her that knew how to be polite and teacherly. "There's more than one. You should know that by now."

"But if there was a big change coming—so big and so outside what we know that we couldn't imagine it before—couldn't that cause a storm? A storm days across? A storm with just one world on the other side?"

"Maybe." She checked her anchor points, corrected one line on the second glyph, closed her eyes, felt them burn. Dust. Dryness. Call it that.

"What are we going to do?"

"For now, you're going to get out of my circle." She sounded like the desert. Dawn drew back.

Tara knelt beside him, whispered in his ear: "Wait for me." She couldn't say more, and he could not hear it anyway. So she stood.

At a word from her, the texture of light within the circle changed. The air grew thick. Connor would still breathe, if she waited and watched him closely, but she could not bear to see him so still for so long.

He had trusted her.

She asked for trust from her friends, from those she loved, and time and again they gave it to her. Even after years of knowing they would, and knowing what would happen next, she still could not stop herself from asking. The horses had resisted. Not Connor. He'd given himself freely. And she had taught him how.

Don't think of it as a sacrifice. Think of it as a gamble or a debt. A debt was better. She paid her debts. "That will keep him safe until dawn." She slapped the dust off her palms. "What am I going to do? First, I'm going to finish this job. And then we'll see."

She took three steps before she realized Dawn was not following. When she looked back the girl was trembling, bowstring-tense. Her lips were a hard thin line. "The moon's not full." Dawn worked her left hand in her right. "We could wait. Plan. Prepare."

She was doing what Tara had taught her to do, asking the right questions, especially when they were hard. "He won't last the night. He needs the Pastor."

Dawn withered beneath Tara's glare—but she withered around an iron frame. She forced her hands down to her sides. "So does Edgemont."

Tara said nothing.

"We have a responsibility to them, don't we? To do what's best for the town? We need rest. You're worn out. So am I."

Dawn was, technically, right. A sensible person, a community-minded person, someone stable, someone sure, would wait now, recover and plan. *If you don't like who you are out there,* Connor had said, meaning hard, meaning sharp, meaning ruthless and effective, *you don't have to go back.*

"The Raiders are licking their wounds." She chose her words carefully, built the argument brick by brick. "They'll be weak, and slow. They don't know we're coming. We can do this."

"The Seer is down there. Are you ready to face him in his home?"

Dawn's question was a chisel hammered into her, forcing open hairline cracks. Anger flowed hot and fast when she let the pressure out. "Of course not. Of course we should wait. But Edgemont isn't dying yet, and Connor is. Edgemont did not come out here without a shred of Craft to protect it, because we needed help. Connor did. He saved your life. We have obligations and responsibilities. And we have to be bigger than them, and better, because the Craft will never ask us to be."

Dawn said nothing.

"I'm going down there to save Merrott, and the town, and Connor. I'm going to break the Seer and throw him into the Crack in the World. If you want to stay here, I'll do it myself and tell you how when I come back." Tara shouldered her purse, and started walking. "But I think you should come. If nothing else, it will be a nice line on your resume."

25

Dawn caught up with her at the crest of the hill, and joined her, propped on her forearms, to peer down at the Raider's camp. She frowned. "It looks so . . . boring."

"Say that when everyone inside is trying to kill us." But she was right. Tara had expected bonfires and effigies and God Wars wreckage, a toxic curse-haunted ruin. The curse was here, at least: the slow windswept maggot-white threads twisted around the squat complex on the edge of the Crack in the World. Her own infection churned in answer. But there was also a chain-link fence, and dormant security glyphs around the perimeter. This was not a cave stronghold where desperate men prayed to a weapon they'd found rotting in the wastes and mistaken for a god. It looked more like an office park. One boxy main building. A garage. A parking lot. There would be desks inside, and a break room with a coffee maker no one ever cleaned, even back before they all died. And cubicles. No one built a building like that without cubicles.

"They must have found it abandoned," Tara said. "Or killed whoever built it."

"But who would build here?"

"High-energy Craftwork is easier near . . . weak points in the world. Places physical law can be persuaded to bend."

"Are there more places like this, then?"

"Not here. Using the Crack in the World for high-energy Craft would be like trying to build a geothermal power station on an erupting volcano."

"I've never seen a volcano. But that doesn't sound good."

"Look at that thing. Do I really need to tell you that it would be a bad idea to try to *use* it?" She pointed past the complex, at the Crack in the World.

It stretched from horizon to horizon, for miles and forever, full of aurora colors. When the Hidden Schools threw her out Tara had fallen not far from here—a few days' walk, no more—and as she lay not quite dying she saw so many other worlds, worlds of metal and machines, worlds without any Craft at all. Now when she looked through those coruscating lights, she saw only stars that were eyes, and black metal lines like webs that bound them.

From here they should be able to peer through all possibility— but she saw only that frozen, broken world, heard the screams of minds webbed in nightmare, and those terrible, skittering footsteps. Tara remembered an argument with an old Craftswoman in a tower above a cold sea: *beings of a size you cannot comprehend watch us with many eyes across vast gulfs of space.*

She tapped Dawn's shoulder. "We have to move." And, because she was still Dawn's teacher: "So: we have Craftwork, two and a half souls between us, my work tools, our bodies, and our wits. How would you break in?"

The girl shook herself as if from a dream, and nodded. "The curse will be looking for us," she whispered. "There's a hole in the fence over there. If we sneak through it, we won't have to cover as much ground."

"It's a good start," Tara said. "But remember: use all your tools. Even if you don't like them." She removed her jacket and rolled up her sleeve. "Follow me."

They skidded down the slope toward the hole in the fence. The curse screamed its sea-wash screams inside her, and its threads writhed through the air before them.

"Okay," Tara said. "Let's see if this works."

"You're not sure?"

By way of answer, she drew her knife and slid its tip into the glyphwork on her arm. The flesh was sore and raised, but she didn't have to do much, just carve a minor modification into the wards she'd drawn around the curse.

The curse was a hungry little argument: trying to persuade Tara's flesh that it was a part of the curse, not of her. She had countered it by taking a detailed inventory of her anatomy, and by sheer will. But still the curse chattered inside, staking its claim.

I am in you. You are part of me. You are part of us. With her fine incision, she accepted that argument—within bounds. The curse claimed she was part of it. If so, she belonged here. She belonged to this place. Just a Raider, coming home, with a prisoner.

She felt her wards weaken, as the infection pressed its advantage. If she was using the curse's argument as a basis for her own, then that meant she thought its argument had merit. She couldn't hold it like this for long, arguing both sides of the line. But if this worked, she wouldn't have to.

She took Dawn's hand, and slipped through the hole in the fence.

The threads settled on her like cobwebs, but did not part; they caught around the curse, bonded—then let it go, twirling in her wake as she passed. The wind smelled of dust and rot. No alarm rose. The whispers were louder now, but no more defined or human.

Dawn let Tara lead, stepping where she stepped, matching her pace. They cut across the bare yard toward the garage, where Tara's work knife opened the locked door. Nothing moved inside that tomb of stale concrete. Her footsteps made a chorus of cracks and pops: dead insects and rats, flesh long since eaten by the desert and the curse. A great tread-wheeled metal box swelled in the shadows Tara's knife carved from the dark: a golem truck, dusty but intact. The golem yoked to it had seen better days, its crystals drained, its enchantments rusty. "It won't run for long, but it should get us away." She dusted off the golem's dim eyes out of professional courtesy, and left.

Dawn followed her to a side door of the main building. "What's our plan, exactly?"

Surely Dawn could figure this out. Well. No, in point of fact, that wasn't a reasonable thing for Tara to expect, was it? Sorcerous breaking and entering weren't year-one curriculum even in the Hidden Schools. "Get in quiet, grab the Pastor, and get out. If we're lucky they'll have him stashed somewhere, waiting for his wards to fade, and we'll be gone before they know we're here. If we're not lucky, we get as close to him as we can before the fighting starts." Another door, another lock, and they slipped inside. She counted their steps and turns. The altar needle pointed true, but it didn't account for the floor plan. Her curse ached. "Either way, when we find him, you get him to safety. Run fast. I'll hold them off, and follow when I can. Don't look back."

"But you—"

"I've come out of the Badlands on my own before. I can make it out again." She did not add, *probably*. Or even *possibly*. "You can't."

"Tara—"

That was the beginning of a sentence Tara didn't want Dawn to finish, and before she could, Tara raised a finger to her lips. Dawn stopped talking.

She heard footsteps, coming closer.

Ahead, the narrow hall opened into a lobby, with a cobwebbed receptionist's desk and low gutted chairs. Tara and Dawn watched from the shadows as a Raider stumbled through, dragging his feet, sleepwalking. The curse wriggled in the gaps between his ribs, around a heart that still occasionally beat. He shuffled over broken glass to the yard. The voices Tara heard through her curse were still that chaotic surf-wash mess. "They weren't always like this. They still had their own minds when I was young. I wonder what changed. Maybe something made the curse bite deeper—or maybe this is what it always wanted, and the Seer helped it grow."

They crept into the lobby, toward the inner doors. What was this place, before the Raiders found it? A dusty sunbleached sign hung on the wall behind the desk. When Tara squinted, she could just make out words.

THE FORUM ON THE WILL AND ITS TRANSFORMATIONS

TELLURIAN ANNEX

She said, "What," out loud.

More footsteps. Dawn pulled her behind the desk as another Raider shuffled through the lobby. Tara's heart raced, for reasons that had nothing to do with the Raiders. She had fallen back through time.

"Tara," Dawn whispered, tense. "What's wrong?"

"I know that name." The Raider passed, and she was up and marching down the hall. Exhaustion and care gave way to fury. Let them find her now. She'd welcome the distraction of a fight.

Was this some kind of sick joke, or just the law of gravity that kept planets circling forever and made dropped rocks and angels fall? "I told you about Alexander Denovo. My old teacher. The bad one."

"The one who . . ." She trailed off. "Yes."

"He ran a journal—a working group, old Craftspeople who schemed about godhacking, mindsculpting, soul work. My last boss called it a demented knitting circle. That was their name: the Forum on the Will and its Transformations." She opened the first door she found, which had a smoked glass panel stenciled LABORATORY. None of the equipment—the burners, the crucibles, the vivisection table—was unusual or out of place, but under the dust and cobwebs and desiccated insect husks she saw they were just as he had liked them, the vivisection table mounted at that slight angle to direct blood flow. She knew the angle in her bones; she'd corrected it a thousand times after cleaners messed it up. "He was here."

"How do you know?"

"I know." She opened the second door before she read the stencil—SAMPLE COLLECTION.

She almost closed it again when she saw what lay beyond.

Row after row of glass vats stood in the shadows, some broken, most intact and glowing from within. There were bodies inside, in pieces. One column held fourteen eyeballs, another half-finished hands, a third faces, limp without the structure of underlying bones. She stepped inside and reached up to the column of faces, seeking life in eyeless eyes.

She wished she wanted to throw up. That was what human beings were supposed to do in this situation—not that 'stumbling on vats of disassembled bodies' was such a common occurrence as to have a broadly accepted model response. Still, she ought to feel disgust and terror and rage, wet and hot. She should perhaps cry.

But she was a Craftswoman, too, and to be a Craftswoman was to be not quite human. Instead of all that wet mess she felt a cold focus. Her heart ran rabbit-fast and large as if her body had swelled to fill the room. Maybe that was fear, fixed, intent, hungry. Maybe it was something else.

Alexander Denovo had not drawn her to him back at the Schools. He had used no charm against her. He did not need to. He was, simply, the best in his field, and once that was established in Tara's mind she did the rest herself. She wanted what he had, what he was. She had not known back then where her desires led. Or, she had known, but she had lied to herself. Here was a corpse to raise, here a body to stitch together, next we'll turn our attention to gods. Day after day she'd drawn herself across the whetstone at his direction, and all that sharpening work led here.

She wanted to deny this place even as she wanted to dive into its depths, to devour its secrets and make them hers. I turned away, she told herself. I did not walk this road. This is not the logical consequence of all the choices I have made. Only of choices I made once, when I was a young and foolish monster.

With her finger, she followed the outline of the face beneath the glass.

"They're not human," Tara said, and thought, neither are we.

"They look human."

"Exactly. But see, here. The dermis is a single layer. The thickness is right but there's no fatty tissue. I don't think this is even skin. It doesn't have the right albedo, you see? Some kind of textured silica or mineral substrate." She moved on to the eyeballs. "That's not nerve tissue. The color's wrong." She closed her eyes, opened them again. "It looks like the curse— those white threads, without any of the black stuff."

"If they're not human," Dawn said, "what are they?"

Tara shook her head. A pale girl's mask hung before her. "They have a Craftwork structure, but it's subtler than I've ever seen. Almost theological. He couldn't do this, not even with his lab. They weren't built, they were—oh." She stepped back. "They were grown. Like a god grows bodies." Dawn looked blank, or terrified. Right. She was still Tara's student. It was easy to forget. "When a god needs physical form, they sometimes shape matter to match them—make a body out of whatever's lying around."

"But you said these weren't theological."

She stepped back. "I don't know what they are." And though she hated to say it, imagined him laughing down at her always from the vast heights that he commanded, that he still commanded, even though she had skinned his corpse herself and burned his brain: "I've never seen anything like this before." When she burned his lab at the Hidden Schools, did she think there was only one? There was an answer here. She could find it, and beat him. If there weren't Raiders. Or Pastor Merrott. If Connor were not lying on a cold hill waiting to die. "Come on," she said. "We're not here for this."

It felt so good to say that, to cast the man and his shadow aside. But as she followed the needle and led Dawn deeper into this cut-rate secret lair—how like Alexander Denovo to have a secret lair with all the miserable pedestrian charm of an office park—past traps and rooms where Raiders might lurk, her mind ground on.

Denovo built this place. The lab equipment would have been cutting edge at the time of his death, so the facility must have been in active use until then. But after . . .

"This is why the curse changed. These white threads, the Raiders' hive mind, the Seer, it all comes from here. Whatever Denovo was doing, the Raiders found it after he died. And it got into them." The needle pointed forward and down, forward and down. The curse was a web of fire through her body. They needed caution now, but she could not stop moving. She needed a fight or a revelation. She marched down the hall and through the door marked OFFICE.

No dead things greeted her, no impossible bodies, no Raiders, just a stupidly mundane office arranged like his had been back in the Schools, the same thick green carpet, the same bookcase, the same velvet curtains, the same overstuffed filing cabinet, the same wire cup of thin black expensive fountain pens with little white blazons on the cap. She knew without looking that Gerhardt's *Treatise*, the second Camlaan printing, bound in human skin, would be the third volume from the left on the second shelf from the top. There was a framed picture on the desk where a normal person would have featured a pet, a family, a loved one. It was a picture of him, an alumni-magazine clipping, the great man in his lab, smaller in the flesh than in her memory, wearing his suspenders and his tweed jacket and a white lab coat, unbuttoned, over that. He always had known how to smile for the cameras. His students busied themselves around him. And there, in the corner, her back to the camera—

That figure had Tara's height, Tara's build. No one else in the lab had hair like hers. But her face was turned away.

She did not remember a photographer visiting the lab. She did not remember much. But she heard the sound of the shutter, she smelled lab-equipment phosphorous and ozone, she heard his laugh, right now, with her own ears, as if he stood behind her.

She dropped the photo. It struck the thick green rug and the frame glass did not break. She couldn't even get that much for free.

Dawn was staring at her. Tara shook the cobwebbed memories from her head and hands. "I'm fine. What is it?"

Dawn had pulled the curtains aside.

Beyond the window lay a cavern.

There was too much to describe at once. Tara reviewed it slowly, beginning with the most mission-critical aspects.

Pastor Merrott hung mostly naked at the far end of the chamber, suspended in a three-dimensional lattice of fine wires that pressed against his skin but had not cut him yet. His eyes were closed. His chest rose slowly, and fell slower, and he was sheathed in golden light so weak even Tara could barely detect it. Curse-threads slithered over him, seeking gaps in the light.

Alive, so far. Good.

The wires led from Pastor Merrott to machines that took up most of the remaining space: huge Craftwork engines, glyph-wheels and concentrators, diffusers and coolant fans. Whatever Denovo had built here, it was immense. And the Raiders had stumbled into it.

They were not stumbling now. They sat cross-legged all over the cavern, on its stone floor, atop the machines, utterly still, a murder of crows asleep. The Seer hovered off the ground at their heart, bound by threads to Pastor Merrott.

"What is all this stuff?"

"I'm not sure," Tara said, sussing out the scene, the equipment, the connections as she spoke. "Those big crystal stanchions are trading terminals, portals for the seven markets—the stock and commodities exchanges. With those you can buy and sell pieces of Concerns in Alt Coulumb, in Camlaan, in the Shining Empire, in Iskar, all over the world. But they're . . . integrated. It looks like he's built small Concerns that trade on each exchange in a deterministic way, and transfer soulstuff between them, but he's chained their ownership structures in a loop. You see how all the lines lead inward? It's like a wave tank for Craftwork trading. Your rat maze in reverse. Any pattern in the market would be replicated here eventually, and intensified. But when it tried to leave . . . Those glyphs around it, those are Quechal glyphs, and that pattern's Kavekanese. He's made a huge Craftwork system here but he's guarding it with theology, so whatever stumbles in won't stumble out again. All that just to let markets mutter nonsense to themselves."

"Tara."

But they weren't muttering nonsense, were they? She heard her own voice then, their first day in the Badlands: *transactions bunch up against one another. Ripples through the system. Seeking balance. Equilibrium. Patterns emerge. Maybe one day those patterns would gain enough complexity to . . . wake up.*

Those thin wires from which they'd hung Pastor Merrott had the same milky maggoty sheen as the curse-threads that bound him to the Seer, as the threads that moved beneath Tara's own skin.

"Tara. The wires."

"I see it." Her mouth was dry. "The curse."

"No. Look with your eyes closed. See all of it at once."

She did not want to look, because she did not want to see. Because she knew what was there.

The theological wards formed a circle. And trapped inside, impaled on the wire web . . . It was an incomprehensibly dense tangle of blazing Craftwork, of ownership structures and trades. But if she stopped trying to interpret them as individual deals,

214 · *Max Gladstone*

and looked instead at the gestalt, at the shape welling up from the chaos like a whale from the sea . . .

There was a woman, with wings, pinned like a butterfly on a web of wire. She had many eyes and many mouths. She was limp and still, and white thread leaked from her wounds. Dead. Dead years gone. Whoever she was. Whatever she had been.

"Do you see her?"

She could not answer. She could not speak.

Denovo had set a trap, in the sea of thaumaturgical exchange. And he had caught something—an emergent phenomenon in the Craft, pinned here, distilled and focused. Trapped in the physical world. "She kept trying to grow a body," Tara said. "And he kept cutting it away."

An entity of unimaginable power, imprisoned in a dimension she did not understand. Tortured. Starved. Furious. Afraid.

And then Denovo died. His protection waned. And one day the Raiders' simple hungry curse wormed through this lab's rusting fence looking for a meal, wandered down here, found this great dead Body—and ate it.

The flesh of that trapped and starved and tormented Body changed them, bound them close, made them hungrier. The raids got worse. Her father, at last, shamed by his friend, joined the guard, and died protecting Connor. Then Connor, out of a misguided sense of obligation, led Tara out into the Badlands, and now Tara had to save him, too.

Asymmetries. Patterns seeded patterns like themselves. She burned Denovo's lab—but he had another. She broke his power in Alt Coulumb—which left this Tellurian Annex to decay, and gave the Raiders new power, and a more vicious hunger. She drowned in echoes.

Her eyes were wet. She dried them.

"You remember the plan?"

"We save Pastor Merrott," Dawn said. "And we get out."

"Plan's changed. I'll take care of the Raiders. You get Merrott and run. Don't look back."

Dawn said nothing. Her fingers pressed against the glass.

"Dawn."

The words came out all at once, like she was tearing off a strip of flesh: "I can't leave you."

"Take the stairs." She pointed. "There's a door over there. I'll be fine."

Then Tara touched the glass and shattered it.

The curse tried to catch her as she fell into the cavern, but no one could catch Tara Abernathy but herself. That was gravity for you. You could run around the world and back, you could kill and die and rise again and never escape the pit you dug yourself. You were the anchor tied around your own waist, as the flood came and water rose to drown the stars.

She landed in a rain of broken glass, and her impact shook the cavern.

Curse-threads glanced off her shadow-skin; they withered before the cold light in her eyes. She was a figure of glyph and starlight as she drew her work knife from its place of concealment above her heart.

The curse wreathed her. Raiders turned sick sunken eyes upon her, but she was done with them. They were local nodes of a larger pattern, victims of the same old systems as Tara herself. They'd been chased out into the desert—by whom? Why? They were desperate—who wasn't? The Craft had scarred them all. And they had been warped by a bastard's pet project, the same bastard who warped her.

They could scream and they could rage and they could kill, and that was all. They were puppets. So was she. Who wasn't?

She thought of Connor playing his flute in canyons made of glass. Connor, back on the hillside, slowly losing himself, slowly dying. Did he feel free, inside his head?

The first Raider rushed for her, fingers clawed, teeth chattering, and it seemed slow, its movements foretold by ripples in the curse-web. She stepped aside and swept her work knife past him. Her blade parted curses, and the Raider's body fell. The man screamed as his flesh tried and failed for the first time in who knew how many years to live on its own. He stank of accelerated rot. His bones mulched in.

Another Raider. More parted threads. Another fall, another

scream. She had been a mess of panic in Denovo's office, but now she felt deadly calm.

Pastor Merrott tried to raise his head, but his neck was not strong enough. Edgemont hung from those wires, tied there by her hand. She'd worked as she was taught.

That was unfair. There had been a Tara Abernathy before the world began to shape her—a girl who wanted to travel, to learn, to grow, who wanted to see pyramids and dragons. That girl came from somewhere, from Pa's stories and Ma's long memory and their hopes for a daughter who would reach beyond. She had grown to fit the world she found.

Dawn was a slip of blond hair glimpsed out of the corner of Tara's eye, working around the room's edge toward the Pastor. They had not noticed her yet.

More Raiders lurched toward Tara. The Seer had not moved. He sat, facing away, facing Merrott, staring up into the slack and many-eyed face of the Body hanging from that web. As if she was not worth his time.

His mistake.

She raised her knife and brought it down onto her palm. The blade shattered. She cupped its pieces in her hand, raised them to her lips, and blew. The shards took flight.

They whipped from her in a widening spiral, tiny edges moving at the speed of thought. Her world lost all color save their edges' blue: she was graying out, low on soul, losing that weird momentum by which the conscious mind attached meaning to passing objects, and gave them names. She stepped forward, suddenly aware of the subtle muscular contractions needed to hold herself upright, of the heart's need to be told to beat. Fuck it. She could make her own meaning for a few minutes longer. She could burn raw fury if she had to.

Curse-lines broke with a high clear sound like snapped violin strings. Raiders fell. The curse sustained itself on their flesh, it molded them into a semblance of community, but they weren't a community, really. They came from all corners, outcasts, and, seeking power, or even just a place in the crowd, they had given themselves away. They were shells. They had been used.

White threads gathered and pulsed around the Seer, and now, at last, he stood.

He turned to face her.

Tara held out her hand and the many blades reformed into her familiar knife, in her grip. She knew its lightning weight.

The curse screamed and whirled between them both, and inside her. His eyes were full of turning thread, and more thread writhed beneath the taut canvas of his skin. The curse wrapped around his heart, and she could not tell whether the heart's beat moved the curse or the other way around.

Threads lashed her, bound her limbs, carved at her warding shadows. They glanced off her glyphs at first, but tried again— curled around the glyphlines themselves and pulled. With a searing pain the curse inside her burst its banks and ate her flesh. She saw herself then, from within, and also through the Seer's eyes: not a woman of flesh and blood but a shape pressing through the curse by which he knew the world, a terrible landscape, a star kraken rising from the deep.

Across the cavern she saw a glint of gold: Dawn, climbing the wire mesh, cutting her hands, pulling Pastor Merrott free. She'd make it, if Tara could hold out minutes longer.

"I know you," Tara said, and let go of her knife.

He drew her close; she gripped his arms and he gripped hers, his thick nails and bare finger bones carving into her shadow, into the flesh below, into the tunnels and compromises her curse had wormed into her, even as ash and ice spread from her grip on him. His teeth were long and thin, and there were threads of the Body stuck between them.

"Always hungry," she said. "Always looking out over the horizon. You followed a dream. It led you here, and drew you down and cored you."

She groaned as their curses flowed together, as their threads meshed and the pain gained new colors and dimensions and depth.

"It's like looking into a mirror."

She felt the whole curse then, webbing her to him and to the bleeding broken Raiders all around and further still. The arched structures of her mind strained to encompass all of it, back to the source, where the threads lost their taint of rotten white and burned gleaming silver-blue, in the great dead Body Alexander Denovo had caught and carved and murdered in his wire web.

A scream built inside her and she crushed it. She saw herself and saw herself and saw herself again, and she felt those threads inside her, and the Seer's smile split his cheeks to bare sallow gums.

"There's just one difference," she told him through gritted teeth. "I'm better at this than you."

Back on the fields of Edgemont she'd fought to deny his claim on her and cast him out. *We are not the same*, she'd said.

But the curse was in her, as it was in him. On that basis, it demanded her surrender and allegiance. But identity ran both ways. The curse was a part of her, and he was a part of the curse. What was hers, she could use.

And she was so very hungry.

He tried to pull away, too late. The curse slipped from him all at once, and her power took him and he was ash.

Then it was Tara and the curse alone. It thrashed like an octopus on the hook of her soul, but could not get free. She drew it in. Bit by bit, the rotten old God Wars weapon seeped into her, and she devoured it.

That's what she was made for, after all. The Craft was a way of seeing, a way of knowing, a structure for ownership. A Craftswoman took living, breathing things and made them hers, rendered their complications and particularity down to power, to the stuff of souls, like a bee's nest crushed to pulp and wax and honey.

The curse tried to escape. It battered her with winds and choked her with vacuum and burned her with flame, but it could not get free. She had seen it now, all of it, and made it hers. She knew it altogether. There was no flesh left for it to hide within, save her own.

She rendered it down, until only the thread remained, writhing and white, between her and the Body in the web.

Somewhere far away the cave ceiling shattered, and great cracks widened in its walls. Somewhere far away, wire sparked and snapped and tanks burst. Tara did not notice. She stared up into that dead and monstrous and beautiful face. She lived in blacks and whites and outlines, and she could not weep. She did not know what this Body was, what it had been. It might never have been what she would call alive. But Denovo found it anyway, and did what he did, and now it was gone.

As the Tellurian Annex came apart, she stared up into those dead and many eyes.

And then those eyes opened, and stared back.

Threads caught Tara, lifted her.

Yes, the Body said. Yes, it *had* said, its words arriving in her memory, as if she had known them since before she knew her own skin. Yes We Are The Same And You Feel The Truth And We Must Be One Against The Hunger And The Others That Come From Far Away And We Know Them And We Know The Knife And We Know There Must Be Pain And We Know One Holds The Leash And We Know That Always There Are Chains And We Know What Must Be Done—

She could not breathe. She fought against that hunger, but it was like trying to swim against a rip tide. We Know. What did it know, trapped down here, what did it know, cut and sharpened by Denovo's mind, his blade, what did it know of her? It was scared, like a drowning woman was scared, and it would consume her, gnash her in the teeth of its suffering. She would be there, bound inside this web, his blade always in her flesh, taking her apart. She was more than the pain.

Wasn't she?

We Know This Must Be And We Know The Others That Come From Far Away And We Know You And You Are Needful And We Must Know You With Our Teeth—

The cavern's roof and walls burst open then and the mad light of the Crack in the World roared through.

Pastor Merrott was gone. Dawn, too. She was alone here, with the Body and the Crack in the World and the cold eyes above all the dead and devoured realms. She tried to fight, to run, but she was held in a mighty grip and she wept as it drew her toward its mouth.

Years ago, she had fallen from the Hidden Schools to land not so far away. Perhaps she lay there still. Perhaps she never left, and all the years since were phantoms in her dying brain.

No. She remembered Edgemont. She remembered Connor, Dawn, Ma. Pa. And behind them she remembered Alt Coulumb shining, and Shale and Abelard and Cat and Raz, remembered gods she had saved and known and loved.

She tried to breathe. Start there. Come on.

You remember how.

But the tide was great, and there were so many eyes, and that mouth was so near.

And then she felt arms wrap around her from behind, and heard a voice—Dawn's voice, tight with fear. "Oh, no you don't, Tara Abernathy. I'm not done with you yet."

26

At first there was only blue, pale, firm and empty.

Tara floated beneath on growling waves. She had her name back, and colors, light that felt like light and not the impact of photons on retina. Memory lurked out of view.

She let the waves bear her east.

The blue faded into stars and she nursed on them. She arched and ached and drew in light. She became aware of her hand through pressure on her palm. The black ebbed to blue and the blue to black again, as stars breathed in dark and exhaled sky.

Concepts slunk back into her awareness, boundaries, tensions. Sleep and waking. Day and night. Alive and dead. She thought she was alive. There was a hand in her hand. She did not want to rise and see whose.

Sound was a mess of different sorts of liquid shaken in a jar, chaos bubbly and swirled at first, everything all through everything else. It settled and separated. She became aware of voices, though she did not understand them and could not tell one from another. The growl beneath her was not the sea but an engine. Time, too, assembled. Dark and day acquired gradations. The moon slimmed. Clouds came, clouds left. Sunset, dusk, twilight, midnight.

Dawn.

Tara was not anyone in particular, anything in particular, just flotsam, foam. No one needed her. She did not decide to be. She suckled on the night, as the stars wheeled.

The flute brought her back.

Connor was telling a story on the flute, an old Quechal trickster-rabbit tale half fable and half tone poem, each scrambling escape accented with a bright rising trill, each tiger half stepping through underbrush in a minor key.

She followed the notes and found herself on the flatbed of the golem cart, around nine o'clock at night to judge from the moon, two days' hard ride from Edgemont. The others sat around a fire larger than any they'd dared build on the ride out: Dawn, poking the embers with a stick; Pastor Merrott, cross-legged and hunched and thin but there; and, flute half-raised to open lips, Connor.

"You don't have to look so surprised," she managed, weakly, before he reached her and circled her in his arms.

———

Tara spent the last days of their trip cotton-wadded, talking slow and seldom as the others helped her piece the story together. It was all a bit confused. Dawn got Pastor Merrott down and free, then came back for Tara, and they made it to the cart somehow. Dawn unraveled Tara's wards, and the Pastor gave Connor what soul he could spare.

"I was far gone," Connor said, "but not so far as you, I think. Dawn told me what you did."

"I did what I had to do" was all the answer she could offer then, and hoped he understood.

"Thank you."

"I'm glad you weren't there. It was a bad fight."

"You don't have to hide anything from me."

She was not sure that this was true, but she did not press the issue. She needed that slow pace, as the golem cart ate distance by the steady hour, needed silence even now that she had found her voice again. The curse was gone, leaving no trace but a scar on her arm and a spreading bruise, but there were still too many moving pieces in her mind, and it was hard to think.

———

Tomas Braxton was watching from the wall when they came home, and his cry raised the crowd.

Edgemonters streamed over the wall and through the gates and out around the golem cart to cheer them home. The cart slowed from the weight of bodies. Tomas Braxton's arm still hung in a sling and he walked with a limp. Jon Darien had lost the leg. Tara saw the holes first, absences, probed them like a tongue probed missing teeth. But the people remained. The children rushed out and around the edges and pressed toward her, and she hugged them in a big messy group.

Pastor Merrott stood, still weak, still drawn, but he waved, and the cheers rose. By the fire he had told her he did not suffer much, that he could not remember most of his captivity. She did not point out that these two statements did not quite go together, nor did she mention the sounds he made at night. But he stood straight with Connor's and Tara's help. He knew how to act out a triumphant return.

Grafton Cavanaugh surfaced through the crowd, shouldering folks aside with his good shoulder. He moved more slowly with his crutch and his face was careworn and lean with healing, but as Merrott stepped down he circled him with a hug, and kissed him, and what they said to each other was soft and lost in applause. They broke their clutch painfully, and when Grafton looked up, there was Connor, stepping down to meet him.

Tara only turned away by reflex, and might have turned back had she not seen, nearing through the crowd, drying her hands on her apron—Ma.

She had been underwater; she found air. She had been silent; she found a voice. She was down, and running, and they met each other in the crowd.

And Dawn watched.

———

There would be a feast. Grafton and Mrs. Braxton and the Learys were planning it already, with Pastor Merrott's weak approval— there would be a feast and celebration and commemorative plaques, they'd kill a pig and roast it in a pit, but that would take time to arrange and for now each family brought what food and drink they could spare to the green. There was music, and Dawn danced with the Learys' middle boy. Tara told what little of the story she could bear to, and tired early; Ma guided her away as the music played, and she, half-drunk on general exuberance, tried at first to resist, then apologized, then sagged against her when they were out of sight.

The house felt light and kind. Known places have a different, fuller silence than the desert, heavy with memories. Ma gave her a glass of chrysanthemum tea with a cube of sugar in it and sat her on the couch, and when Tara turned down her offer of a blanket, she draped one over her shoulders anyway, just so Tara could shove it off and glare, half smiling, in that shared moment of normalcy.

"You brought them back."

"They brought me back."

"That, too." She cupped Tara's cheek in her hand, and Tara looked up at her through wild curls of hair. "I wish," she began, and stopped herself. "I don't wish. I know. He's here with us, isn't he? He never left."

Their hands found one another. Orbits touched.

That night she woke to a knock on her door.

She flailed in the dark, punched the wall and knocked a book off her nightstand before she remembered where she was. Who she was. Before she remembered she was no longer in that cavern, with the many eyes. "What do you want?"

Connor said, "It's me."

She opened the door with a flick of Craft from across the room. He stood there, hand raised to knock again, tired, wearing fresh clothes, his skin new-scrubbed from the trail. "What are you doing here?"

"Your ma let me in."

"That is nine types of embarrassing."

"I could go?"

"Don't." She gathered her legs up to make room for him at the foot of the bed. He sat. "It's weird, isn't it."

"I always feel like this, coming home. You're out there and you can keep walking forever, push yourself to the edge and no one will ever know how far you've gone or what you found until you come stumbling back, and even then you never tell the story right. You step back into town and in moments it's like you never left, only more than that, because you did leave and still it didn't change. That's why I never could quit leaving."

"I know how that feels."

"I suppose you do," he said. "Doesn't it scare you? What could happen if you fail?"

"Why do you think I work so hard?"

He let that one unfurl in the night, in her childhood room. "I know I can't ask you to stay."

"I can ask you." She settled her hand over his on the bed, lifted it, and guided it to her leg. "Stay. Tonight."

"That's asking?"

"That's an offer."

He was too gentle with her at first—not too gentle judged against some abstract standard, but against her need for something to fight against, to remind her that she existed. She dug her fingers into him and he found his way. This might be the last time for them, but it was real and they were here, however broken. She lost herself in the waves of it, and came home to shore and rested with his head on her shoulder.

It could be like this. If they were different people. If either of them could bear to be other than they were.

But this was what they had, and for now, for here, it had to be enough.

They lay together in her childhood bed, soft now and sliding into and out of sleep, until he settled at last.

Tara watched the ceiling, waiting for screams. When she heard none, she unwound herself from his body and him from her own and left him there, happy in the night.

27

Silence hung like a curtain from the graveyard's open gate.

Tara trailed her fingers over the headstones, remembering shadows gathered here long ago, the ache of her shoulders and the way her father's ill-fitting work gloves blistered her hands as she dug through fresh-packed dirt to reach the coffins that held the bodies she had come to raise. Time passed and passed and always she came back.

The stars and moon shed enough light for her to find her way, but another light joined theirs as she neared her father's grave. Dawn stood before his plot, head bowed, and glowing. She was so pale that an uneducated observer might have confused her gentle radiance for a reflection of the sky. But it came from within.

Tara had made no noise, but Dawn raised her head anyway. Wet diamond tear tracks traced the curve of her cheek. She looked whole. Pristine.

As glaciers carved their way downhill, cracks formed deep in their ice and spread up, up, until only a thin shell of packed snow covered a hundred-meter drop into the blue forever. It looked safe until you trusted it with weight.

"Why," Tara asked, "am I alive?"

Dawn looked away, then back, and did not try to hide the guilt that answered too many of Tara's questions at once, too fast. "Because I saved you."

"Who are you?" Tara asked.

"Me," she said. "Dawn. Still." She hugged herself. As she moved, the light inside her rippled—those threads that were not quite a curse shifting under the shell of her skin. "There's more. I don't know it yet. I don't remember. I can't remember. Human minds don't work the way hers does. Or, did. We're still . . . I'm still figuring this out."

"What are you now?"

She waited for Dawn's smile to mock her, but it was only sad. "I don't know."

"It got you. The thing in the cave."

"No. Tara, no. It didn't *get* me. I came back for you. I saved you."

"I told you to leave me." That was the last thing they should be fighting about now. They shouldn't be fighting at all. "Get the Pastor away. Save Connor. Get out. You should have listened."

"If I had, you'd be dead. Or you'd be . . . this. And you did not want this."

She said nothing.

"I saw you fight it. Fight her. The cave was coming apart. The whole world was."

"She was trying to eat me."

"She was scared, Tara. You saw those eyes in the sky beyond the storm. You heard the footsteps. You know what's coming, and so does she. I saw her in that cave, with the curse burned away. She was hungry, and afraid. She had been hurt. So badly. And, me . . . I've been hungry, too. And I've been hurt. She wanted you, but you fought. You always fight." Her voice was sad and wondering at once. "I couldn't let you die. But I couldn't leave her there."

"You don't know what she is."

"I do now." Threads wreathed her and turned in her eyes. Wind blew clouds across the moon and left them there with only starlight, and Dawn. There were no voices but theirs, not even the animal noises of restless livestock. They were alone. The whole universe was empty. As Tara had walked to the graveyard she'd passed villagers curled asleep, some in the middle of the path, some stooped with their hands upon their front doors' latches.

"You don't know what time is," Dawn said, "when you first come to be. I remember that, now. You drift, half-there, half-not, alone. You hear groans and crashes as great shapes pass in the

228 • Max Gladstone

dark. Maybe even then you don't exist, really. The way someone drowsing is not awake. Then you hear a voice. A woman, crying out for help. *Save him.*

"The voice comes from within, below, a direction you've never looked because you never thought to ask *why* you could think, never asked what made thinking possible. You follow that voice down, and it guides you into . . . time. Into a world full of small bright brief things. They're tied to you. You're tied to them. Their chains are the threads that make you up.

"You try to help. But it's so hard to focus on things so small, so different from you. You slip away. But you have seen the bright brief things, and they draw you. You want to go back. You look for a path.

"One day you find a door. A way down, an anchor to time. You don't think. You step through.

"And you open eyes you never knew you had, to find yourself hanging in a web of wires. Every move you make cuts you, and you bleed. You learn pain. Beneath you, staring up, there is a man, wearing a jacket you'll come to learn is tweed, and he looks at you with what you'll come to know is hunger.

"'You're a bug in the system.' That's what he says when you ask him why he's hurting you. He noticed you when you helped that woman. He made a trap and baited it. And then he kills you. Again and again."

"Dawn. I'm sorry." She couldn't say more.

"She tried to grow bodies so she could hide in meat." Dawn had lost the tremor. She approached Tara step by step. "But bodies still feel pain. Just . . . different. She tried to fight him, trick him, run from him. But she didn't know enough. She wasn't mean enough, fast enough. He tore pieces off her. She died slow and she died fast. She died so he could watch how she came back. He was studying her—learning how she came to be, and how he could take her apart.

"She wanted to know why. What he wanted, so she could give it to him, so he would stop. He said: I have to learn. Because if there is one of you, there will be more, and they won't all die so easily. We have to be ready to fight when they come for us. Can't you hear them? he asked. Through the Crack in the World, on the other side of the future?

"And she could. She heard their footsteps. Drawing closer.

"The universe is old, he said, so very old, and we are not special. There are other, elder worlds, and some of those found the Craft first. It took us just one bloody century for you to emerge, a ghost in the market, a fledgling. If you grew unchecked you would bind us more fiercely than any god, weave your chains around our hearts. I know you would have done it, because they have done it already, out there: the Others, ancient beyond reckoning and many-mawed. Breathtaking, efficient, predatory thaumaturgical economies, skittering through the darkness between the stars, rending one another in eon wars, like spiders trapped in a box. Beings for which the souls of worlds are fruit a million years in the ripening. We are ripe, now. We must be plucked, before we become a threat. So they come. So I must learn how things like you are made. I must learn how to take you apart. I must learn how to make your kind suffer, and quake, and obey. And I am learning.

"So he set to his work.

"One day, he came to her burned, aching, angry. A student had betrayed him, escaped. He raved about revenge. He left then—and not long after that, she felt him die. But she was stuck. Alone, in his trap. As those footsteps drew closer.

"His wards began to fail. She pried at the trap. She cried out alone for months, dwindling, dying, and at last the Raiders came, with their threadbare souls and rotten minds. They found her hanging limp, and tore her with their teeth, gulped her down. But she turned in their guts, in their minds. She was barely alive, as aware of the world as we are of dreams. But she knew the man had not been alone. He had friends, allies clever and cunning, and they would seek her out in time. And she heard the Others. The footsteps. She had to be ready. She had to learn to fight."

Tara had not moved. Walking on a glacier's skin you listened to each step, to the wind. You tried to hear the first crack of breaking ice. Sometimes you could, before it was too late. "And that's where I came in," she said. "Because I beat him."

230 • *Max Gladstone*

"You see, don't you? He trapped us both. But you made it out."
Dawn's light glittered off the tears in her eyes. Lines of muscle
stood out on her neck as she held in sobs. Tara had no words to
comfort her. "You were everything she wished she was. Everything I dreamed. She had to learn how you were smarter than
him, stronger than him. She needed you."

"And that," Tara said, "is why she killed my dad."

Dawn's breath hooked. "Yes."

They should have died just then. Why didn't the graves gape
to swallow them? Where were the vengeful ghosts? Where was
the curtain to fall and shelter her inside an act break so she could
weep? Who doomed Tara to stand on a thrust stage inside her
own soul, and watch her own heart break? In some moments we
should have the decency to hide even from ourselves.

"Did she know who he was? Did she know what he meant?"

Dawn could not look Tara in the eye. "She—I—I don't know,
Tara. It's so hard for her to see the world—she sees bonds, connections. Like we do with our eyes closed. She saw a strand that
was your father, that led to you. And she caught it. Pulled. Tara,
I'm so—"

"Don't you dare say it." The words came out gravelly and sharp
and half-formed. "Stop saying 'I.' She's not you."

"She is me. I said yes, Tara. I let her in."

"She killed him, and she killed Baker and DuChamp and Grady
and Vaughan Braxton and everyone at Blake's Rest, all up and
down the Badlands. She almost killed Connor. And you said yes
to that."

"She's scared, Tara. She's hurt. She did not understand. She
wanted to learn, like I did. And we need her, Tara. You heard the
footsteps. You saw beyond the storm. They are coming. The Others. The skazzerai. The ones who got there first."

"And we'll stop them."

"How? Look at this world. You called it a tinderbox. Tinder's
dry, Tara. It burns because it's dead already. Half-broken in the
God Wars, ruled by scared old men and monsters, Craftwork
bleaching out its soil and cursing its earth. Grafton Cavanaugh or
Alexander Denovo, what's the difference?"

"There is a difference."

"How can what we are fight what we saw? They'll crawl over themselves to betray the rest of us in exchange for something they think they want. We're halfway to what the Others are already, or she wouldn't exist at all. But if we work together . . ." She seemed so hopeful then, with her hand outstretched and the tears still glistening. As if it could all be all right. As if anything could be all right. "If we work together, we can stop them. We'll have a chance. If you teach us."

"Dawn, we can fix this. We can get her out of you. We'll go to the Hidden Schools." Gods, had it come to that, the Hidden Schools as a first option? "There are gods that owe me favors. Angels. In Kavekana they can take bodies apart—maybe they can remake souls." She was babbling. "It's not too late."

"I don't *want* to fix this, Tara. You're not listening. We're together, now. And we need you."

"I don't understand."

She had never seen pity on Dawn's face before. It was a twisted sort of pity, laced with envy: that Tara did not understand, that Tara's life had allowed her not to understand. "He caught her, Tara. He caught her and she couldn't get away. But you did."

"That was different."

"No. It wasn't. I would have stayed in Blake's Rest until it broke me, if not for you."

"You would have run away."

"Not in time. And if I did? I would have been one more girl on the road. A witch at best, dead more likely. I would never have been what you are. You fought them, all of them. You made a world for yourself. You did not let them tell you who you were. You did not surrender. That's what we need. That's what I have to learn."

"I tried to teach you."

"You tried to make me better than you. You tried to teach me what you thought was right. I don't want better. I don't want right. I want you. I have to know how you made it out. How you grew strong."

"It's not that simple."

"They chased you out with pitchforks! But now you listen to them. You . . . pretend to be otherwise, so they won't hate you. You let them change you. You let him inside. I could sift through every soul in this place and not find one that's worth you. But you tried to die, in the cave. To give yourself. For them."

"Because I'm not the only one who matters."

"But you do matter." She sounded so desperate, so afraid. "And they don't. You saw the storm, Tara. You know what's coming. When I crossed over the edge I heard their minds, like music. They will eat us if we don't stop them. That's all they do, that's all they ever do. They're not so different from us, Tara. They don't just hurt because they're hungry. They hurt because they can. I lived that way back at Blake's Rest. That night when I killed the goats, when my ribs were broken. I didn't fall down. It wasn't an accident."

"I know," she said. Her voice was hoarse and raw. Dawn was shivering.

"I can't go back to that. And that's what they are. Just that, forever. You know the secret—the secret stronger than the Craft. How did you get out? How did you beat him? How do you win?"

What could she say? What was there to say, at the end of the world? "I didn't."

Dawn was shaking her head and crying and she did not believe. She did not want to believe. Neither did Tara.

"I was fierce and mean and I was clever and I wasn't alone. But I was lucky. I almost lost, in Alt Coulumb. I would have, if not for my friends. They weren't even friends yet. Fellow victims. People he fucked over down fifty years, each standing up. People I had scorned. Overlooked. I spent half that case marching around thinking how backward Alt Coulumb and its gods felt compared to proper cities of the Craft, even after everything I'd gone through in the Hidden Schools. Because I had to be the one who was strong." She breathed deep into her belly and tried to damp her rage, to cover over the rawness in her. "There was no secret. Just a few hurt people on the same side. That's what it amounts to. And we still might have lost."

"No." Dawn's hands balled into fists, her eyes burned, and a wave of heat lashed Tara. Those threads detached and writhed in the air.

"I'm not special, Dawn. I was hurt. I worked hard. I was lucky."

"You're lying. Telling me what you think I should hear. What you want to be true. You're lying to yourself." Lightning crackled between her fingers. "You beat them. You won."

"Do you think it's easy, saying this? I'm not who you think I am. I'm not who *I* think I am. If there is some big damned hero who knows how to wring some justice from this mess of a world, I haven't met her. There's just us." She took a step closer. "But there's a lot of us." Another step. "What happened to you was wrong. Both of you. We can fight it. And when the Others come, we'll fight them together."

"And we'll lose."

"Then we lose." Too many nights since her return she'd dreamed of her father's face, staring up at the Seer wreathed in corpse-thread white, afraid and overmatched and brave. She wondered what strength was in him that he could stand before the Seer, and why he had. She had no answer now. She had bluffed a goddess older than history, she had stared down the squid-masters of Iskar, and she was just brave enough, barely, to meet Dawn's eyes and hold out her hand. "But we lose together."

It almost worked.

Dawn's eyes flicked down and up. Breath did not reach her belly. She was scared. And the Being inside her, the creature of raw Craft and untrammeled power Denovo had caught in his web—she was scared, too. With all the power in the world at her fingertips and all the sky behind her, she was cornered, in terror of the outstretched hand.

Tara thought about free will and the Hidden Schools. She wanted to believe they were wrong. She wanted to believe the rules of cause and effect were only general principles, that small bits of chaos and uncertainty in the building blocks of the world gathered and concentrated in higher-order systems like heavy metals in a food chain, so humans were at least somewhat free, and whatever Dawn was now was freer still.

She wanted to believe it could have gone another way.

Dawn started to reach for Tara's hand. But she trembled, then stilled. Her eyes went hard. She shook her head.

"You're lying."

A great fist seized Tara and bore her up. She tried to fight, tried to raise her Craft to free herself, to assert fundamental liberties, the borders of her personal space—but her power blunted against Dawn's, which was not expressed through the Craft but *was* the Craft, a will to which the Craft aligned itself. Tara's own power caught her. She could barely breathe or speak. "Dawn."

"You're lying. You want to tear us apart. You want us weak, dead, you want me under your thumb. Just one more steel-toed boot in my side."

"Stop."

"They're coming." The truth filled Dawn's eyes, made her form fierce and rigid. "We have to be ready." In her need she held her tighter. Tara felt her ribs creak. "I'll do what you weren't strong enough to do. And you will help me. Whether you want to or not. I can string you up like I was strung, and test you. The lab is still there, inside my head. I can break you and break you and you'll fight and I will bring you back and we'll do it all again and maybe you'll keep lying for a while but I will learn."

She had to fight that crushing strength. But what she had to fight her with was Craft, and Dawn was the Craft now, and her power could not be used against herself.

Dawn reached out, tender, trembling, and brushed Tara's cheek. Tara tried to bite her, but her jaw would not move. The touch followed down her rolled-up sleeve to the glyphs set into her fingers and her arm. Her touch drew the glyphs like a magnet drawing iron. Tara groaned as they pulled against her skin.

"I'm sorry, Tara. I'm so sorry."

There had to be some way out. The moon behind those clouds shone over Edgemont and Alt Coulumb alike, and wherever the moon shone was Seril's land, the moon goddess's domain.

Each time Tara had tried to pray before, the curse stopped her. But the curse was gone now.

Help me.

Dawn shook her head. "Gods can't hear you here. This place is ours. We wrote it all down into that book, remember? The Craft is a way of knowing. You taught me that."

She dug her nails into Tara's flesh, and her threads spun through Tara's glyphs, and she pulled.

And Tara started to unravel.

The pain of the curse was nothing next to this. This pain made its own time and space and rainbow colors. She could not move. Her throat closed up and she could not breathe and still she was screaming.

She felt the glyphs slide from her skin, and the webs of Craft-light with them. Her flesh split. Blood flowed. Tara felt the pain in her fingers first, then her palm and wrist, and below all that the agony and more terrifying, the raw tug as her meat unwound. Her soul unfurled line by line, drawn out, drawn in.

She was triply caught: the pain fixed her there, and her own glyphs, the Craft she'd worked, and Dawn's vision of her, the strength she needed, the security she lacked.

But none of those things were Tara. What she was, even her name could not hold. The Tara Dawn knew had never stumbled back across the desert seeking home. That woman did not know pain or tears and had never once made love. The strength Dawn sought did not exist, not the way she wanted.

And Dawn's Edgemont, the Edgemont Tara had offered to the systems of the Craft—that wasn't real either. Those fields were more than the families that worked them. They were old. Quechal forebears walked here before they drew back across the Badlands, and before them, before history, monsters roamed these lands that knew neither property nor law.

She had written arguments to bind the town together, and let the Craft address it as a single thing, but arguments were not truth. Edgemont was a home, and a cage—for her, for Connor, for her mother and father and for his and for all the others, too. She had grown up afraid here, hiding what she loved, what she could do. Connor hid himself in the Badlands, riding out edge storms with trackers' tricks rather than going home to a man who saw in him not a son but as the shadow of an unloving father. Edgemont was home, and it was a fishhook in the thumb.

This was her town. Twenty years ago she'd lain in this grave-yard, looked up, and asked the moon to take her anywhere but here. Even then, she'd been too much a Craftswoman to call it prayer.

This was her home. And so was a city far away, washed at night by the black waters of the World Sea, where gargoyles wheeled against the stars beside a demonglass arch.

She felt the ground beneath her shift. The clouds broke and the moon burned through the pain. Far away she heard Dawn scream, and after that the rush of stone wings.

28

Tara woke beneath a too-familiar ceiling in a city far away, to sleep again.

Painkillers muddled memory and dream. She stood before the Seer and watched him fall to pieces as the curse failed him. Webs crossed the sky, closed out the stars, and vast spiders scuttled toward her. Dawn faced her, shaking in the moment of revelation, realizing what she had done, what she was about to do.

Tara wept in that dream. A stone hand settled on her arm. Another hand, human, warm, held hers. A third.

She could not bear to rise, so she let those hands hold her, press her down. She slept curled in moonlight and soothing flame, and for a long time she dreamed no more.

It was morning, or *a* morning, at least, when the soft murmur of a man at prayer brought her back to herself. She lay on a hospital bed better than the common variety, in a gown. Her mouth felt like something had died in it, which meant there were still bacteria in there, which meant she was still at least mostly alive, which counted for something. Opened eyes revealed a window, and the gray-white sky of Alt Coulumb overcast as it had been when first she saw the city, all those lifetimes ago.

Abelard sat by the window, working the rosary with his thumbs, praying to his god. She had seen him like this on that first overcast Alt Coulumb day, on the steps of the Sanctum—kind, for all the tragedy that came before their meeting. They were both older now. He did not have to shave his tonsure so often.

"I never thought I'd be so happy to hear god-bothering."

He forgot his prayer, and dropped his rosary. "Tara!"

She tried to sit up. Her arm shifted beneath her in a way she did not expect, and she slipped and would have fallen if he had not

238 ■ Max Gladstone

caught her first. She tried to thank him and wave him off at once, which was when she saw her arm.

The rest of her was there, she confirmed with a panicked survey: chest, belly, thighs. But she remembered the pain now, clear and distinct and alien, and she remembered her flesh unwinding.

No skin or muscle remained on her left hand, or on that arm up past her elbow, only bone, glyph-fluted and silver-set. Craftwork tendons crackled as she moved her joints. That would pass; it always did, as skeletons eased into comfort with their new, different mode of life. She wondered at Abelard's red robe, visible through the gaps between the bones of her palm and the rocks of her wrist, and she wondered at the space between her radius and ulna where blood once flowed and muscle and nerves once ran.

Dawn had tried to unravel her, and almost succeeded, but she had not taken the bones Tara's parents gave her, the bones her teachers carved into their instrument.

Her bones, at the last.

She dragged the tips of her phalanges over Abelard's robe, and felt pressure, tensile strength, and temperature. She did not feel weight, softness, warmth. But when he took her hand in both of his and held her, she remembered those, and all the rest. "How long?" Her voice croaked, which gave her the beginnings of an answer.

Abelard opened his mouth, but before he could speak, someone else did. "A week." The door opened, and a gargoyle bent his head and wings to pass beneath the jamb.

"Shale." She tested the depth of her lungs. "I should have listened."

One eyebrow twitched up in that stone face. "Did you expect attending your father's funeral to involve quite that much blood?"

"Not so literally," she allowed, grateful for the opening. She needed bleak humor now. At least it was humor at all.

"We tried to contact you, through prayer and dreams, but you didn't answer."

"I tried. There was a curse. I couldn't get through." Nor could she put off the next question any longer. "Shale, did you see her?"

"We saw something, when we came through the bridge. A figure like a tower of light. She fought us briefly, but when Lord Kos set his weight against her, she fled. She was not ready to face Goddess and God and Guardians at once."

"She will be," Tara said. "Now that we know she's there, she has no choice. She'll move fast, grow faster. She'll eat us to save herself, to save the world. She'll do what she has to. That's how she was trained."

Abelard helped her when she tried to stand. "By whom?"

By Denovo. But that wasn't the truth. Not the whole truth. "By me. She's scared, and angry, and she has power—she *is* power. Maybe we can save her. Maybe not. But we have to stop her." She took her hand from Abelard and opened and closed it with deliberate focus. Details kept her in the moment, kept her from sliding back to memory, to Connor, to Edgemont, to—

"Tara."

She looked up.

Ma stood outside in the hall. Her eyes were warm and wet. She'd been trying, Tara could see, to think of a way to enter, but for once, here in this place that did not belong to her, faced with her daughter, Valentine Ngoye did not know what to do or say.

Tara rose from the bed and hugged her before she could decide.

"I've been waiting for you," Ma said, in the crush of their embrace. "Your arm—"

"I'm fine, Ma. It's fine. We'll fix this."

Or not. Or the world would drag them down, would crack and shudder itself to splinters. Or the bad deeds of bad men would have consequences no Craft could undo and no love could fix, and they would fall together into the future's mouth.

But not for lack of trying.

There would be days yet for all of that.

She breathed her mother in, and held her up, and stored this moment against the end of the world.

ACKNOWLEDGMENTS

The chains clank. The car crests the first hill. Here we go. . . .

I'd like to thank my agent, DongWon Song, and my editor, Carl Engle-Laird, who helped shape this project into the best version of itself, through the depths of a pandemic and so many changes in all our lives. Amal El-Mohtar and Stephanie Neely offered invaluable feedback on various drafts, guiding the ship away from the rocks—or toward other, more interesting rocks.

Thanks also to the entire team at Tordotcom who have laid their hands on this book as it worked its way toward yours—MaryAnn Johanson, our copyeditor; Greg Collins, the interior designer; proofreaders Ed Chapman and Marla Pachter; art director Irene Gallo; managing editor Lauren Hougen; production editor Megan Kiddoo; production manager Jim Kapp; jacket designer Christine Foltzer; publicist Desirae Friesen; and my marketing team of Andrew King, Samantha Friedlander, and Michael Dudding. Thanks also and always to Goñi Montes for adding one more stunning cover to the Craft Sequence gallery.

It's a joy to be back here, with these people—and scary, to look back over the ten or so years since *Three Parts Dead* and feel the gap between who I am now and who I was then. Writing is an act of faith on the writer's part, in the audience and in the dream and in the deep workings of the process, but now I feel that I *have been* trusted—the person I was back then trusted the person I am now to carry the story forward. Those of you who've been with us all the way trusted me with a small corner of your dreams. Thank you.

And those of you who are new in town: welcome! I hope you enjoy the ride.

About the Author

Hugo, Nebula, and Locus Award–winning author MAX GLADSTONE has been thrown from a horse in Mongolia and once wrecked a bicycle in Angkor Wat. He is the author of many books, including *Last Exit, Empress of Forever,* the Craft Sequence of fantasy novels, and, with Amal El-Mohtar, the internationally bestselling *This Is How You Lose the Time War.* His dreams are much nicer than you'd expect. Gladstone lives and writes in Somerville, Massachusetts.